Recipe

Melissa

Recipes *for* Melissa

TERESA DRISCOLL

bookouture

Published by Bookouture

An imprint of StoryFire Ltd.
23 Sussex Road, Ickenham, UB10 8PN
United Kingdom

www.bookouture.com

ISBN: 978-1-909490-87-1
eBook ISBN: 978-1-909490-86-4

For my mother…

CHAPTER 1
Melissa – 2011

Melissa Dance had two tics.

When under extreme pressure her right eyelid would flicker. This would then kick-start the second tic, which was an involuntary movement of the head – a sort of chin twitch, which she fancied, *on a good day*, distracted people from the eyelid nonsense.

But this was not a good day. Not good at all.

'Are you all right, Miss Dance?'

It was the handwriting. Working on her other muscles like an anaesthetic now so that while her eyelid and chin continued in the infuriating world of their own, her mouth – in sharp contrast – was completely frozen.

Nothing would come out.

Melissa pulled her hair up into a ponytail, using a band from her pocket, while across the desk the tall and now clearly awkward man, who had introduced himself as James Hall, poured a glass of water and pushed the drink along with the book to the edge of the splendid stretch of mahogany in front of her.

He seemed to be staring at her eye. Or was she imagining that? And then suddenly he plunged onward, speaking much too quickly, about his client's instructions. About how very specific they were. *That the client had specified an expectation of some discomfort but that his duty, under the terms of the agreement, you understand, were to persuade her – Ms Melissa Dance – to take the* *book. And to consider it, please, in her own time. Yes?*

Those were his very specific instructions.

Still Melissa's right eyelid flickered. Still she could not speak.

Mr Hall cleared his throat to add that his client had urged that Melissa *should be reassured at this initial meeting that the* *purpose of the book was to be a comfort. A guiding hand. Not so* *much recipes, per se, as recipes for life. There were letters in the book.* *Also photographs. Did she understand this?*

Melissa stared again at the cover. She stared so hard that both her eyes – the twitching and the non-twitching – were now beginning to water.

It was the handwriting. The black ink.

The main title **RECIPES** was pre-printed in bold but her name had been added by hand – and Melissa knew the handwriting instantly. She glanced to the corner of Mr Hall's office and could see her sitting right there. At the old desk in the corner of her bedroom with the fountain pen in her hand. Beautiful, sloping writing in shiny, black ink.

…for Melissa.

Mr Hall shuffled in his seat and asked if she would like the book back in its envelope?

In her head Melissa replied that she did not mind either way, but whether the words came out of her mouth she had no idea. Whatever the case, Mr Hall placed the book back in its padded envelope and held it out to her.

He clearly knew who the book was from. And Melissa did too.

It was the sloping, haunting hand of her mother.

The mother she had not seen for 17 years…

Gran's Cupcakes.

4 oz self-raising flour
4 oz butter
4 oz caster sugar
2 beaten eggs
Zest of one orange (crucial...remember?)

Preheat oven to 180. Cream butter and sugar. Slowly add eggs (room temperature or it will all split!). Fold in flour gently then mix in orange zest. Pop into bun cases. 15-20 mins in oven. Great-gran recipe... sorry for old money!

(Lovely topped with cream cheese goo + a chunk of strawberry or more orange zest. For the goo – mix equal quantities of cream cheese and soft butter, then add icing sugar until the right thickness and sweetness. Sorry to be so vague.)

Oh, my darling girl. You will be shocked. Yes? Even as I begin to paste this first recipe and photograph into the book, I can feel it. Your shock.

I have paced and paced and there is a waste basket full of screwed up paper. Starting this over and over. So worried about getting it right. Putting it right.

I have worked myself into such a state – truth be told – that I feel worried this is not the right day to start at all. But what else to do? Try tomorrow? The day after that?

When I get wound up like this, I have this really annoying thing. My eyelid twitches. Yes I know. Embarrassing and completely weird. It's doing it right now. Bloody, stupid thing.

I keep meaning to see an optician or something. Your father insists he can't see it; that no one else notices either, but I find that hard to believe and the whole business makes me feel like some kind of freak. You see. This is precisely the kind of stuff I would have lain on a bed and talked to you about, grown-up to grown-up, if I had just got the chance. The very reason I am doing this.

So.

Anyway.

I have given up throwing pieces of paper into the bin. Decided – no more editing. I am just going … to keep going. To write what I am thinking – exactly as it comes into my head. So all I can do as I sit here, worrying that I am starting this on the wrong day, is to hope and pray and plead with you, my darling, to *please, please*, take a deep breath. To forgive me for the shock and to go with this – with an open mind – and try to understand why I have waited so long to talk to you in this way.

I simply don't know what to say to comfort you except that, to me at least, there feels a good reason that I have done this.

Waited, I mean.

The date as I start here is August 1994. You will know better than me what that means, timing-wise, and I must tell you, in fairness, that your father and I are not at all in agreement over this. I don't mean this book because he **doesn't know about this book**. I mean about the rest of it.

By now you will not need me to tell you what a magnificent man he is. That is why I have not the slightest fear leaving you in his wonderful hands. But he is in shock too, poor darling, right now and does not realise yet that he is going to manage so very beautifully without me.

He wants us to do the whole 'memory box' thing. He wants us to see some counsellor woman. Some charity which has bears and balloons. And though I know that they are the experts and they all mean terribly well and they have studied *ologies* and all of the rest of it, I just know that is not the way for me. And you will understand by the end of this book how very stubborn I can be.

What I have decided is that I do not want you to know a thing about all the shit that has become my life. As I write now, you are eight years old – asleep in the bed next door in princess pyjamas, with a fairy costume discarded on the floor. I am sorry but I cannot do it to you.

I want to have some time with my darling girl – just one beautiful corner of my life and yours in which I can pretend that everything is going to be completely all right.

Is this selfish? Possibly. Probably. I have no idea what you will think. But would it really have been any less painful for you to have known? To have been warned?

Max thinks so. Maybe you will too.

In which case 'sorry' will not help.

All I can tell you is I have a very strong instinct that this is the right way for me to do this. I cannot speak for others and I do not want to criticise the charities and the people who advise otherwise. Maybe they are right. Maybe not.

So if I got it wrong and you are very cross with me then will you please just give me the benefit of the doubt and at least walk with me through these pictures and these thoughts? If not now, then some time very soon?

Please.

I did wonder about telling you. Trying to prepare you just a bit, but last night I looked at you when you were sleeping – so very beautiful and so very calm and I thought – what's the point? You will be shocked and sad and angry, whether you are prepared or not. The way I see it, telling you will just start the sadness sooner.

Anyway. It's done now. Too late.

So I am putting this book together instead. My original idea was just recipes which were handed down to me by my own mother and grandmother and which I wish very much to pass on to you. They are not so very special or rare. Just simple, solid recipes I cooked with my own mother and she with hers – and which I hope, one day, you may get to cook with your own children. You will need to jot down the conversions. It always felt rather sweet to me to leave them in 'old money'. Then later I decided that it would be nice with each recipe to put in a picture of you and I cooking – and to share a few thoughts. Just stuff which may help you now that you are all grown-up. OK. Deep breath.

Twenty five years old? You will be wondering why now? Why wait so long? Oh my darling – I did think about the usual milestones. Eighteen? Or twenty one? And then I remembered the complete state I was in at eighteen and how twenty one never felt grown-up at all.

And the whole idea of this – the point of it – is to be really open and to talk to you woman to woman.

And so I decided to pick the age I truly grew up myself. Twenty five. The age I had you, Melissa...

God. How I wish I could see you. Wish that I was just the slightest bit religious. Believed in heaven. Something. Anything.

Anyway. Whatever. I have been careful over the details, in case you are wondering. The plan is to leave this book in the care of a very good lawyer who will be instructed to check that both you and Dad are fine before this comes to you. This way I can write – knowing you will only be reading if you are both OK.

I am imagining shorter hair. Did you get it cut? Secretly I hope not, but I rather think it will suit you, however you wear it. You have that sort of face.

Oh God. I'm rambling already.

So – yes. I picked twenty five, Melissa. The age our story began. And the age, I hope, that will see you truly ready for the things that I need to say to you.

Grown-up honesty.

How weird is this? Woman to woman, as you sleep next door. Leg lolling out the bed, with Elizabeth clutched in your arm. Do you still have her? I hope so. Such a pretty doll and you do so love her.

Goodness. Rambling again. Sorry…

Focus, Eleanor. So what then is the first thing – the first really important thing that I need to share? And now this sounds like preaching and it's not meant to be that either. Oh, Melissa. It's just there is all this stuff.

So. Much. *'Stuff'.*

I guess you must make of it what you will. And I will trust my gut and start with the simplest but most important piece of advice I feel that I can give you, my darling girl. Which is how every single day of my life, I wish more than anything on this planet …

CHAPTER 2
Eleanor – 1994

Eleanor heard Max's footsteps on the stairs and quickly tucked the book into the top drawer of her desk.

'You home already?' She tried not to sound flustered as he kissed her on the forehead before sitting on the bed, alongside the desk, which doubled as a dressing table – a homey mess of paper and envelopes and old ink bottles which she collected from car boots and junk shops. A myriad of colours and shapes made of thick glass, which in the summer months caught the morning sunshine to sparkle patterns on the wall which Eleanor loved.

'So how did it go?' He was swinging his right foot to and fro very fast as he spoke. To. Fro. To fro. He had very much wanted to go with her today but she had point-blank refused.

'What?' Eleanor twisted her mouth to the side, then tilted her head as she put the lid carefully back on her fountain pen.

Her husband still looked like a boy. It was his hair. Unruly curls which had never learned to behave. Often these days she looked at him and tried to burn all of these images into her brain so that she could pull them out at random when he was away at work. The mad hair. The way he fiddled with his hands when he was nervous.

'The consultant, Eleanor. The trial. Did we get the trial?' He was playing with his wedding ring, moving it up and down between the knuckle and the base of the finger.

It was only in that moment that she realised that she had made the terrible mistake of letting it matter so much. That tiny flicker of hope. She had tried so hard to chant the mantra of the 'long shot'. The 'outside chance'. To remind herself that the odds of her case being a fit for the drug trial were slim.

As indeed they had turned out to be.

She shook her head fast from side to side, fighting the hot stab at the back of her eyes and then closing them, not wanting to see his.

'**Shit,**' a long exhalation of breath and again he was pacing. Left, then right across the room. Left. Right. 'So we appeal. Yes? There must be some appeal. Some second opinion? They surely don't let one consultant play God over this?'

It was the last option. A tiny splinter of hope. Two letters. Consonant. Vowel. And it was over. No.

They were all so very sorry, Mrs Dance, but she had not been suitable for the trial…

She had known that Max would not accept it.

When finally she opened her eyes, he was sitting on the window seat pinching his bottom lip with his thumb and index finger. Over and over. So hard that the lips were turning white where the blood was disturbed.

'Don't do that. You'll hurt yourself. There's no appeal.'

He continued pinching and then he got up suddenly to walk into the en-suite shower room where he ran water and splashed his face.

Then very quickly he was back in the room, pacing yet again.

'America. I read somewhere that there are new things in America. We should go. I can take a sabbatical...'

'Stop it, Max. Please. I am not taking Melissa to America. You need to sit down.' She patted the space beside her.

He paused for a time, fiddling with the buckle on his belt before sitting right next to her on the wide wooden stool in front of the desk-cum-dressing table, leaning his head onto her shoulder now as they watched each other through the mirror. Embarrassed then at his reflection – trying to smooth down his hair.

'You know what I've decided. Please, Max.'

And now it was his turn to close his eyes.

'No, Eleanor. If you stop everything. Stop all the chemo and all of it—'

'It won't make any difference. All that shit.'

'But if you stop *everything*—'

'You heard what they said. Buy an extra month or two at most. So what's the point?'

The pinching again.

She moved her hand up to still his own and clasped her fingers through his.

'I'm tired, Max. I just want a bit of normal. For Melissa. *Please.*'

He looked away to the window and then back.

'She's not going to get normal – Eleanor. You know that. She's going to get a whole heap of shit.'

'So let the heap of shit wait. Because it's coming anyway.' She kissed him on the forehead and then tilted her own head in so that their skin was just touching.

'It's the only thing left I have to give her. A little bit of normal. Please? For me. And for Melissa?' She was thinking of a blanker page. No more appeals and letters. No more hiding from Melissa – fixing sleepovers so she wouldn't see her after the treatments. 'No more, Max. ***Please.***'

He would not look at her. He looked instead at the wall, leg swinging faster and faster again until she reached out to hold his chin and to turn his face back towards hers. His eyes at first off on some other planet, buying tickets to America. And writing letters to consultants and health boards and strident appeal letters over obscure drug trials…

'Please, Max.'

And then coming slowly back to her. Eyes which filled her heart and broke it all at once. Eyes which at last said that he could not say no to her.

Would not say no to her.

CHAPTER 3
Melissa – 2011

'You are seriously not taking that suitcase.'

'What's wrong with this case?'

'You really need me to tell you?'

She frowned.

'It's too big, Melissa. Way too big.'

Melissa looked at the case and then back at Sam, pulling her head back into her neck.

'And please don't do that,' he was smiling. 'You look like a tortoise.'

Normally she would tease him right back. Poke out her tongue. But not today.

'It won't fit in the car, Mel.'

'Oh don't be silly. Of course it will fit in the car. How do you think I got it home,' Melissa continued to place neat piles of clothes on their double bed – T-shirts in one, jeans in another and dresses, folded perfectly, into a third pile. For some reason she was now unfolding the dresses and starting the whole process again. She was trying not to think about this morning. About the book.

'I don't mean our car. Or your dad's. I mean the hire car at the other end.'

Melissa now tilted her head to reappraise the grey, shiny case. In truth, she hadn't thought about the hire car. Shit. She tried to imagine the boot of a Clio. Or was it a Fiesta? 'It'll be fine. Surely? Anyway – this way we share.'

Sam craned both arms over his head. 'Why can't we just take two soft bags as usual?'

Melissa stopped then, blushing and readjusting the band on her ponytail. There was an awkward pause; both looking away.

'Oh – I get it,' the penny dropping as Sam's expression finally changed. 'So – this is to reassure me?'

'Sorry? I don't know what you mean.' She did.

And now they were both staring at the case.

'You don't need to do this, Melissa.'

'What?'

'Gestures. We talked this all through the other night. Closed it down. I thought we were OK.'

'We are OK.'

'Right. Good. So you're not pissed off that I asked you to marry me. And I'm not pissed off that you had a panic attack.'

Melissa tightened her lips.

'You do know I didn't mean now. Get married now. I mean, I completely realise you're young still. I just meant get engaged. Have a plan. I honestly didn't mean to put pressure on. To…'

They both continued to stare at the case.

'Look – I borrowed it from Lou. If you really hate it, I'll give it back to her. I just thought it would be more convenient. You know – one case. It's no big deal, Sam. Honestly. If you would rather we pack separately as usual, we can pack separately.'

Each of them stopped then, conscious of the other's breathing. It had been like this for the last forty eight hours. Ever since the debacle of the birthday dinner.

The ring box.

Melissa had handled it very, very badly and was more sorry than she could explain. She had been winded in the restaurant

– just as she had been winded this morning in James Hall's office – so that everything had come out all wrong. She hadn't seen it coming. Not at all, which she realised, looking back now, was naive of her. OK – so she knew that he was smitten. That he had been smitten pretty much from the off. But Christ – wasn't she now smitten too?

She looked at Sam now and could see that other, younger version. Longer hair – ever so slightly sun-bleached. Sawn-off shorts. Awkward teenage smile but perfect teeth. She could feel that pull in her stomach – the strange contraction that happened every single time she turned a corner to catch sight of him unexpectedly.

And OK – so it had taken her longer than him to see it. Believe in it. Their story the cliché of kids growing up together; that same smile across so many rooms across so many years. But Melissa truly loved Sam now, even if this fact paradoxically and inexplicably frightened her. So was it really so terrible that she wasn't into the whole marriage thing? She had tried so hard to explain in the restaurant. Why couldn't they just be in love? Why did they need a piece of paper? It wasn't personal.

'Not personal, Mel? You don't know if you want to marry me – and you think that's not personal?' He had looked completely broken.

She really couldn't find the words to explain it because she didn't even understand it herself.

And now Melissa could not help it. The picture of the padded envelope. Her mother at a desk.

Black ink…

'So what was the solicitor thing all about?' He had brightened his tone for her. She looked at his face as he changed the subject, and deliberately his expression also, and felt it. That sharp pull of a muscle, right in the bed of her stomach.

'Sorry?' She turned away to smooth and refold a shirt now, hoping that he would not notice that her hand was ever so slightly trembling.

'You said it was today. The solicitor thing. The mystery letter. So what was it? A will hunter like you thought?'

'Yes it was a will hunter. But – it wasn't me. Wrong family. Long shot; trying to trace someone from some family in America.'

Melissa had no idea why she did not want to tell Sam about the book. She had read just two pages. Overwhelmed.

Her mother had got one thing right at least. She was in complete shock. So badly needing now to press pause. To go on this holiday and find some freeze-frame; some place to work out how on earth, on top of everything else, to hold on to him. How to show this lovely and much too kind man that the fact she wasn't sure about the whole marriage thing did not mean that she did not love him. And yes – if she were honest – it was precisely the reason she had borrowed a case the size of a small country. Stupid. Clumsy. Panicking.

'I can take the ring back if you like.'

'Oh, Sam.' In the restaurant she had asked for time to think about it. Begged him not to be hurt by this.

'It's OK. I'm fine about it, Melissa.'

'Really?' She sat down on the bed, a fresh wave of guilt washing over her.

'Yeah – really.' He turned to look at her properly. Not fine. 'I got carried away.'

'It's not that I don't care. You do know how much I care, Sam?'

He nodded very quickly – the kind of rapid nodding which didn't mean yes at all.

Melissa stood back up and for a moment then was very, very still – the familiar tightening in her chest, wishing she could say something which would trigger in him the same happiness he so effortlessly triggered in her. But when she paused like this; tried to analyse what it was she was supposed to feel or to say to make things OK for him, it just made things worse. Made her feel so inadequate and guilty, as if something inside her was jammed. Yes; that was it.

As if something was *jammed.*

She turned away again and continued sorting the items for packing into their neat little piles. Melissa, who felt safer and calmer in an environment of complete order – all her clothes hanging right this minute in neat sections in the wardrobe, according to colour and length.

Darks to the right. Brights and lights on the left.

'OK. So how about we just go on holiday as we planned, Sam. We celebrate both our birthdays in the sun. We get a tan. And we have a lot of sex? Yes?' And now she was talking much too quickly. 'Which is actually the real reason I think the whole marriage thing is overrated,' clowning. 'Given that when people get married they stop shagging. Proven statistically.'

He was silent.

'Big pants, rows over the dishwasher and no sex. Is that really what you wanted for us?' She turned to pull her tracksuit bottoms high up her waist, gesturing the shape of very big pants.

'Don't Melissa.'

'What?'

'Please stop.'

'Stop what?'

'Trying to turn it into a joke. To do what you always do when you don't want to talk to me.'

'I don't know what you mean.'

'You do. And it won't work.'

'It will.' She pulled a face, stretching the jersey even wider from her hips until he was fighting a smile and then turning away from him again to take a deep breath. Trying very hard not to think of it. The ring box. The decision she was supposed to make on this holiday over her career.

But most of all – the book.

That beautiful fountain pen. The click of its lid. And the memory of a strange chemical smell which until today she had completely forgotten.

*Of **ink.***

CHAPTER 4

Eleanor – 1994

'Have we spoiled her?'

'Of course we've spoiled her. Why wouldn't we spoil her?'

'You know what I mean. Am I trying too hard?'

'Eleanor. This is Disneyland Paris. Hardly the place to start worrying about spoiling a kid.'

She had done this at Christmas too. Bought too much and in a panic put some of the boxes back in the loft.

'You're right. I know you're right.' Eleanor glanced at Melissa in her Snow White costume, staring through a window.

Of course it was too much. They were staying in a pink froth of a hotel, for Christ sake, and tomorrow were booked in for croissants with a mouse in tails.

'*I thought it had to be a birthday to meet Mickey Mouse, Mummy. Sophie in school said that—*'

'*No. It doesn't have to be a birthday, honey.*'

'You look tired, Eleanor.'

'I'm fine.' She wasn't. 'Though I might just take a little break. I've told Melissa I need the loo. Would you mind doing the rides for the next hour and I'll meet you at the restaurant for lunch? I'll grab a nap.'

'You sure you don't need us to come back with you?' he was leaning in to check her face more closely. 'No. No. I'm not happy to leave you. Your eyes look a bit bloodshot to me.'

'Honestly, Max – it's fine. Mel's on a high. She wants to see the dragon under the castle. I'm just a bit tired. I'll be right by the phone. Don't worry. Don't fuss. She won't mind. I can ring reception if I need anything.'

'You promise me?'

'I promise. And you have the list of rides – suitable for her age, I mean?'

He tapped his top pocket to confirm the rustle of paper.

Back in their room, Eleanor lay down on the bed and surprised herself by drifting, almost immediately, into a deep sleep. She woke – forty minutes later, with a heavy, dragging ache low in her abdomen. She checked her watch, took two more of the stronger painkillers, with water beside the bed, and closed her eyes as she struggled to swallow them. Two days it had been like this. So very difficult to swallow her tablets. She was starting to worry that she had misjudged the timing. The book.

For this reason she had brought it with her – hidden it in a large soft zipper case containing Melissa's hair paraphernalia – bands and ties for her ponytails.

Eleanor opened it at the first picture. She had taken it just two days earlier, baking the cupcakes with Melissa from her mother's recipe. They had decorated half with cream cheese and strawberries and half with strawberry pink icing – the colour of this hotel. Eleanor wondered whether Melissa would remember the story of the orange zest. What she would think when she got to see this picture. The book.

Would there be time? Was she doing the right thing?

She took her fountain pen from her handbag and took a deep breath to continue…

…which is how every single day of my life, I wish more than anything on this planet that…

...I was more like your father. Kinder and more forgiving, I mean. You will probably have fathomed by now what I knew within weeks of meeting Max. That he is probably the kindest man you will ever meet. Well – actually, cancel that. On reflection, I hope not. I hope that you will find someone as kind as your father to share your own life with. But I am biased, of course, and I think it will be a tough call.

What I burn to tell you is a truth that I am not terribly proud of; that it took me a long time to learn from him. So often I would do the wrong thing, Melissa, before I met your father. Think the wrong thing. Say the wrong thing. I never deliberately hurt people or anything like that. I don't think I am a bad person. I certainly hope not. But too often I simply opted out. Failed to do things which could have made a difference. And then somehow, time with Max just softened me and taught me to stop and think a bit more. To open my eyes.

And now, in this awful chapter of my own, I keep rewinding to times when I wish that I had behaved differently. Before some of your dad rubbed off on me, I mean. For some reason I keep thinking of this girl in school. She was called Monica and she was exceptionally clever but also terribly thin and terribly shy. Don't get me wrong. I was never unkind to her. I would smile at her and try to talk to her. But I never really knew how to handle the fact that she was on the outside of *everything*. By the third year, I think I realised deep down that it was more than shyness. Her hair started to thin and she began to dye it as if by way of disguise or distraction. Dramatic red, then blonde. But I still didn't say anything or ask anything. I just sort of gave up trying to talk to her. Opted out. And then many years later she turned up on a talk show. Turns out she had anorexia nervosa – all of her life. Very nearly died at one point and talked about how lonely she always felt. Soon after that all the papers went

completely mad about eating disorders. You couldn't open a tabloid without some feature about it. And I remember thinking
how awful it must have been for Monica through all those years
in school, living with such terrible sadness in the days when so
little was known about it. And I wish I could go back – Melissa.
To try at least to talk to her. Just to try that little bit harder to be
that little bit kinder.

Max would have done better. You know that and I know
that.

You may well, by now, take more after him than me, and I
hope so. But this book is about honesty and so I will be frank.
Be kind, my darling girl. Always try to be kind. It sounds so trite
and I know that you would not be intentionally otherwise, but
sometimes it is as simple as deciding not to sit on the fence. To
do something instead of nothing. Am I sounding like a lunatic?
Like some terrible God squadder? Or do you understand what I
am trying to say to you?

Eleanor looked at the page of handwriting, skimming through
the last few lines. Was she preaching too much? Would Melissa
see it as criticism? She blew on the ink and bit into her bottom lip.
This was so much harder than she had thought. The decision not
to edit. To write straight into the book. She felt a frisson of panic.

And then the phone startled her. Max.

'Hi – honey. I just woke up. Phone made me jump.'

'Sorry. You OK?'

'Yes. I feel better for a sleep. Where you ringing from?'

'Ice cream shop.'

'Oh right. So how was the dragon?'

'Best not to ask. Rather too realistic for a girl of eight.'

'Oh dear.'

'It's taking a lot of raspberry ripple'

Eleanor laughed. She could picture them exactly – Melissa persuading her father into double scoops. Sauce. Chocolate flakes. 'So – she's twisting you around her little finger again?'

'Moi?'

'I take it we need to bump lunch back?'

'No. No. Twelve thirty still OK. You know Melissa. Always hungry.'

Eleanor glanced at her watch – just past noon. 'Meet you there. I just hope it's as good as the write-ups. Got a river with boats – right through the restaurant. The picture looked gorgeous.'

'Not that we would want to spoil her,' he was teasing.

'Shut up and tell her I'm on my way.'

'Tell her yourself. Here, Mel. Come to the phone. It's Mummy.'

There was a fumbling with the phone and some unintelligible spit whispering. *Go on. Go on. It's Mummy.*

'I wasn't scared.'

'Sorry?'

'The dragon. I wasn't scared of the dragon. I don't know why Daddy said that. He shouldn't have said that.'

Eleanor felt her shoulders move and closed her eyes.

'He's a silly Daddy. Of course you weren't scared. You're my brave, brave girl.'

CHAPTER 5
Melissa – 2011

That one man's snoring could make so much noise was unbelievable. Partly her fault, to be fair. Way too much red wine.

Melissa stared at the clock – just past four a.m. – and then stared at Sam, well aware that it was not healthy to so often watch him like this when he was sleeping. To think and think and sometimes whisper in her head; to tell him things in her head only that felt too dangerous. Out loud.

She closed her eyes and leant back on the pillow, exhaling very slowly. Normally when she could not drift back to sleep, she would tiptoe through to the kitchen for a cup of tea but the door needed oiling and she really didn't want him to wake so, instead, lifted her handbag from the bedside chair and padded through to the en-suite bathroom. She clicked the light, wincing at the glare and turning to check there was no movement from the bed. Nothing. The snoring continued, which for a moment made her smile.

I do not snore, Melissa.

She put the seat and then the lid of the toilet down and sat, carefully taking her mother's book out of her bag as she pushed the door to. Just shy of the click. There was that same hollow feeling in her stomach now as she examined the title again. Her name in the familiar slanting hand.

Melissa paused, took a long, slow breath and turned the title page to look again at the photograph alongside the first recipe.

She was wearing a green-striped top, but what was strange was she remembered the jumper very well and yet did not remember the photograph being taken at all. She looked down at her arm and could see it really clearly. The soft wool with hoops of green and cream.

In the picture she was holding a baking tray of cupcakes, half covered with cream and strawberries and half covered with vivid pink icing and tiny silver balls. The feeling in her stomach changed now, her fingers twitching…

Sprinkle them gently, love. As many as you like…

Melissa turned her head towards the shower and back again, narrowing her eyes. She was remembering a wooden spoon. The coolness of the tiny silver balls as she picked them from the container. Yes. She was allowed to lick the spoon. Melissa could feel a strange tightening in her chest and a change in the movement of the air around her. She must have been beaming right at her mother as the photograph was taken and yet she could not call this up. The image of her mother standing there with the camera. Why? If she could remember the wooden spoon and the silver balls, why not that? And then she was suddenly unsure if they were real memories at all – the spoon and the decorations – or if she was taking them from the photograph. Wanting it to be so.

Why did she not remember any of this before?

She skimmed down the page and was then drawn back to a section, to read her mother's words more slowly…

So if I got it wrong and you are very cross with me then will you please … at least walk with me through these pictures and these thoughts? If not now, then some time very soon?

Please…

Melissa took a while to register that the discomfort she was now feeling was from holding her breath. She exhaled. Breathed in and out more slowly. Had to concentrate for a while to get this natural rhythm going again.

She closed her eyes and leant back against the wall.

More stillness now as Sam's snoring softened. Melissa stood up for a moment to examine her face in the mirror, narrowing her eyes at the large, dark circles. She sat back down on the toilet seat and tried to resist them. Other memories. The head teacher in school.

I'm fine. Honestly, Mrs Pritchard. I just don't want to talk about it. OK?

Pluto with a very large tongue in Disneyland. Scones with jam and cream in Cornwall. Some debate over whether it was cream first or jam first. And now she was unsure if these images were real either. From memories or conjured from her father's photo albums?

She could feel this terrible sadness seeping into the room and with it the beginning of a panic. The familiar tight, tight knot of anger. She closed her eyes but it was still there. An image suddenly of kicking and screaming. Something dropping to the floor. *A doll?*

She was starting to feel just a little bit dizzy and was thinking that she could probably do with a hot drink after all. Sweet tea, maybe. Yes – *sugar, Melissa*; when…

'Aaaaagh!'

'What the…'

'Shit, Sam.' Her heart pounding instantly from the adrenaline rush – only just stopping the book falling from her knees, the door now a foot ajar. 'You scared the life out of me.'

'Sorry. I'm sorry. But what on earth are you doing, Melissa? Do you realise it's four o'clock in the morning? What's that?'

Through the gap in the door, he was staring at the book. She shut it and put it quickly into her bag.

'Oh nothing. Just some notes for work. Something I forgot to do. It was on my mind.'

'Work? At four o'clock in the morning?'

'I'm sorry. Sorted now. You know me. Worry bunny. I couldn't sleep.'

Sam was now running his tongue around his mouth, glancing back at the bed – alongside which was a glass of water. Frowning. Eyes heavy.

'You sure you're OK, Melissa? You look a bit odd.'

'I'm just tired. Too much wine. Sorry. I didn't mean to wake you.'

'Look, I really need a drink. You want some water?'

'I might make tea actually,' Melissa stood up, clutching her bag, and to avoid his eyes moved quickly through to the bedroom and then the kitchen, the door squeaking as she called back over her shoulder. 'Quick cup of tea then we really must get some sleep.'

CHAPTER 6
Max – 2011

Max Dance ran for his life. He ran for his sanity and he ran for the sake of his colleagues. An in-joke at work. On any day that he did not run, he was apparently out of sorts.

'Missed your run, did you Professor?'

Max knew very well that this had nothing to do with endorphins and everything to do with the same OCD nonsense that saw his grown-up daughter display the mugs on her kitchen shelf in neat sections according to their colour.

'You do know that we are a pair of bloody misfits,' he said regularly to her over their monthly dinners as she fiddled with the cutlery until it was perfectly straight. All the angles and spacing precisely to her liking.

'Yeah – but it works, Dad. You run. I tidy. This is what we do. Why fix it when it isn't broken?'

Not broken?

That they were close was never in any doubt in Max's mind. He saw far more of Melissa than many of his friends seemed to see of their children once they left home. It was only the taboo that troubled Max.

Your mother would have loved this.

At their monthly dinners – always an Italian restaurant by mutual preference – he would keep it up. Dropping in the little asides.

Your mother loved seafood.

While in turn Melissa would resist. Distract. Clown.

Only once had he pressed it. *Why is it, I can't even mention her in front of you without all this defensiveness? This atmosphere?*

And you really think it would help if we wallow?

'Do you think I wallow?' he had asked Sophie just last month. 'Is that what I do over Eleanor? Wallow?'

Sophie was the other symptom along with the running which made Max worry about his life.

Sophie was an artist with an unusual eye for colour and a most unusual take on the world. For the last five years he met her once a month for dinner and sex – a no-strings liaison (strictly her terms) which, in its limitations, was both perfect and completely disastrous all at the same time.

This morning Max set the alarm for six thirty to get his run in before taking Melissa and Sam to the airport. It had taken some persuading – to get Melissa to accept the offer – but what was the point of working your way to Dean of Faculty if you could not wangle your way out of lectures?

The truth? Max hated that he was no longer the one to share a birthday dinner with his daughter. Spooky that they had the same birthday – her and Sam. But there it was.

He liked Sam actually. He liked especially that he made Melissa so happy. But it had still been a huge adjustment after so many years when it was just the two of them.

In the shower after his run, Max checked his watch and realised he had pushed it. Tight for time now. In the car, his shirt was sticking to his damp back as he listened to the latest on the Eurozone Crisis. Greek's plea for a second bailout was still at stalemate. Max was thinking Cyprus could well be next. Maybe he should warn Melissa to take some dollars or sterling? Just in case. No. *Stop panicking.*

Max switched to a music channel, checked his watch then and prayed for no hold-ups south of the river. He texted ahead to say he should be no more than 15 minutes late, but they were still watching out anxiously from the window as he pulled up outside the block, and appeared almost instantly on the pavement.

'What the bloody hell is that?' Max kissed his daughter as Sam struggled behind her with the most fantastic piece of luggage he had ever seen.

'Don't you start. I have had enough grief already from Sam.'

'I'm not surprised. So what's the plan here?' Max stepped back to examine the case more closely. 'To live in it?'

'Shut up,' she punched his arm playfully as Sam wheeled the monster toward the boot.

'And belated happy birthday. To both of you.'

'Thank you.'

It was only then that Max clocked just how exhausted they both looked.

'Heavy night on the juice, was it guys?'

Melissa grimaced.

Max checked her face more closely and knew to ask no more. Max knew all his daughter's faces.

They made good time – the traffic light – and Max felt the familiar anxiety as he pulled into the drop-off point. 'You'll text me when you land?'

'Sure.'

She wouldn't.

'And we're on for our regular dinner when you get back?' He would track the flight online.

'Yes of course – Dad. On the calendar.'

'And we'll talk then. You know – about the freelance contract. You haven't made a decision?'

Melissa, only just finishing her training as a journalist on the local paper, had the unexpected offer of a try-out on a national. A big call. Local job with pension versus freelancing.

'I'm bumping it until after the holiday. In fact I'm bumping everything until after the holiday.'

Max got out briefly, brushed imagined fluff from his trousers and eventually stretched out his hand to Sam. 'You look after her.'

'*Dad.*'

'Sorry, darling.'

Melissa then kissed him hurriedly on the cheek, checking her watch. 'Look. I really am sorry but we need to dash.'

Max glanced again at the huge grey case and shook his head. 'You have a lovely time.'

'We will.'

At the university later, Max made himself the treat of a large cafetière of coffee and tried very hard not to worry; to prepare himself instead for Anna's arrival.

Anna was the school's newest seminar leader. She had started in the summer term and was now grappling admirably with a timetable chock-a-block with freshers. A couple of times each week she touched base with Max to talk through progress and the following week's plans. Max had been right about her appointment. She was keen, bright and ambitious; though there was now a problem he had not foreseen.

Max braced himself, closing his eyes to the smell of the coffee. Ten to noon and right on cue – the click of her heels in the corridor, then the knock on his door which was already ajar.

'Come in.'

And then – there it was again.

'Morning Max.'

The *lurch*.

'Sorry. Good afternoon, I should say. Christ. Where does the time go in this place?' she was staring down at a single sheaf of paper.

Max had tried to convince himself that it was his imagination. The lurch to his stomach. But no. It had happened three times now for three consecutive meetings. First sighting. Cue lurch.

Today she was wearing cream linen trousers with a burgundy wrap top. There was the tiniest flicker of a thin pink silk bra strap showing on her left shoulder as she tightened a large tortoiseshell clasp holding her hair up.

Max shifted uncomfortably and looked away. Never again would he date anyone at work.

'You got time for a quick run through this, Max?' she was now leafing through more paperwork in a black zipped case in her hand and Max guessed it would be more on the plans she was championing for a series of lectures she was hoping to lead the following year. He approved; this ambition – the very reason she had got the job. The proposal had both academic merit with the welcome (and these days essential) bonus that it would almost certainly be a hit with foreign students. Keep the money men happy.

But that was not what Max was thinking. What he was thinking was that Anna Merrivale smelt of baby's talcum powder. He had noticed that last week also. Not grown-up perfume – but baby's talcum powder.

'Won't take five minutes. Promise.'

Max took a very long slurp of coffee and glanced to the window, trying very hard not to look at the peak of bra strap. Not long until take-off and now he was working out in his head what time he could relax. Check online that Melissa had landed safely.

'Sorry. Is this not a good time, Max?'

Cheese Straws

4 oz plain flour
2oz butter
2 oz mature cheese (best you can afford)
1 egg yolk
Salt and cayenne pepper to taste
Cold water

Preheat oven to 200. Season flour with the salt and cayenne pepper and rub in the butter. Mix together with cheese, egg yolk and water to make a stiff dough. Roll out pastry thinly and cut into narrow strips. Place on greased baking tray and cook for 10-15 minutes until a pale golden colour. Cool slightly on the tray and then transfer to wire rack to finish cooling.

Second recipe and I am feeling a little less panicky, Melissa. I am hoping that, by now, you will be calmer and more understanding of what I am trying to share here.

Do you like the picture? It's from a while back – the first time we made these together. I have chosen the cheese straws next because I am hoping that you will remember the 'Jaw's Straws' saga?

A recap – just in case. Cheese straws have always been one of your Dad's favourites. He likes them to 'bite back' so I tend to go heavy on the cayenne. So the first time that you and I made them together I came up with this little joke. The 'Jaws Straws'… which would bite him back a little harder than he bargained for. (You will recall it was your father who 'accidentally', ahem, let you see *Jaws* far too young. Enough said.)

Is this coming back now?

We made the usual couple of dozen straws and then to three of the strips I rolled inside a *huge* quantity of really strong cayenne – right through the middle.

Oh Lordy! I thought we had given him a heart attack. Of course we hadn't. Though it was so worth it. Can't tell you how happy it makes me, Melissa, to think of how hard we all laughed. Your dad too…

And that's the point of this second scribbling. I really don't want you to be hanging onto all the sad bits. Especially with me popping up out of the blue like this.

I do so hope you will remember how much we laughed. And that I hope your lives – both you and Dad – are full of it still. Laughter.

Tricky for me this because I write, assuming that he will be with someone else by now and I want to tell you that I am completely OK with that. More than OK. I have tried to discuss this with him but it's too hard. So if he is being too fussy, **have a word – won't you?**

And while we're on the topic of princes (and frogs) – I rather wonder where you will be? Much too young to be worried if it has not come good yet, of course but be reassured that – well – we all kiss a few frogs. Gawd. I did.

Eleanor leant back in her seat to review the page and, as always, blow gently on the ink to dry the final lines. She twisted her mouth then and felt suddenly guilty. She had promised honesty. The truth? It made her physically sick to even think about it. Max with someone else.

Eleanor went over to the window to see him appear around the corner. As always, he stopped just shy of the door to bend down, palms on bent knees. She smiled, taking in every little bit of him. The mad hair. The slightly dodgy shorts. The huffing. The puffing.

Max did not realise that she watched from the window as he did this – tried to recover his breath, and with it his pride, before he came inside. He had taken up running soon after her diagnosis. At first he ran to burn off his anger. Now he ran every single day, setting off earlier and for longer during the spells when chemo put the physical side of their marriage on hold.

It wasn't rocket science.

Eleanor badly missed making love too. Only now – watching him and wishing that she could run it off also – did she feel it properly. The realisation there was only one thing worse than imagining Max with someone else.

And that was imagining him alone.

CHAPTER 7
Melissa – 2011

They met as children – Sam and Melissa – a story that so pola-
rised people that on that long flight Melissa again watched Sam
sleeping and did what she could never help. Overthinking.

Turns out he had been mesmerised by her from the very beginning. He had watched her and befriended her and quietly
looked out for her right through their schooling – Melissa bliss-
fully unaware it was anything more than friendship until very
much later.

One camp of friends saw this as romantic. Others not so
much: *'So you two took precisely how long to get together?'*

One of Melissa's journalist pals had just a month back said
out loud what others were clearly thinking. 'Are you sure you
haven't – you know – *settled* for Sam?'

Melissa was thrown, not because she cared a jot what other
people thought but because she suddenly worried that, deep
down, this might be precisely what Sam thought. The upshot
was she had in recent weeks made a point of at least trying to say
more often how much he meant to her.

'*You do know that I love you, Sam...*'

Small wonder he had suddenly proposed.

Melissa crossed her legs, adjusting the lever holding the
food tray in place to a perfect 180 degrees and then reaching
across quietly to do the same to Sam's. *Shit.* She had wanted to

reassure him and ended up doing precisely the opposite. She took out the flight magazine from the pocket and again began to not read it.

She was trying now not to think about the dreadful kerfuffle at the check-in desk. Melissa closed her eyes. All her fault – the giant suitcase rejected on the grounds it exceeded the maximum weight for a single item of luggage. Her swearing and distraught then – certain the holiday was now off. Sam rolling his eyes but then quickly solving the crisis by buying a soft bag from the nearest kiosk and transferring all the heaviest shit from the case. This had, alarmingly, included the grey silk zipper pouch containing her mother's book, and Melissa had panicked. Almost told Sam about it on the spot because she didn't want the journal crushed in the smaller, bright pink bag. But no. She very much needed to read it on her own first. To work out, also on her own, how the hell she was going to tell her father…

The words on the in-flight magazine now blurred. A metallic jangling sound then drew Melissa's eye to the end of the aisle where the cabin crew were setting up the drinks trolley.

Four and a half hours…

The other shock. She had no idea the flying time to Cyprus was so long. That had amused Sam also, as she had grabbed the flight magazine for the map when the pilot confirmed it over the intercom.

Did you not check the map when we booked this, Melissa?
Of course I checked…

Melissa glanced again at Sam, now so deeply asleep that even the noise of the trolley did not stir him.

The truth?

Her reaction to the whole proposal thing was irrational, confusing and a bloody mess. Melissa did not understand herself why she was so unsure about getting married and so had not the foggiest chance of explaining it to anyone. In the restaurant, she had argued that it shouldn't matter. *Only a piece of paper.* But she could see this now stirring the same old doubts about their history.

Only for her, it wasn't about doubt; at least not doubt over Sam. It was about something else. Something she couldn't quite put her finger on yet and didn't actually want to think about…

Melissa was aged precisely four and a half when she met Sam – enrolled in the Sacre Coeur primary school as a sop to her mother's Catholic guilt. Eleanor was what Max frequently described as a 'lapsed catholic'. Not quite an atheist but certainly heading that way.

But Eleanor, Max explained, had made that first sacrifice of principle, so common among parents picking schools for their children. The Sacre Coeur was the best state school in their area and so what was a little hypocrisy when it was your child's future? Eleanor and Max apparently reasoned that Melissa should make her own decision about faith when she was grown up herself. Meantime she should be taught the Catholic way with her parents on hand to dilute the scariest bits.

The strategy inevitably backfired. Melissa decided she was to become a nun – an obsession that lasted alarmingly into the third year, trumped only by the arrival of a striking new altar boy called Michael. This first infatuation came around the same time an older boy in the school called Samuel Winters began inexplicably to accompany Melissa on her walk to school, offering to carry her satchel.

'I don't need you to carry my satchel. It's not heavy.' Melissa liked Samuel very much but had not the foggiest idea where his sudden interest in her blessed satchel came from. Still. He was funny and could do impressions of all the teachers. He was kind and popular but he was four years older than her – hanging out with the big crowd, which rather scared her.

After Eleanor's death, Melissa finished her stint at the Sacre Coeur then sat the 11-plus early to progress to the nearest girls' grammar school, which was a forty-minute bus journey.

Michael the altar boy went on to the mixed Catholic secondary school, which was a temporary source of conflict between Melissa and her father. Samuel the Satchel, as she had come to know him, had long since gone on to the boys' grammar school and she saw him only occasionally when they caught the same bus. On these rare occasions, Sam would sometimes sit with Melissa for the journey home, only desisting when his friends bombarded them with whistles.

'I've no idea why they do that,' Melissa complained. 'It's not as if we like each other in that way. Is it?'

It was not until the agony of A levels that Melissa bumped into Sam more regularly again. He was on the long haul studying Architecture at university and so was around only during the holidays when he managed to get a job at the local music shop. Melissa and her friends would often hang out there, using the booths to listen to CDs, and to her surprise, a number of her friends seemed to be in thrall to Samuel the Satchel.

'Why didn't you tell us you knew him?' her close friend Emily whispered one Saturday.

'Who?'

'Him.'

Melissa had glanced across at Sam who was smiling in her direction.

'I think he likes you, Melissa.'

'Oh don't be ridiculous. We've been friends since we were in primary school. That's all.'

'You think?'

'I do.'

'Well, good. Because I am hoping you can get him to notice me.'

'You saying you fancy him?'

'Duh, Melissa. Of course I fancy him. Everybody fancies him.'

Melissa would remember this moment always. She put the CD in her hand back in its slot on the shelf and looked again at Sam. By this time he was serving an older woman, who was in animated conversation about the soundtrack for some musical. Melissa noticed with no little amusement that even this older woman was trying to flirt with him.

Why it had not occurred to her before then that Sam would be a target for this kind of attention, she had no idea. She examined his jawline and felt her head shrink back into its neck.

Do you know that it makes you look like a tortoise when you do that…

Melissa listened to the echo as she watched him serving the customer across the record shop floor.

Good God. He really was quite striking these days. It was not so much that she had not noticed this, but rather that she had not registered that it had any significance for her.

'So do you not fancy him then, Melissa?'

She did not know how to answer this. Sam was Sam. Sam was the older boy who walked her to school. The boy who helped her with her roller skates in the local park sometimes. The boy who did great impressions of the teachers. How could she answer a question like that?

Sam was Sam.

And then everything changed when Melissa started university herself. She was reading English Literature, which her father had actively encouraged, despite others around being a good deal less supportive. *And what precisely is she going to do with a degree in English Literature? Read for a living?*

Max, of course, had been a nightmare when it came to UCAS. He knew all the rankings and he knew all the insider gossip. And so on the grounds of teenage conflict alone, Melissa resisted every single piece of advice and plumped for Nottingham. The course looked good and the shops looked good. Also it was one of the few universities that Max had not actively promoted.

'Why would you want to go to Nottingham? This is not about some bloody boy is it?'

'Of course it's not about some boy. I just like the sound of the course. Very traditional.'

Max didn't know any of the professors at Nottingham University.

And so that settled it. Melissa would go to Nottingham.

What she did not know until two weeks into the term was that Samuel the Satchel was finishing the first part of the slog that was Architecture at Nottingham.

'You're here. Good God. I didn't know you were here.'

She happened across him near the library, still thick with fresher's flu, dark bags under her eyes and a messenger bag containing her laptop across her middle.

'If you offer to carry my bloody bag, I will have to hit you.'

She gave him a hug, shocked at the very physical pleasure at her face close in to his neck for the very first time. Then instantly embarrassed. Awkward and surprised also that he smelled so very good.

'Goodness. Nice smell. Is that actually aftershave?' She was now pulling back and fidgeting with her hair.

'Present from my mum.'

'Well it makes a change. All the guys in my house stink.' Wishing now that she had done her face. Washed her hair that morning. At least put on some mascara.

'And that's not sexist at all?'

'So how the hell are you? Oh God. It's good to see you, Sam.'

'And you. A very nice shock. So – you settling in OK?'

'Loving it. Though dog-tired. Can't hack the hours yet.'

'Fancy coffee?'

'Yeah, I do, actually.'

And so it finally *began.*

Melissa sat there over coffee, watching, as he told her all about his course, about the university and about all the best places to study and socialise and which agent to use for a house in the second year and which bars had the cheapest drink prices and where he was planning to do his year out before the slog of the second part of his Architecture studies. She was sort of listening and sort of in some kind of daze. Because in reality she was right back in that music shop, looking across at him, at the perfect line of his jaw and the unusual shade and the warm and very open expression in his eyes. Green. Yes. Looking at him again with a completely different lens on the camera.

'I really had no idea that you were here. At this uni? Did you ever mention it to me, Sam? That you were coming here? Nottingham?'

'Don't think so. Why do you ask?'

'I don't know. It just feels really weird.'

'Nice weird or horrid weird?'

'Nice weird.'

'Good. So does that mean that I can finally ask you out for a drink without you doing your tortoise impression…?'

A very loud clearing of the throat suddenly… 'Excuse me. I'm sorry, madam. But I was wondering if you would like a drink?' The steward's raised tone confirmed this was not the first request. Melissa physically started. A couple of passengers turned as her foot hit the back of the seat in front.

'Sorry. I'm so sorry. Miles away. Two bottles of water, please. Oh – and some crisps. Any flavour. Doesn't matter.' She turned back to Sam who stirred momentarily at the noise but then rolled his shoulder over, trying awkwardly to nestle into the headrest of his seat, still asleep – mouth now gaping.

Melissa felt her pulse in her ear. The trolley trundled noisily past. A man stood up in the now vacant aisle to remove a small case from the overhead locker which made Melissa think again of all the luggage in the hold. The soft pink bag they bought at the kiosk. She was staring at the little cartons of crisps and then at the passengers across the aisle who had pre-ordered hot food. One older woman was tentatively dipping a plastic fork into what looked like some kind of pot roast. Or moussaka. Or lasagne. Or God knows what. It smelled terrible.

And now Melissa was thinking – why food? Why had her mother filled a journal with recipes? Melissa was a pretty average, basic cook but not an enthusiastic one. She did not understand why people made such an unholy fuss in the kitchen. Did not really have the patience for it, or understand why people devoted so much time when there were so many good restaurants and takeaways. And Waitrose. I mean – why had her mother not simply written letters? A diary? When there was so very much to say?

She twisted the cap from her bottle of water and took a swig.

Why food?

Easter Biscuits

8 oz self-raising flour
5 oz butter
4 oz sifted castor or icing sugar
1 medium egg
Dash of good vanilla essence... or a touch of cinnamon is nice too.

Preheat oven to 180 and grease baking trays. Sift flour and salt and rub into butter. Add sugar, plus your choice of flavouring, and mix. Add sufficient beaten egg to give a very stiff dough. Knead the dough lightly on a floured board until smooth. Wrap in foil and chill for 30 minutes. Roll out thinly and cut out circular biscuits. Place these on baking trays (not too close as they expand a bit) and prick with a fork. Bake for 12-15 minutes until pale gold.

These are firm favourites, Melissa, and you just have to make them. Why they are called Easter biscuits as opposed to Christmas biscuits or Halloween biscuits, I have not the foggiest. Gran just called them Easter biscuits and so that is what they are (though very happily eaten all year round).

I have my own particular memory of these and I am hoping you will too. For me they conjure up a very strong picture of a red, square biscuit tin which my mother kept on the second shelf of her larder (never the first or third; always the second – note). I guess that is what this book is partly about for me. Sharing and passing on to you things that I want to stay important. Family traditions and family memories. The continuum of stories at the stove, if you like. Generation to generation.

My mother was a very good, basic cook, who was indignant, and quite possibly a little snobbish, about the arrival of packets and freezers and anything which carried a 'convenience' tag. True – she came from a generation who had the time and had not yet experienced the chaos of juggling career and family which made mine rather rethink the whole equality battle (that's a whole chapter, for sure. I've started a big section on modern motherhood at the end of the book. I am imagining it may not interest you yet which is why I have set it apart, but I like the idea of leaving my thoughts and tips for when they become relevant to you). Anyway, Mum, bless her, had both the will and the *time* to cook and so cook she certainly did.

These biscuits seemed to be available in our house as I grew up pretty much all the time – although the strict rule was that we had to ask for access to that red, metal tin on the second shelf.

In our home, as I write, you may well remember they are a holiday treat and always gone in a flash.

The photo I have included alongside this recipe is from one of our trips to Cornwall when baking these cookies with you was a given. Insanity, your father always said, to bake when there was a wonderful pastry shop along the seafront and I was supposed to be on holiday. But that was all down to the juggling. The guilt at trying to combine a career with being a halfway decent mother, Melissa, which was not as easy as I had anticipated and there were not as many cookies baked in our house as I would have liked, that's for sure.

But as you see from the picture, you loved to help me from quite a young age and so it felt like the perfect thing to do on holiday. It made us so very happy – you and me. And your father certainly never complained about helping us to eat everything.

And then there is this other, less pleasant thing I have to tell you. It is not that I want to upset you and I am hoping that you can set it apart from the whole recipes thing. I don't actually like to link the two at all. The pleasure of the cooking… and this other stuff. But you know I promised honesty in this journal and one of my motives here is to be open and also to try to keep you safe.

It was on this holiday in Cornwall that I found the lump. The truth? I was brushing down flour that I had managed to sift all down my front while baking and as I smoothed down firmly, brush after brush, I felt this knot at the top of my left breast, near the armpit. I thought it was the bra at first and I didn't want to let you see that I was concerned. As the cookie dough was resting, I went to the bathroom to check properly and there was no mistaking it.

I really don't know how I had not felt it in the shower before then? A knotty little lump on the surface but which went much deeper in when I had a proper feel around.

Anyway, the point is I was stupid, Melissa. I worried and worried for the rest of the day and then I just sort of pushed it aside – blanked it, if you like – and got on with the holiday. Most stupid of all, I did not go to the doctor immediately when we got back. What I decided to do was to monitor what I assumed was some fluid-filled cyst or the like. I remember convincing myself that if I waited long enough it would surely just 'resolve'. Go away – like some inflammation.

I 'monitored' it for a quite a lot of weeks before I finally accepted that it wasn't going to go of its own accord and that's when I took myself to the doctor.

I wonder now, of course, if it could have made any difference if I had acted sooner. Probably not. Let's hope not. But I am telling you, woman to woman now, the truth because I need to be sure that you would never be so silly yourself, Melissa.

Dad will probably have told you the facts already – that my illness, both in nature and the unlucky speed of spread was extremely rare for someone my age. I do not want to worry you unnecessarily, but with that said you really do need to look after yourself, Melissa. To check yourself properly and often. My understanding is this is not familial, and the last thing I want is to instil paranoia. I don't know of any other case of breast cancer in a close relative so I refuse to believe you are at increased risk.

But for all that, I have talked to Dad and asked him to press upon you the need to be sensible, *just as all women should*. He will obviously find it difficult – talking about it. So this feels like the right time, as you move properly into full-on adulthood, now to have my own loving, little nag.

Eleanor, as usual, read through her words as the ink dried and wondered if this was too much too soon.

She tried to imagine how it might feel for Melissa skimming the very same page, and suddenly felt the need to touch it. The page. She kept her hand there for several minutes – reluctant to lift it.

Eleanor had allowed herself to cry only once. It was at the appointment when the dreaded word 'metastatic' was added to her vocabulary. She had started out shocked but almost aggressively optimistic when the 'c' word was first mentioned. A spell of disorientation and then full-on fighting spirit. She was so young, she babbled to Max in the car en route to the clinic as they awaited the results of more tests and scans. *It would be an early diagnosis and it would be fine. Wouldn't it? And I mean – they could do absolute wonders these days. With reconstruction, people would hardly be able to tell. She had seen this programme where a woman had actually felt she looked better after surgery than before. No. Seriously.*

She would not share with Melissa how badly the shock had hit her when the consultant explained about spread. And staging. They say that patients hear nothing after the word 'cancer' but that was not how it was with Eleanor. Not at all. She heard cancer on the first confirmation of diagnosis and she thought – OK. Shit. But we fight this? Yes? So tell me how we fight this.

It was not until that later appointment, when they had taken chunks and put a wire right into her breast and checked the horrid bits of tissue in their horrid little labs. No. It was not until she heard the words 'stage four' and 'metastatic'; not until they were looking at scan results and talking inexplicably about her liver and her lungs that she stopped listening.

Her doctor had warned her not to turn to the new internet service which he knew she had access to via Max at the university. 'If you have any questions ask me and not this new world wide web? OK?' But Eleanor had already been reading up. Anything and everything that she could find. Pamphlets. Features. Research papers. And so while Max listened intently to the consultant, starting to talk treatments and timelines, Eleanor was already in her mind's eye back at home – among the sticker books and fairy wands; among the biscuit cutters and clouds of icing sugar; staring at her beautiful daughter.

CHAPTER 8
Melissa – 2011

As Sam put the hire car forms into the glove compartment, neither of them mentioned the case – squashed now into the back of the Clio. Much too big for the boot. Melissa took out a guide book and map.

'If you'd let me get a new sat nav, Mel, we could have added the programme for Cyprus.'

'I can map read. I hate sat navs.'

Sam was grinning – brighter-eyed from his sleep on the plane. 'What?'

'Nothing, Melissa. You are a great map reader. I'm very much looking forward to it.'

She was pleased to see his spirits lifting; feeling more positive now. With the new pink bag and her mother's journal safely in the boot, she was thinking that perhaps the trip was going to be OK after all. Time for her to deal with the journal and to build bridges also.

Melissa turned to Sam as he suddenly frowned at the new dashboard.

'So when would you like to do Troodos, Sam?' Yes. The break could be what they both needed.

'Hadn't really thought about it. Don't mind.' Sam pulled away, turning down the sun visor and experimenting with the indicators.

Just so long as the pact held. Their agreement after the restaurant was no spiralling into dramatic heart-to-hearts during this holiday. Sam had agreed to give Melissa time out on the proposal and she was thinking the Troodos trip could help them both. A distraction.

The route to their resort further north was, in the event, straightforward. Good signposting and the convenience of driving on the left meant Sam was adjusting more quickly than usual to the unfamiliar car.

Melissa reached out to stroke the back of his neck. 'Well how about we settle in for a couple of days. Flop. And then do Troodos – say Monday?'

Sam turned to catch her eye, his expression softening.

Cyprus had been his idea from the off. They had each wanted somewhere hot to recharge their batteries after a busy stretch at work. But Cyprus meant Sam could also include a very personal gesture for his Grandfather Edmund. He had died eight months earlier, but in the weeks before his illness had been sharing with both Sam and Melissa his ambitious plans to write an autobiography.

Much as she liked Sam's grandfather, Melissa had to bite away a smile as he asked how one went about acquiring a literary agent. *And did she think it would sell well? His autobiography?*

Diplomacy aside, the many ensuing conversations about his project became more interesting. The story was to include details of his time serving in the army in Cyprus in the late 1950s. After his grandfather's death, Sam gained access to the files on his computer. He was very close to his family – Sam – and was very shaken by the story Edmund had wanted to share. He had shown Melissa all the research material and notes and there was one episode in particular – written up in draft form only – which had deeply moved them both.

During the Cyprus troubles of that period, the British Army was deployed to try to put down anti-British insurgents operating in the Troodos mountains. Edmund's story centred on an early summer's day when several different British battalions were operating in the same mountain area. On this particular day their boundaries became confused. Edmund never quite got to the bottom of it but the outcome was that one group of British soldiers fired on another and he witnessed a young soldier's death as a result of this friendly fire.

'I held him in my arms,' he wrote. 'Just a boy. I really had not noticed how young we all were until that very moment.'

Edmund's notes explained that as a child in school he read a book on the First World War in which observers said soldiers often called for their mothers at the end. He had disapproved of the remark, dismissing it as sentimental. Pacifist propaganda designed to undermine recruitment. An insult to bravery. But in the draft of his story, Edmund's attitude completely changed.

'I must tell the truth here and the truth is this. He was just a boy – that lad in the Troodos Mountains. Nineteen tops. And it completely broke my heart because, in those final moments, he was very, very afraid, for all that we tried to do for him. And there is no shame in my telling you this, that he wanted one thing and one thing only in his final moments. Which, indeed, was his mother.'

Melissa became conscious of the discomfort from staring as she turned this line over and over in her head. She blinked several times at the dusty vegetation – just a blur as it raced past the car window.

'Of course I don't know where Granddad was stationed and where exactly it all happened,' Sam was fumbling with the controls to try to find the windscreen wash. 'But that doesn't really matter, I guess.'

Edmund had written of his plan, once the book was finished, to revisit Cyprus and lay flowers for the soldier and his family. But that of course had never happened.

Sam's idea was to make a trip into Troodos on his Grandfather's behalf. He was explaining now to Melissa more details from his research; that the official British Cemetery was tricky to access and, in any case, the British dead were apparently buried in the 'no-man's' land controlled by the UN, twixt the Cypriot south and Turkish-controlled north.

'All a bit sensitive these days and I'm not for rocking the boat or upsetting anyone. I was thinking of something low key. You know – find a church. Light a candle. Pay respects. What do you think, Mel?'

'Definitely. I told you. I think it's a really lovely idea.'

'OK then. Monday.'

Melissa still felt very tired herself on the drive but was surprised by a second wind as they arrived in the small and largely unspoilt resort of Polis to find their apartment even better than detailed online. It was spacious and had been completely refurbished since the photo shoot, with an airy sitting room, a vibrant colour scheme and a huge, modern bathroom tiled floor to ceiling. It had a small shared pool with cafe alongside and was walking distance from the beach.

There was just one problem now dawning as Melissa got her bearings, moving swiftly from room to room. The apartment was entirely open-plan. No door to separate the bedroom from the sitting area with its additional sofa bed. She had not noticed this when they booked and was wondering now how she would find the space and privacy to deal with her mother's journal.

Melissa still felt uncomfortable keeping it from Sam. But she needed the space to get her head around it all before deciding if it was right to tell him before her father.

Sam liked a lie-in but could easily surprise her as he had last night, and any light, even the lamp, was bound to disturb him.

Melissa frowned and glanced through the patio doors. There was no way she would take the book to the pool. It could get wet; damaged. Also the terraces and sunbathing area were clearly visible from their balcony. She felt nervous suddenly, even thinking about the journal. The image of her mother writing it.

'So you don't mind, Mel, do you, if I take a stroll into town? Check out where to eat later?' Sam, standing behind her, sounded sheepish – entirely unaware that this, their familiar arrival dynamic, was now to be a gift. Melissa liked to swim before unpacking while Sam liked to get his bearings. Did not settle until he had worked out the lie of the land.

'Sorry?'

'I was wondering if you minded me taking a recce? Earmark a restaurant.'

'Oh right. No. Not at all. You go,' Melissa smiled and then watched from the balcony as he turned the corner, pausing for a moment to run his hand through his hair – that familiar little gesture of self-consciousness. As ever, he was also looking upwards. Even as a child, Sam, the born architect, had done this – walked with a permanent tilt to his chin, forever checking out the buildings, the balconies and the rooftops. And now he was noticing the signposting to the town square, turning to disappear from view. Melissa took her mother's book from the zipper case in the foul pink bag, heart racing to find that – no; it had not been crushed.

Cheese straws...

...and then to three of the strips I rolled inside a huge quantity of really strong cayenne...

Oh Lordy! I thought we had given him a heart attack. We hadn't of course, and then how we laughed. That made it all so worth it. Can't tell you, Melissa, how happy it makes me to think of it.

I do so hope you will remember how much we all laughed...

Melissa had been reading for ten, maybe fifteen minutes tops and closed the book on the shiny, pine table by the kitchenette – aware of the oddest sensation of *returning*. Back suddenly in this strange room. She stared down at the unfamiliar wood – a little too orange, its heavy lacquer stamped with circular stains from hot mugs – and was again struggling to find the scene that her mother had been describing. Jaws? She remembered some body board with a shark – at least she thought she did. There was a photograph of her carrying it in a frame at her father's house, so maybe she was just remembering that? But – no. Try as she might, she could not work it out. Did not remember the joke with the cheese straws at all.

Melissa stood up and paced. She went over to the window, hands on her hips, to watch the activity by the pool. There was a father teaching his son to dive. Holding his stomach as he bent his back to the right angle, stretching out his arms straighter and pressing his hands together.

Melissa paced. To and fro, searching for the memory. But – no. She turned back to watch the child complete the dive, the father applauding as the boy surfaced.

So – where was it? Her picture?

She thought of Sam, always babbling with stories of larks and of laughs as kids with his older brother Marcus.

Melissa had read somewhere that most people could recall events from around the age of three. That technically gave her five years of memories with her mother. So where precisely had she put them?

Melissa placed the book quickly back into the zipped case and concealed it among T-shirts, which she unpacked from the monster case into the shelves of the bedroom wardrobe. She then found her swimming things and headed out to the pool. Five lengths of breast stroke. Five of crawl. Five of butterfly stroke.

By the time she had returned to the apartment and fully unpacked, Sam was back – looking for a nap ahead of their evening out.

Later they enjoyed their first dinner at an excellent taverna – right on the town square, with children playing in a disused fountain nearby. Melissa watched them mesmerised, at first smiling and then her expression changing as a ripple of discomfort and realisation began slowly to move through her.

Sam watched the children also but pointedly made no reference. Instead they each talked – only upbeat – about the food and the wine and how lovely it was that Polis was so unspoilt. Not high-rise. Neither of them mentioning the subject now temporarily taboo.

Their future.

The children playing in the fountain.

They spent the weekend relaxing and mostly reading – talking very little – and then rose early on Monday for Troodos. It was impossible to know precisely where Edmund had been patrolling and so they chose a church at random on the map, some forty minutes within the forest. The journey took longer than they had expected – unable to resist regular stops for photographs of the spectacular views from the winding mountain roads. En route to the village originally earmarked, they happened upon an utterly charming and particularly atmospheric hamlet, with women crocheting and gossiping around a neat, village square.

After coffee and pastries at a cafe, they headed through a stone arch off the square to find a cool and quiet Byzantine church where Sam decided there was no need to travel any further. This was perfect. He lit two candles – one for his grandfather and one for the man he had held in his arms all those years ago. Melissa watched the blokey awkwardness as Sam stood utterly still, hands on his hips. He had been close to his grandfather who taught him to fish and in his will had left him all his kit. It was in the garage and Melissa caught Sam just staring at it some days. Standing ever so still for a moment. Hands on hips. Just like this.

She waited, saying nothing, until he walked ahead outside and then, as a memento for him, took a picture of the two candles against the background of the stained-glass window before quietly lighting a third candle for all the Cypriot young men who had been lost. And one for her mother also.

They had parked the hire car on a steep road on the outskirts of the village, unsure how difficult it would be to find a spot in the centre and it was as they walked back to the vehicle, around a wide bend that everything changed.

From the quiet and the stillness of the church there was suddenly the intrusion of a tremendous roar. Melissa was walking a few steps behind Sam who had struck up a conversation with a young, local man as the roar registered. She turned to see a great swirl of dust as the motorcycle lost control on the bend. With tremendous screeching, it then slid at an angle directly towards Sam.

And then everything happened very, very quickly.

And also in slow motion.

CHAPTER 9
Eleanor – 1994

Eleanor flipped down the sun visor to check her face in the mirror and in leaning forward caught a glimpse of Melissa in the back – the new body board still across her lap.

'You can put that down, you know – sweetie.'

'I'm going to call it Jaws.'

'You haven't seen *Jaws*,' Eleanor glared across at Max as he indicated to overtake. 'At least – I hope you haven't?'

'Daddy let me see the nice bits. The bit where the little boy copies his dad. And the bit where they're all on the beach and—'

'I thought that was our little secret, darling…'

'Tell me, you didn't let her see *Jaws*?'

'Only a very little bit by accident. No gore.'

'So that's why she wanted the body board with the shark?'

Max shrugged.

'I'm surprised you haven't put her off the sea completely. Oh Max. Really.'

'The sharks are only in America and Australia, Mummy. Not in Cornwall. And in the film they killed it. Daddy was watching and I was doing colouring.'

'I switched channels, Eleanor. It's no big deal. I didn't even realise she was looking. As soon as I did, I turned over. It was ten minutes. Maximum.'

'Unbelievable.'

'You let her watch *Dr Who* videos.'

'Yes – but not the Cybermen.'

'Excuse me?'

'Oh come on, Max. *Jaws*? She's seven, Max.'

'I'm nearly eight.'

Max and Eleanor exchanged a conciliatory glance.

'I'm sorry, Eleanor. I'll be more careful. She didn't see anything gross, I promise you.'

'How long till we get there, Mummy?'

'One more coffee stop and then about an hour.'

Twice a year they made this trip. It was Max's idea. He had been taken to Cornwall for bucket and spade holidays by his own parents and wanted Melissa to know the ups and downs of the old-fashioned seaside break. The zip of a wetsuit in a cold wind. Tea in flasks. Sand in sandwiches. Eleanor, whose parents had both taught, spent every summer in France as a child – gîtes mostly – so was less convinced, but Max's knowledge of the best coves and beaches around the Lizard peninsula very soon won her over.

By the time Melissa was toddling, Max had taken up a new post at the university and, with a more flexible timetable, they often managed a long weekend in addition to a week at Easter and during the summer. Eleanor and Melissa, over time, became as enthusiastic as Max – loving the coastal walks, the steep streets of cottages tumbling down to the sea and the early evening spent watching children race crabs on the shoreline.

Melissa would watch, mouth gaping – just that little bit too shy to join in – but shrieking with laughter when some of the competitors set off in entirely the wrong direction.

She also grew to love all manner of seafood, just like her mother – with Max knowing exactly where to buy straight off the boats.

They stayed, wherever possible, in the same cottage overlooking the beach in Porthleven – a small and unspoilt fishing port with art galleries and a good choice of restaurants, cafes and gift shops where Melissa loved to buy shells and polished pebble pendants while Max watched the boats returning with their catch.

Sometimes Eleanor wondered if they should cast their own net wider but was so tired by the end of each term that the familiarity and the rhythm of the same cottage was too much to resist. Beach View, the three-bed they rented, was owned by a couple in their late fifties – the Huberts – who lived in the centre of Porthleven themselves and used the income to boost their early retirement. They were sweet and considerate – leaving a tray set for tea with scones, home-made jam and clotted cream in the fridge for every new visitor.

'Yay! Cream tea!' Melissa would chime as they opened the stable door into the kitchen to clock the treat already set out on the table. And Eleanor had come to love the rhythm and the echo of all these things. The sense of a memory being etched deeper and deeper with every repetition.

Truth was, she hoped and prayed that the Huberts would never sell the place; that they would leave it to their own children to let – so that one day Max and Eleanor would come here with Melissa and her husband and grandchildren, and they would tell the story of how they found the place – just the way Max's parents would talk when they sometimes joined them for a few days. Stories about Max on the beach when he was a little boy.

'You OK?'

'Yeah. Just daydreaming,' Eleanor smiled as Max deposited bags in the hall while Melissa headed straight for the fridge to check for the cream.

It was only later as they unpacked Melissa's small bag that Eleanor caught herself trying not to look at the second single bed in her daughter's room. The agreed pact was that they didn't dwell on it. Her and Max. They were still trying – *technically*. Had been trying for more than three years now, but Max felt there was no need to be panicked into fertility treatment. Not while they were still so young. And Eleanor was trying very, very hard not to panic.

Technically.

'So tomorrow we go shopping for food. And I was thinking we could get the stuff to make cookies. Give us something nice to do if it rains, Melissa?' Back in the kitchen, she was watching Melissa spread an alarming quantity of jam onto half a scone as Max rifled through a drawer for more cutlery.

'Do you know that in Devon they put the cream on first?' Max interceded.

'Can we get pink icing?'

'For the scones?'

'No, silly Daddy. For the biscuits we make.'

'Cream first would be ridiculous,' Eleanor pulled a face secretly to Max as Melissa used a knife to smooth cream from a spoon onto her generous puddle of jam. 'Pink icing? Sounds lovely darling.'

'You know there is a pastry shop right along the front? If you want biscuits and cakes…'

'You don't get it, do you?'

'What?'

'Four days with no head of department having kittens over when these new Ofsted inspectors are going to rock up. Four days with no emergency investigations into how a teacher could get locked in a bloody cupboard by second years.'

'That really happened?'

'That really happened.'

'And you think – let's bake?'

'Yes I do. Bliss.'

'Mummy said bloody.'

'All right, Melissa. Mummy is very naughty.'

Max pulled a face. 'I'll never understand women.'

'It's the penis, Max. Gets in the way.'

'Mummy said penis.'

'No she didn't. She said it was a heinous crime not to under-stand women. Now how about we finish this cream tea then we can get the beach stuff together and try out Jaws.'

It was not, in fact, until Wednesday that the baking tins came out – the weather being kinder than was fair to expect for Easter. Two full days of glorious sunshine and then a downpour so that Max was out fishing under a large umbrella – Eleanor reflecting that she did not understand men either – while she and Melissa left the cookie dough in the fridge to rest.

Eleanor sprinkled flour across the kitchen table as Melissa selected cutters from the plastic box she had brought.

'I like the snowman. Can we use the snowman?'

'Well, it's not really the season for snowmen, is it honey? Why don't you look for the rabbit. There are some heart shapes too. Should be in there somewhere. Have a look.'

And then Eleanor noticed that she had managed somehow to sprinkle more flour over her jumper than the table and began brushing it down off her chest – the rhythm fast and firm, wishing she had brought a full apron, and then suddenly interrupted.

She paused and brushed the left breast downwards again. Eleanor frowned. She must have caught her finger on some twist in the bra fabric. She used three fingers to press the fabric smooth. But it would not be stroked smooth.

'Can you just give mummy a minute? I just need to wash my hands.'

In the bathroom – a complete change in her body temperature as if she was outside suddenly. A cold draught through her whole body. She wanted to look. And yet she didn't want to look.

Eleanor moved across to the larger mirror above the fitted towel rail, pulled her sweater quickly over her head and moved her bra down on the left side. She felt softly at first and then more firmly. That draught again.

She sat down on the edge of the bath.

'I've found the rabbit, Mummy,' Melissa's voice was right outside the bathroom door.

Eleanor's pulse in both her ear and in her fingers too as she felt under her left armpit. Another bulge.

'OK, honey. Mummy's just coming through.'

She washed her hands, put her jumper back on and splashed her face with cold water.

'You look funny, Mummy. Your hair's wet.'

'I was just a bit hot.'

Eleanor began to fuss with the selection of cutters, picking out a star, a heart and a gingerbread man, her hand trembling slightly as she sprinkled more flour right across the table.

'What's the matter with your eye?' Melissa was still staring intently into her face.

'Nothing. It's fine.'

Eleanor could feel it clearly. The intense and infuriating flickering of her eyelid. Like some tic.

'So come on, then. Let's get these biscuits sorted, shall we?'

CHAPTER 10
Melissa – 2011

Melissa in her mind watched the bike hit Sam – full on. In that first slow-motion version, she saw the scream of metal and dust explode right into him. It was the version that for weeks and months she would replay in her dreams.

But that is not what happened. That image was the raw terror born of prediction and fear and dread. That was the version in which everything ended, right there on that mountain. What actually happened seemed impossible. The bike slid through the dust and the gravel, and the young Cypriot man who'd been talking to Sam as they strolled down the hill suddenly moved at a speed which seemed to not quite fit the picture. As if his movement was being replayed and overlaid within the scene at a different speed. Yes. That is what it was like.

The young man hurled himself impossibly through the air, slamming the full weight of his body into Sam, thrusting him with the momentum towards the other side of the road so that at the point of impact it was his own right leg which remained directly in the path of the bike.

Melissa had to move very quickly herself then, backing into the shade of trees at the other side of the road to avoid the bike and rider as they continued on their slide, stopping eventually much further down the hill while she then ran back upwards towards Sam and his dark-haired saviour – both now lying in the road.

'Oh my God. Sam. Jesus Christ!' kneeling down alongside them – taking in the blood and the ugly rips through flesh into white underneath the stranger's leg but taking in also the relief that they were both wincing. Both sufficiently conscious and OK to feel the pain. Which she was remembering was a good thing. Pain. Consciousness.

And then Melissa became aware of two new sounds. From the top of the hill three people had appeared – an elderly man and woman and a younger very tall and thin man – all shouting in Greek over the roar of a second motorbike.

The shouting continued as the two men hurried down the hill, the second motorbike passing them to join the first and its rider, now on the ground, much further down.

'Stay still. Help is coming,' Melissa had her arm on Sam's shoulder as he and his injured Good Samaritan lay side by side, in shock still but straining now against the immediate pain. She watched the helpers getting closer, waving their hands and shouting even more loudly, again in Greek, to the two motorcyclists as the second was now helping the first back onto his bike.

And then Melissa watched in disbelief as both motorcyclists simply rode off. Just a few more seconds. More dust. And gone.

'Bastards,' she couldn't believe it. 'Hey. What are you doing? Come back!' shouting pointlessly. Randomly. Over and over. 'Come back here, you bastard!'

It was the two men from the village who were now taking charge, the younger producing a phone from his pocket while the older woman walked more slowly towards them. 'I phone for ambulance. Yes?'

'No. No ambulance,' the Cypriot man, who had dived so bravely to push Sam aside, was now biting into his lip. 'Just a bad cut.'

'For God sake, Sam. Look how deep it is. We need to get you both to a hospital.'

The courageous stranger had a long gash, deep to near the bone, it seemed. Sam's injuries were ugly also – a nasty patch of shorn flesh where the gravel had sliced the surface, some of it embedded. Superficial but nasty all the same. They would both need stitches.

'You could have broken something. We need an ambulance,' she was taking out her own mobile, her hand shaking.

The helpers were now talking quickly in Greek to the other injured man before translating for Sam and Melissa. 'He wants to get it stitched at the nearest medical centre. He is saying the hospital will take hours. What about you? Do you want an ambulance?'

'I could get this seen in Polis, Mel. They're right. It will be much quicker. There's a centre right near the apartment.'

'I don't know. I'm not happy about that. And I don't think you should be sitting up. We need to check your neck? Your bones? Jesus…'

'Mel. Please. You need to calm yourself. We're going to be fine. There's no serious damage. Just a rugby tackle. And a very bad landing.' Sam was now reaching out to the young man who had clearly come off worse. 'Are you all right? I am so grateful. So very grateful.'

'But you might have broken something. Fractured something. There could be something internally—' Melissa had her hands up to her head.

'They have gone to fetch my brother – Alexandros. He can help you,' the youngest of their helpers was again on his mobile, speaking in Greek briefly before putting it back in his pocket, then speaking again in Greek to the older man who was nodding. 'He is home on holiday. Alexandros. Working up at the cafe. You need to keep still, I think. He will only be a few minutes.'

Melissa hated that she could not follow the phone conversations – her face betraying her continued panic. Failing to see how a waiter…

'He's a medical student. My brother.'

'Oh right,' she blushed. Still she would have preferred an ambulance but had no idea how long it would take for one to arrive.

Melissa was now looking at Sam's injury.

'It's OK, Mel. These guys are right. An ambulance and hospital will take hours. We're gonna be fine. I'll get this all washed and cleaned up back at the resort. We're all just a bit shaken. It's going to be fine.'

'You want police?' the young Cypriot helper was looking at his watch.

The younger injured man shook his head then turned to Sam who shrugged his agreement.

'OK. No police.'

'But it's a hit-and-run, Sam. The guy should have stopped,' Melissa still couldn't believe what she was hearing. 'We can't let him get away with that.'

'It was an accident.'

'He lost control because he was going too bloody fast.'

'Look. None of us needs it, Mel. The police. The paperwork,' Sam's eyes were wide. 'The whole circus. These guys are tougher. And they're right. We'll be stuck here for bloody hours. Please. Just let it go. We're all right.'

It was at this point that Alexandros joined them – an immediately calming influence who urged everyone to step back while he very methodically checked them over in turn. Their eyes. Their limbs. 'Does this hurt? And this?' flexing their legs and arms and feeling very carefully the flesh at each of their joints. Also their chest and ribs.

'You have both been very lucky. Nothing broken. We can wash the wounds here. Clean you up a bit but you both need stitching.'

'Yes I realise. We will get it done in Polis. There's a medical centre not far from where we're staying. But what about the other guy?'

'There's a place not far from here also. I'll arrange it.' Alexandros had now stood back up and was talking in Greek to the two other men who helped both Sam and his saviour to their feet.

'Let's get you both back up to the cafe to get you washed up. Then – we'll see.' Alexandros' tone remained both calm and kind and Melissa was now placing him. He was the one who had served their coffee and pastries just an hour earlier.

'This is very kind of you, Alexandros. Thank you. Very kind.'

'No problem. But I warn you. I'm only in my third year,' and now he was grinning. 'So – no litigation?'

Sam now managed a smile as he let the men help him further down the road to the hire car which they all decided was a better bet than trying to help the two injured men walk back up the hill. They moved beach towels from the boot to protect the seats from the blood and Melissa drove very slowly with Sam in the front and the other man across the back seat, while Alexandros hurried ahead on foot. By the time they accepted the shoulders of volunteers to guide the patients slowly into the cafe, Alexandros had set up a table through an alcove at the back, with hot water in a bowl into which he had poured some foul-smelling concoction. He had also set out bandages and some sterile dressings from a large, zippered first aid kit.

The older woman, who Alexandros now introduced as his mother, was meanwhile producing small cups of strong coffee.

'Sugar,' she was saying, pointing at the cups. 'Sugar.'

'It's sweet. Please drink it. My mother is right. The sugar will be good for the shock,' Alexandros was smiling as he lifted the Cypriot's injured leg onto a chair to examine the gash more carefully, narrowing his eyes at first and then nodding. 'It's pretty deep and will need several stitches. But – you'll live. I can tape it and arrange a lift. And you two want to get this properly dressed in Polis. Yes?'

'Yes,' Sam broke in before Melissa could fuss further.

'OK. But this must be done today. You'll need to get back to Polis before 4 o'clock. I will ring them. Tell them to expect you?'

'Would you? That would be great. Thank you, Alexandros.' Melissa was sitting down at a second table as his mother brought her a coffee also along with a small pastry – nodding her head and smiling.

And then Alexandros was asking questions. What they were doing in the area? How long they were staying in Cyprus?

'We were just exploring up here,' Melissa said finally, feeling a little guarded about their true motives. 'We heard it was very beautiful.'

'Yes. But no one told you about the problem we have with the motorbikes?' Alexandros was shaking his head. 'They go off road through the woods at night too. Madness.'

He went on to explain that he was studying medicine at the University of Nicosia under a collaboration with the University of London. The scheme involved the early years in Cyprus and then later secondments abroad. He was still working out the terms for his studies overseas.

'Alexandros is going to be a doctor in London,' his mother was beaming as her son sighed.

'Maybe. We'll see,' and then lowering his tone for Melissa and his new patients. 'They have sacrificed a great deal – my family – to help make this happen. So let's all hope so.'

'Well you get top marks from us,' Melissa said, beaming her thanks to his family and friends, more of whom were now crowding into the room, word of the drama having apparently spread.

With the wounds properly washed and dressed, Melissa was feeling a good deal calmer – revived also by the sugar in the pastry.

'So – are you sure you're OK to drive, Mel?' Sam was looking right into her face. 'I know you don't like mountain roads.'

'Yeah. Yeah. Of course. If Alexandros is sure this is OK, we should get straight off. Soon as possible.'

She said her own thanks again to the young man who had so bravely swept Sam out of the bike's path, offering her business card if he was ever in England. Melissa then tried to offer money for the drinks and as a thank you to the cafe, but Alexandros and his mother shook their heads and so she took a business card from the counter, thinking of an online review at the very least, as volunteers helped Sam back out to the car.

He had been given painkillers plus a little local anaesthetic and temporary butterfly stitches but was still pale and clearly pretty uncomfortable.

She drove very slowly – Sam silent with his eyes closed now.

'Hang in there. Should only be about an hour.'

And then she was embarrassed as she made it back onto the main route and had to fight hard to keep it in: the wave of delayed shock which had not yet evolved into relief. Reaching into her pocket for a tissue. Feeling it all over again – that terrifying split second in which she was sure of a different outcome.

Melissa had to let out little puffs of air, making a strange noise. Her breathing all over the place. In the end she had to pull into a layby.

'I'm sorry, Sam. I just need a minute.'

CHAPTER 11
Max – 2011

The lurch again.

Max tried very hard not to even look at Anna who was entirely oblivious and utterly professional, shuffling papers, her reading glasses on the top of her head like sunglasses. He glanced at the phone in his hand and put it quickly in his pocket. Still no return text from Melissa. *Why was it she couldn't just acknowledge a text? One second it would take…*

He looked back up. Could actually not fathom it at all – this ridiculous reaction every time Anna walked into the room. She was not the kind of woman who dressed for attention and Max was, ordinarily, no kind of flirt at work – most especially since the debacle that was Deborah – his one relationship at the university.

So why the hell was he sitting here right this moment, fighting the urge to examine, again, the little dip at the base of Anna's throat? Did other women not have precisely the same biology? Why this neck? Why now?

No, Max.

He was ashamed to find his gaze darting to her hand. No wedding ring.

Stop this.

'Is this a bad time again?'

'No. No. Absolutely not. Fire away, Anna.' He lifted his jug of coffee by way of invitation and began fussing with the milk as she began to discuss her seminar group. By the time he had swung back around with a second mug, she looked for a moment startled. Max had very deliberately not offered her coffee on any of their previous weekly encounters.

No wedding ring.

And then – as he was pouring the coffee, she was suddenly both smiling and apparently, for the first time, actually relaxing. It was a broad and full-on smile of genuine relief with absolutely perfect teeth.

'Do you have any plans for lunch, Anna?'

'I'm sorry?'

Shut up, Max.

'It's just I was planning to grab a sandwich at the Panier Cafe and if you wanted to join me, we could talk some more then?'

Jesus Christ, Max... Do you learn nothing? He was remembering Melissa's face when he shared with her the debacle over Deborah.

Anna was meantime now looking at her watch. 'Well. It's just – I normally do a run this lunchtime actually.'

'Oh right. You run, Anna?'

'Well. More walking with bounce – but I'm in training for a half marathon with my son. In danger of rank humiliation.'

'Oh right. Well. Good for you – for giving it a go, I mean. That's excellent. Really. Jolly good.'

A son? Of course she's spoken for. Just because she doesn't wear a bloody ring, Max, doesn't mean that...

'Though – the sandwich was a nice offer. Thank you.'

'No problem. We'll finish up here then.'

'Right.'

'Good. Excellent.'

That evening Max put in an extra run of three kilometres before supper. He pushed himself really hard, bending down for rather

longer than usual to catch his breath before facing the steps up
to his front door.

And then, as soon as he was inside, he couldn't help himself
– standing sweaty and still out of breath as he dialled.

'Hi. It's me.'

'As in Max me?'

'Yes. As in Max me. You OK?'

'Yes. I'm fine. Just finishing a new watercolour for the gallery.
I've been a bit lazy lately and they've been nagging. Anyway. It's
come out rather well so I'm rewarding myself with a second glass
of extremely good Sancerre.'

Max glanced at the sofa, then down at his sweaty shorts and
walked over to the window. The light was just fading and across
the park he could see the first warm glimmers of a sunset over
the grouping of three oaks. He suddenly felt very hot, wishing
that he was back out there. In the breeze. Beneath the oaks.

'The sky's good here. How about you?'

'Not so special. Cloud cover.'

'Shame.'

'So you were right about Greece. More trouble, I mean.'

'Yes. Absolute shambles. But someone will blink soon.'

She paused for a time.

'OK. So are you going to tell me what's the matter, Max, or
am I going to have to guess?'

'I was thinking – wondering actually if I could come and see
you tomorrow.'

'Oh right. I see,' there was a distinct change now in Sophie's
tone. In Max's head one voice wanted to suck the words back in.
Another wishing he had faced up to this long ago.

This was breaking the rules.

Max and Sophie saw each other on the first weekend of every
month. Her suggestion. Her rules. They had dinner, they went

to the theatre and sometimes to an art exhibition and afterwards they had extremely enjoyable sex. But they did not ring each other in between these encounters and Max no longer asked questions about the rhythm of the rest of her life.

Sophie was intelligent, beautiful and like no other woman he had ever met. She did not do commitment or conventional relationships, eschewing all the usual conventions over how liaisons might normally progress.

Max had broken off their 'connection' as she called it once before when he had experienced the disaster of dating Deborah at the university. Melissa had met Deborah. Quite liked her. But Max did not discuss Sophie with anyone…

'Is this what I'm thinking, Max?'

'I don't know'

'You don't know?'

'To be honest – I don't know what I know any more. That's why I need to see you.'

'I thought we had talked this through, Max. The last time. I thought we were both OK?'

'Yes, I know. And so did I. But I'm not sure if I really am OK.'

'I see.' There was a pause. 'OK, Max. If talking is what you need to do then talking is what we will do. Tomorrow at 7 p.m? I'll cook us something nice.'

'Oh don't cook. Please don't go to any trouble. I'll book somewhere. Hartleys?'

'And now I am really worried.'

'I'll text you. Pick you up around 7 p.m.'

Max put the phone down and stared at it.

He had no idea if he was doing the right thing but the truth was Sophie had become a paradox in his life, making him both very happy and terribly sad. The very reason he had not told Melissa about her.

They had met at the Tate of St Ives gallery in Cornwall – admiring an exhibition to champion local artists' residencies. It was years after he lost Eleanor - in the phase when friends felt Max should be 'moving on'. But he did not. Later that same day Max and Sophie bumped into each other again at the nearby Barbara Hepworth museum. They talked very easily and so walked on the beach and shared coffee which turned into lunch. It was not until they were parting reluctantly and several hours of excellent conversation later that Sophie shared that she was an artist herself.

A very good one as it turned out. Her paintings – mostly watercolours and charcoal sketches – sold well, especially, she confided, since she had hit upon a darker streak. Sophie began to weave shadows into the water and skies of otherwise bold and bright colour ways – an effect which always seemed, to Max at least, to be terribly sad and also rather brilliant.

For the most part, Sophie reflected the vibrant shades of her work – a torch beam in the room. The kind of person who always had some fascinating titbit from Radio Four and the Sunday papers, which she seemed to find the time to read from cover to cover every single week.

Max had for a short time imagined that this might be the relationship which could surprise him. But – no. It was not many weeks before he realised that the very thing that had drawn him to Sophie – her enigma – was the key. She had a switch. On. Off. And while she was very happy to 'connect' for their dinners and the occasional weekend, she did not want a conventional relationship.

Those dark shadows through her paintings.

Max had wondered if he might help her with this. If they might help each other? But Sophie did not see her situation as anything that needed solving. And so Max simply went along with her rules. They enjoyed each other's company. They enjoyed each other in bed. She was kind and funny and made the best fish soup he had tasted outside of France. But – sorry; she did not ring and she did not need to talk in between their monthly dates and very soon Max realised it was precisely why he was both drawn to her and had stayed with her.

With Sophie he had found a place where he did not need to '*move on*' from Eleanor.

Which was – yes; perfect and completely disastrous all at once.

CHAPTER 12
Melissa – 2011

Melissa woke with a start – at first disorientated and then, slowly registering the new anchors. The hum of the air conditioning. The shutters instead of curtains at the window. The large and ridiculous case casting a shadow in the corner of the apartment.

And then her mind was moving somewhere else – slipping back for just a second into the dream so that she had to close her eyes tight to it. Turn her head away towards the wall. She felt her right hand flinching. Imagined the wet sand between her toes. The sound of the ocean.

Melissa opened her eyes and sat up quickly to shake herself fully awake. To try to compute what was happening.

Jesus. She hadn't had that dream in years. Relieved now, heart pounding, that she had moved during the night onto the sofa bed. Sam had felt guilty – tossing and turning and keeping them both awake.

I'll go on the sofa bed, Mel.

No, Sam. We'll both sleep better if you stay in the bedroom. You need the space for your leg. Just for a night.

Melissa kept very still and listened. No sound from the room next door. He must finally have dozed off.

Melissa picked up her phone from the floor alongside the sofa bed to check the time – three a.m. She tightened her lips at the message tag reminding her of two unanswered texts from her father – her eyes slowly adjusting to the half-light as she leant back now against the wall to slow her breathing. To wait for her heartbeat to settle.

She didn't want to wake Sam but badly needed a drink and so, after a few minutes, swung her legs ever so carefully from the bed. She tiptoed then to the kitchen area and poured water from one of the large bottles on the surface. It was unpleasantly warm but she daren't risk the fridge door – couldn't remember how noisy it was.

Sam, if he woke, would want to sit with her. And talk. And because he knew her face better perhaps than anyone, he would very soon work out from that same face – her hands and her demeanour also – that it wasn't just the accident that was disturbing her.

Melissa glanced over to her bag, zipped tight in the corner, now containing her mother's book which she had retrieved from the wardrobe.

Just four days since she had first set eyes on it in James Halls' office. How could it possibly be just four days?

She had so far read very little but now that Sam was safe, she couldn't quite understand her reluctance to read on. Felt guilty about it.

Shouldn't she want to devour it? Page after page? To finish the book.

How could it be normal that she didn't want to do that? Read on. Somehow couldn't.

Melissa closed her eyes again to the familiar prickle behind each one. She remembered how in school she would do arithmetic to control this.

Eight eights are sixty four. Nine nines are eighty one.

She had the dream a lot back then. Once she had asked a friend if she ever had the same dream over and over and her friend – Laura – had said – *absolutely*. She had this dream about sitting a test and not being able to do it because it was all in a foreign language. *Seriously. Like Russian or something.* Other friends much later at university said they had recurring dreams about being naked in public. Or having to re-sit their A levels without having done any revision.

Melissa never told anyone about hers. Most especially not the woman back in school with whom she met once a week and then once a month for 'special chats'.

She wouldn't understand. No one would understand. They would all think, you see, that it was quite a nice thing. Comforting. They wouldn't understand the confusion. That Melissa did not actually want the dream. No.

For in this dream, Melissa was walking on the beach with her mother. She was holding her hand and Melissa knew for certain that it was her mother – not only because she could feel the wedding ring on her finger as she gripped her hand, but because she knew deep inside from how completely happy and how utterly loved and safe she felt.

They were at first walking along the beach and then running and laughing and Melissa could feel the wind in her hair and she could hear the roar of the waves and taste the salt on her lips.

She was *so happy*. And that was actually the problem that no one would understand. They would think it odd – that she was some kind of freak – that she did not want to feel that.

But here was the truth: Melissa did not want to remember just how good all that felt. And the more often she had that dream the harder she had to work not to look up into her mother's face. Because Melissa knew that if she let herself do that in the night – to look up at her mother's beautiful face, smiling right at her – she would not be able to cope with the next morning. Or the next day. Or the next week.

And so she ran along the beach in the dream over and over and over. *Do not look into her face, Melissa. Look at the sand.*

Eight eights are sixty four. Nine nines are eighty one.... Eleven times twelve ...

Melisa wiped her cheeks. She looked again at the bag containing the book.

How was it she could have something so very precious and be so terribly afraid to read it?

CHAPTER 13
Max – 2011

Max settled into the driver's seat and reached into his jacket pocket for his glasses. He then completed the ritual of checking the car as thoroughly as possible for anything with wings.

The truth was there was very rarely anything to find – just occasionally in the summer when a tiny fly might need squatting against the inside of the windscreen – but Max was not for taking any chances. He sighed, remembering the time when it was just a joke. When it did not trigger this flicker of dread.

All their marriage Eleanor had ribbed him about it. 'Oh for goodness' sake, Max. It's only a fly. It can't hurt you.' Melissa had learnt to join in too, laughing as Daddy once waved an ice cream so frantically at a fly while on holiday in Cornwall that the sphere of raisin and rum had plopped straight onto the floor. Before he had enjoyed even one lick.

And then came the day – eight weeks into the numbness of his new life post-Eleanor – and it was a fly which brought it all to a head. A single, sodding fly pointing up just how thinly the thread now stretched for Melissa.

It was June – loads of flies about – and he was fed up to the back teeth of them; waving them away from his food out of doors and from the surfaces in the kitchen. Max just couldn't help himself, unable to relax and ignore them as other people, including his young daughter, seemed to do. He couldn't bear the thought of them landing on his skin. His face. His arms. Anywhere.

It went back to childhood when Max had watched a programme examining whether it was true that flies puked and pooed on you when they landed. Turned out they did. Flies, Max learned, had no mechanism to chew solid food and so their strategy was to vomit enzymes onto anything they fancied to break down the solids before slurp, slurping it up. They also drank big time compared to other species which was why so much came out the other end.

Thus began Max's hatred of flies and on that fateful morning, some two months after Eleanor's funeral, he was in a rush – late for the university, having dropped Melissa at school en route. Max had arranged flexible working but was still struggling to adjust to his new circumstance. He needed to get in earlier than usual to sort a presentation for later in the day and was stressed. Not coping well enough. For his daughter and for his job.

The motorway was completely clear and so he had his foot down. First mistake. And he was going over the plans for the presentation in his head. Second mistake. And then suddenly there was this tiny fly flitting to and fro right by his face. Max couldn't help it. He took his hands right off the steering wheel to bat it away and in that split second the car veered completely out of control. Unbelievable, when he looked back on it, that from cruising straight, albeit very fast, in the inside lane one second, he could be veering across towards the central barrier the next.

He very nearly clipped the barrier, swerving alarmingly as he struggled to regain control, still terrified of where the bloody fly was. By the time he had things back under control the car had swung through 360 degrees and he pulled up, horrified and disorientated to discover he was facing the wrong way.

Still – thank Christ – nothing coming.

Max, his heart pounding almost out of his chest, executed the fastest three-point turn of his life and pulled up into the hard shoulder. He had read somewhere that you shouldn't get out of your car on the hard shoulder unless in an absolute emergency but Max had no choice. He got out, walking around the front of the car, stepped over the low barrier and sat on the grass on the other side. And then, to his horror, it came.

The one thing he tried so hard, for Melissa's sake, not to do.

Max completely lost it.

He lost it for Eleanor's last breath and his last words to her in the hospital. '*Please don't go… I'm not ready.*'

He lost it for Melissa who now followed him around at home like a frightened puppy.

He lost it for the vanilla-scented soap he would not throw out at home because it was the last soap Eleanor had used.

He lost it for all the baking tins and recipe books that he had packed into a big box because he could not bear to **bloody… look… at… them**.

Roaring his fury. Kicking then at the bracken and the twigs and the metal barrier. Picking up rocks and a discarded Coke can to hurl them, still roaring, into the undergrowth.

All over a frigging fly. A stupid, puking, poxy insect which could have left his daughter to face all of this shit all alone.

And so – yes; Max now went over the top every single time he got in the car. He checked for flies and he would not pull away until he was absolutely sure there were no sodding, stinking distractions; at least none that were in his gift to control.

The journey to Sophie's took just under an hour and a half. He had allowed 15 minutes for traffic and so was under no pressure.

Hartleys was her favourite restaurant – a tiny place with a huge fireplace and sloping floor of original flagstones. Just half a dozen small tables, which created exactly the relaxed and intimate environment they both so loved. Sophie was an excellent cook herself and hence quite a difficult customer to please, but Hartleys had never failed them and Max needed the meal, at least, tonight to be good.

They had not spoken since the phone call to arrange this and Max guessed exactly how this would go. They would both be sad. On edge. And he would add guilt and nerves into the mix, hoping that she would not try so hard this time to make him change his mind.

Max had broken things off with Sophie once before. Over Deborah. They had not seen each other for the eighteen months of that relationship, for Max, try as he might, could not be like Sophie.

When everything had imploded with Deborah – he winced at the thought, clutching the steering wheel very tightly – it had not occurred to him to get back in touch with Sophie again. What kind of person would that make him, for Christ's sake?

No. It was Sophie who found out. Sophie who called. Sophie who soothed and supported and coaxed him back. And yes – it was weak of him to rewind. No strings. No stress. No future.

Tonight she looked wonderful – a turquoise Chinese-style dress, sporting deep blue dragon motifs with tiny pearl buttons down the front and a deep blue shawl. But she was unusually quiet as he drove them the twenty minutes from her place to the restaurant. And then as they sat at the table and he ordered only sparkling water for himself, she tilted her head. 'So – you really aren't staying tonight, Max? This is really it?'

He wanted to take her hand and was trying to remember the script he had rehearsed on the way but it was gone now.

'You know your problem – Maximillian Dance?'

'No.'

'You are way too nice.'

'Don't, Sophie'

'No. It's true. Someone less nice would keep their options open.'

'I hope that's not how you think I see you. An option? I really never meant—'

'No – my lovely man. I know that's not how you see me,' she topped up her wine and then ran a finger around the rim. 'You do know, Max, that I still see other people. Just occasionally. And I have no problem with you doing the same.'

They had discussed this before and Max had never quite known how to feel about it.

'I really thought that I did not want to be in love again, Sophie.'

'Ah. That old thing.'

'Yes. That old thing. I really did think that after Deborah and the way that all went so horribly wrong, I would face up to it. That Eleanor was IT. And that you don't have to keep on looking.'

'And now I hear the but?'

Max looked down at their plates. He had finished his already – sea bass fillet with ginger and spring onions. Light. Lovely. Sophie had chosen partridge roasted with juniper and thyme and was toying with the final slithers. There was a bleep from his phone then.

'Sorry. Very rude but do you mind if I quickly check this? I'm waiting on a message from Melissa.'

'Not at all.'

It was a text from her at last. **All fine. Stop worrying xx** He shook his head.

'Everything OK?'

'Yeah fine. She's fine.' He put the phone back in his pocket.

'Look, Max. I know I've said this before but there are so many kinds of caring, and the version we have isn't wrong.'

'I know that, Sophie. And I have treasured it. And I have gone over it a million times in my head. But I know that all the time that I am seeing you… Well. It just doesn't feel right any more.'

He wanted to add that there was this void; this gaping hole right inside him which he just couldn't fill up no matter how many rocks he threw and how far he bloody ran.

Sophie put her cutlery together on her plate and patted her mouth with the crisp, damask napkin. She looked away to the roar of the fire and then back.

'Is there someone else? Another Deborah?'

'No. Not really. Not yet. The problem is that I have surprised myself by feeling again lately that there could be. Or rather that, if I am being honest with myself, I would still like there to be. Does that make any sense?'

'I gave up trying to make sense of you a long time ago, Max.'

He smiled. 'And now you are sounding like Melissa.'

'You sure you don't want to stay friends, Max? To wait a bit. See how this maps out?'

He shook his head slowly and so she took a deep breath and reached into her embroidered purse to produce a card. 'My next exhibition. There's a painting I would like you to have. A little parting gift, if you like.'

'No, no. I couldn't. Sophie. Absolutely not. This is hard enough…'

'You will like it. And if you care for me at all, Max, then you will listen. These have been happy times for me. We are very different. I always knew that, but I will miss you and it will make me feel better if you will take this. I will leave the painting for you to collect on the Friday. I won't be there. But I would like you to see the exhibition. Will you do that for me?'

He looked at the card. It was a few weeks away – at a gallery nearby.

'And don't look so worried. It's not a trap. I'm not trying to lure you back. I'm just trying to say goodbye properly, Max,' she clinked her wine glass to his water glass and tilted her head. 'To say thank you.'

CHAPTER 14
Melissa – 2011

The second night on the sofa bed and Melissa was relieved again for the space to think. Sam's leg was still very sore but, with the strong painkillers, he was at least getting by. But he was unhappy with the separate sleeping – also the excuses she was making to buy privacy for the journal. Melissa had no idea what to do about this.

During the day, Sam now sat mostly in the shade by the pool and Melissa had taken to hiding behind novels, insisting that he needed to do the same. To just chill to get over the accident. The truth – that she badly needed space herself to digest all that had happened. The accident. The dream. The journal. But Sam was unsurprisingly both agitated and uncomfortable in the heat and she would often catch him watching her and frowning. She was now worrying he would go stir-crazy if they just stayed in Polis and so put forward some ideas for trips. But this had not gone down well either.

Sam clearly wanted to talk. She didn't.

Over the past couple of days, Melissa had found herself, on top of everything else, obsessing about a box in their garage back home. It was one of three which Max had brought over from his own outhouse storage when they moved into the flat. Two of the boxes contained useful bits and pieces – lamps and bedding and old schoolbooks and mementos which she had unpacked long ago. But the third, to her surprise, contained her mother's old cooking equipment. Max had packed some of it away soon after Eleanor died. His argument was there was way too much of it for the cupboards – the truth obvious even to the young Melissa. It all upset him. When he brought the boxes over, he said that Melissa should feel free to give anything she didn't want to a charity shop. Even before the book, she had found the sight of her mother's kitchen equipment unsettling and upsetting. The old tins and boxes and the familiar Kenwood Chef mixer, wrapped for protection in a towel. She didn't want to bring them up to the flat. But there was no way she could part with them either.

Now, smoothing the cover on the sofa bed, she was trying desperately to picture the contents of the box in greater detail. Melissa turned her head and for a moment had this sudden glimpse – a clear picture of her mother chattering away while holding a damp cloth, wiping splatters from around the switch of the mixer. She would do this every time she finished with it. Wipe over the white surface and the pale blue trim until it gleamed, folding the dishcloth carefully over so that she could run it around the joins and the very edge of the switch, to tease out any stray flour or sugar.

Melissa felt the now familiar paradox. The knot deep inside. Not knowing if she wanted to think of this. Or not. She waited until there was the gentle rhythm of Sam's snore then moved slowly and quietly out to the balcony, taking her mother's book with her.

She kept the grey silk pouch close by the rattan chair so that she could conceal the book if Sam stirred. Melissa sat for a while not quite ready to read. She stared at the cover, wondering again if at home she would have simply thrown a sickie from work. Read it straight through. Cover to cover. Maybe.

Probably not. Still she was so very disorientated by all these emotions it stirred.

All day she had been thinking about the dream. Wondering if it would come back again if she read on? Again unsure if this was something that she wanted now. Or not?

Melissa kept very still and listened. Nothing. And she would hear the sliding door if Sam stirred and came through from the bedroom.

She looked out across the dusty vegetation to the sea in the distance – the half-moon low in the sky. Normally she loved this abroad. The warmth of the night. The faint scent of the ocean and the hum of the crickets. But tonight it brought no calmness at all.

Melissa was not religious. She did not believe in interventions or fate or anything of that kind. But she was wondering about timing and about chance. That they should have been there on that road in the mountain at that precise time.

To think that if they had drunk just one more coffee before they left Polis. Stayed a few more minutes in the church.

Melissa closed her eyes again to the scenes from the other version of the accident – the one in which there was no stranger and no dive – pulling her wrap tighter around her waist until her knuckles turned white. And then she looked down, took a very deep breath and moved the postcard she was using as a bookmark, to turn the page.

Strawberry Jam

2lbs strawberries (not too ripe)
1.5lbs granulated sugar (no need for jam sugar)
Juice of one lemon
Three saucers placed in freezer
Confidence!!!!

Chop strawberries in half and leave coated in the sugar
for a few hours or overnight (this will help them keep
shape). When ready to make the jam, use a large and
sturdy pan. Warm fruit + sugar very gently over a low
heat until ALL the sugar has dissolved. Then add
lemon juice and turn up heat to a rapid boil. Time for
8 mins and take off the heat. Use one of the cold saucers next: put a teaspoon of jam on the cold saucer and
leave for a minute. Push with finger... if there is a soft,
wrinkly skin you have a set. If not? Rapid boil for 3
mins and try again. And again if necessary. Once you
have a set, allow mix to cool for 10 mins and then put
into jam jars which have been washed and warmed in
an oven to make them sterile. Ta dah!!!

My lovely girl. I know exactly what you are thinking. Jam? Are
you mad? This is not the WI. I am 25. There is no way I am going to make jam.

Please, I beg you, go with me on this one! I decided to try
making jam after a few of those splendid holidays to Porthlev-
en. Do you remember? The owner of the cottage would always
leave out a cream tea set on a tray with home-made jam like
nothing we had ever tasted. Anyway. I persuaded her to share
her own recipe, which is a take on a classic apparently. She

makes it in small batches as she enjoys it so much. So this is a cheat… not some family secret but rather something special from our past.

The first time I made it, it took 8 mins + 3 mins + 3 mins. The second batch was different: only 8 mins + 3 mins. So it's not an exact science and that is partly the appeal. I can't recommend highly enough the sense of achievement when you get it right. So I am passing it on because I hope it will remind you of very happy times.

And I have decided this entry is to be cheerful only. No sorries. No sadness. Just a little nudge to point you to the things we so loved.

Oh Melissa – do you remember cricket on the beach in Cornwall? Do you remember how terribly seriously Daddy took it all and how wound up he got that we both found it so hard to hit the bloody ball?

'If you would just CONCENTRATE, girls!' And then, poor darling, he would be so offended. 'Why are you laughing at me? I am trying to teach you something important here. And you think this is funny?'

Do you remember those enormous pasties from the bakery along the seafront? With huge chunks of swede and potato. Very, very peppery. Daddy would always buy three exactly the same size (for which read HUGE) and I would always say – *shall we get a smaller one for Melissa?* And he would say – *oh, no. I'm sure she's hungrier than you realise* – so that he would have the excuse to finish yours as well as his own. Bless.

Do you remember the Snow White costume I made you for the fair day competition in school? God – I was so proud of that costume. You looked just edible, Melissa, and then the stupid judges thought that we had bought it so you didn't get a prize and I was so disappointed for you… and I was thinking we may as well have let you wear the costume we bought in Disney. All those hours at the sewing machine!

What else? Oh – yes. I am hoping that you will remember the skittles. Cue the child psychologists – but this is actually quite interesting. You see I read somewhere when you were very little that working mums need to be very careful not to fall into 'later, darling' speak. Always so busy, busy, busy. Always a million things to do. As I said before, I am writing a special section about modern motherhood (the warts 'n all version) at the back of the book. But this reference belongs here.

You see I wanted to set a good example to you by working and doing something I am passionate about. For me that is education. Continuing with my teaching. But even with all the school holidays sorted, it turned out to be busier and much, much harder than I had expected. To work and mother, I mean.

So back to this 'later, darling' tip. I read that it is important to regularly play with your child until they are sick to the back teeth of you. Not every time (because you just won't have time) but often enough for the child to get the message that they are your priority (which I promise you are).

So I picked skittles. You had this really beautiful painted wooden set given to you by my father. Every week we would set them up in the long hallway and I would earmark the time to play until YOU wanted to stop. That's the trick apparently.

And what a revelation.

I admit that with a lot of other things, I had to take the lead on moving on. Putting games away to get the supper. Putting the book away to get you to sleep. Turning off the television, to help you with your homework. Sitting you in front of a video while I marked books.

But with skittles, I made sure you were the boss. *Again*? Of course. *And again*? Why not?

Melissa closed the book. Her pulse in her ear again. She was entirely surprised now by her surroundings. The veranda. The temperature dropping just enough for her to notice the breeze. Until now, she had completely forgotten about the skittles and so it was just like the cupcakes picture. The cue. She was remembering how her mother's knees cracked sometimes as she stood up to set up the skittles once more. Over and over. And the fact that she had not thought of this before – not ever – made her feel both disorientated. Smiling inwardly and yet also guilty somehow.

Why did she not remember these things before? *Why?*

And then, for just an absolute blink, she became conscious of another sensation. Turning the page back to the recipe and at first remembering the noise. *It's a rolling boil. Look, Melissa.* The bubbling and the sweet stickiness of the jam. The memory of the smell. And then it was exactly like that moment when you are trying to remember someone's name and it almost comes to you and you turn your head, trying to grasp the information. Suck it back to you.

Melissa turned her head once more and felt it again but only very fleetingly. Gone before she could hold it. Acknowledge the sensation properly. A shiver ran through her then, and not from the breeze, as Melissa closed her eyes to the realisation of what it was.

For one fleeting and tantalising moment it was like remembering what it actually felt like to have her mother in the same room.

Not a memory. Not a picture. The actual *feeling.*

Melissa quickly placed the book back into the grey pouch and zipped it closed. She cleared her throat. She stood at the balcony railing for a short time, taking in the cooler air to temper her breathing and then moved back into the sitting room and set up her laptop on the coffee table.

She clenched her right hand and could feel the nails pressing into her palm. But it was not like the dream, this. The voice of the book made it feel different somehow and Melissa found now that she very much *wanted* the feeling back. Yes. She was thinking that she could Google the cottage in Cornwall. Find a picture of the kitchen. The tray with the scones and the *jam*… She typed into the search bar quickly but then the external light on the balcony – visible through the patio doors – suddenly began to flicker. Instantly the internet connection died.

Shit.

Melissa tried quickly to reconnect.

No Wi-Fi detected

She tried to set it up again – fumbling for the apartment information folder and the password. But nothing.

It was gone now. The moment. The frisson. The memory and the scent of the jam.

All of it.

Gone.

CHAPTER 15
Max – 2011

Max left early for his run to put in an extra two k. He set off feeling that a weight had been lifted from his shoulders, that he had finally done the right thing and that he was capable of putting things back on track. OK, so he might be lonely for a bit. OK, so he would miss the sex. He was human. He was a guy. But he had been thinking about this for a long time and he felt better. Lighter. Yes. He had absolutely done the right thing.

Fast forward an hour and Max sat staring at his stopwatch at the kitchen table in abject disbelief. He could not possibly have taken that long to do just 5 k. Christ. If it really took him that long, he was going backwards.

Max closed his eyes, feeling the sweat running down his back. Nice one. You are past it. Losing it. Not just your physical fitness but the plot. You have waved goodbye to possibly the only decent woman who is going to give you the time of day, let alone climb into your bed. You are going grey, you are losing fitness, your daughter no longer answers your texts ipso facto you are now one hundred per cent on your fucking lonesome.

For a full ten minutes he sat, numbed by the pendulum of these emotions, staring blankly at the knots in the oak of the wooden floor. He wondered if this was what depression felt like – this ability to sit still for so very long without any inclination to move. Or was this just another symptom of true middle age? The dreaded slide.

For just one moment of panic he considered phoning Sophie and confessing that he had made the most terrible mistake but – no. That, he reflected, would not help either.

The truth was very simple because Max was actually quite a simple soul. He still missed Eleanor…

Even after all these years, he missed simply being with her. He missed all the little and everyday things about their marriage that he had so taken for granted.

Max looked across the room at the large frame which featured a montage of pictures from that other version of himself. Max on his wedding day. Max with Melissa asleep on his chest as a tiny baby. Max in charge of cricket on the beach in Cornwall. He remembered with a pang of discomfort how sometimes in that other hectic life he had both longed for and luxuriated in the small windows of time to himself. His run. His drive in the car to the university.

And now? When your child finally outgrew you and those small windows of solitude got bigger and bigger and bigger?

Fuck you – fate.

Just *fuck you.*

In the shower, he turned the heat up too high so that his flesh was scalded an alarming red by the time he realised – *shit* – that he had pushed his luck and would now, on top of everything, be up against it for his first lecture.

In his office, realising there would be no time for coffee, he was just thinking that things could not possibly get any worse…

'So are you going to tell me precisely what the problem you have with me is?'

No knock. No warning. No – *do you have a moment.* Just Anna standing in his office, face fuming.

'I'm sorry?'

'I was wondering, professor, if you were going to have the decency to tell me to my face precisely what I have done wrong?'

Max was temporarily struck dumb.

'No?' She had widened her eyes – a ripple of lines on her forehead as her brows stayed high. Furious.

Oh right. The email.

'Look, Anna. If you're unhappy about the email, I can talk to you later about that. It's just I'm running late…'

'And funny how you are always running late. Every time, every single Wednesday for as long as I can remember when I have been trying my very best to make a fresh start and a good impression here. Putting in God knows how many extra hours to try to make a real go of this. Looking to you – my supposed mentor – for some support. Some feedback. Some small encouragement. And not only do I get none of those things but I get in this morning to a one sentence email bumping me to another mentor. To Frederick fecking Montague. And we both know precisely what that means.'

'Frederick is a fine professor. And a respected colleague…'

'And two years off retirement. With no influence, no ambition, no interests in the politics of this place, which we all know is everything these days – and absolutely no interest in my future. Which is clearly something you have in common.'

'I think that's enough, Anna.'

'Well for your information, I have only just begun. I'm taking this straight to HR, Professor Dance. You are not going to get away with this.'

And now Max felt the blood drain from his face. H fucking R.

'Look Anna. I transferred you to Professor Montague's team precisely because I have a real interest in your future here. I just felt I was not the best person to take forward the enormous effort and enthusiasm you have shown already for this new role. My other responsibilities make it difficult, at this time, to give you the time you clearly want and need. I'm not the right person. The right mentor. Professor Montague has more time.'

'And why couldn't you have at least discussed it with me?'

Max took a deep breath. He looked at Anna and for a split second considered saying it out loud.

'Anna. Can I ask you to just give me some time on this? Before you take it to HR. To allow me to properly explain myself.'

She looked at him intently – no sign of calming down at all.

'Can we meet back here, Anna? One o'clock?'

She looked away towards the window and then back at him – eyes still fuming.

'I will not be fobbed off. I may have come from what you all sneer at as a former poly but I am a good lecturer.'

Shit. So that was what she thought.

'I will not have my efforts and ambitions here compromised just because of sexist, cliquey, old-school—'

'I think that's quite enough, Anna.'

And only now did she finally flush just a little bit.

'One o'clock, Anna? I am running late for a lecture,' he stood up, reaching for his jacket from the stand alongside his bookcase, deliberately keeping his eyes turned away from her. 'Back here at one o'clock.'

And then she was gone, slamming the door behind her.

Max went on to deliver what was quite possibly the worst lecture of his life. A comparison of anti-trust laws. Different approaches by different countries to trade and monopolies. A lecture so badly focused that even his favourite students looked bemused. At one point, Max lost his way so very obviously that he had to feign the symptoms of a cold to excuse the fuddle.

Never mind, he was thinking whether legislation should or should not be controlling the growth of Google – what the hell am I going to say to explain myself to HR?

Sorry Mrs Bramble but I had a crush on her. I kept getting distracted by her bra strap so I decided it would be unwise for me to continue as her line manager and mentor.

Holy shit, Max!

Eleven thirty and he retreated to his office. He checked back through his emails to find no fewer than ten recent, detailed and yes – impressive emails from Anna outlining her suggested changes to improve the course, which had prompted very short and one might even say, dismissive replies.

He hadn't even realised that he had been doing it. Blanking her.

He pictured Giselle Bramble going through these same emails and wondered if there was no other option than to come clean with Anna. No. Shit. That would only make things very, very much worse.

One o'clock arrived very much too quickly and as the knock came at the door, Max was mortified to realise that he still had no intelligent strategy in place. And then to his surprise she was in the room looking quite different. Not just calmer but actually cowed. Head down. Flushed.

'About earlier?' She sat down on the chair opposite. Max held his breath. Maybe she had already been to HR? Maybe she looked cowed because he was about to be suspended. His prospects and his pension – all gone already.

'I may have been a little more direct than I intended.'

And now Max was winded. This was good. Completely unexpected but good. Also disorientating. He took a deep breath and opted for silence – repeating inwardly only one mantra. *Don't dig, Max. Do. Not. Dig.*

'I realise that it is wholly unprofessional of me to bring my personal life to work. Unforgiveable. Unlike me. I really would not want you to think—'

'Your personal life?'

'I had a very bad weekend and your email, which felt to me as if it was shutting down all the plans I had in place for the course. Well – it was the straw and the camel. Which doesn't mean that I am not disappointed. Hugely disappointed and you need to understand that I am not prepared to let it go. Give up on all my ideas, I mean. But I realise that the way I spoke to you earlier. It's not the way I normally like to deal with things. The reputation that I want here. The hysterical woman.'

'I see.' Max did not see at all.

And then something completely appalling happened – something which Max had never known how to handle. With Eleanor. And Melissa also.

Anna began to cry.

Oh no. Please, no.

She struggled hard against it and was clearly mortified – raising her arm and turning away as if to head to the door.

'Don't go. Please – Anna. Sit a moment, at least. Please.'

She now chose very oddly to sit on a chair in the corner of the room by the door, turning away from him and fumbling in her bag for tissues while Max wondered what the hell he was supposed to do now. Were he to make any attempt whatsoever to comfort her, he was in danger of giving himself away. Worse – he would be marched off to HR for the inappropriate laying on of hands. Fail to comfort her and he was the cold, callous and disinterested bigot she believed him to be.

'I'm sorry about this, Professor Dance. Very unprofessional of me.'

'Don't be ridiculous. We all have our moments.'

Moments. What a bloody ridiculous word, Max. Think of something.

She blew her nose and then twisted her mouth to the side as if weighing something up.

'It's just…'

Max was now thinking bad thoughts about Anna having a tiff with her husband or partner or whatever he was. This man whose ring she did not wear.

She plunged on. 'My son. The half marathon?'

'Oh yes. You mentioned it.'

'He's pulled out.'

Max was still not following.

'Oh I see.'

'He's going to stay with his father instead. Abroad.'

And now something in Max's stomach physically moved as if a muscle had contracted involuntarily while Anna stood up, shaking her head.

'Which is clearly of no issue here. To my work, I mean. And I should not have let it affect things – or even mentioned it. But there it is. It upset me and I allowed myself to be unprofessional and to overreact. For which I feel I should now apologise.'

CHAPTER 16

Eleanor was born an only child late in the marriage of teachers Michael and Susan. That she would become a teacher herself was no great surprise. For starters, she wondered why anyone would want to work in a job which did not accommodate the whole summer in France. Slowly she became aware of the snide putdowns – *those who can do, blah blah* – but Eleanor watched both her parents take pride in their careers. She watched the huge range of expression from tutting to beaming as they pored over great piles of books lined up for marking on the dining room table – and she listened to them bicker about the meddling politicians; the education secretaries who *knew nothing about education.*

Michael taught Biology in a respected comprehensive. Susan taught French in a girls' grammar. Eleanor decided on English Literature on the grounds that permission to read full-time seemed like some kind of joke. Right through university she wondered when someone was going to find her out.

Her first job was every bit the trial her parents had warned of – a large and underperforming comp where getting the girls to exam year without a baby in tow was considered an achievement.

There were many lows. Once when four students stunned her by disappearing through a ground-floor window during one of her classes she stunned the rest of the class back by hopping out the window to sprint right after them. Not too bad on her feet, she caught them easily, marching all four back to the head, on pain of suspension. To be frank, she had rather expected them to tell her to piss off and keep running, but they seemed more shocked at her agility and speed to do anything other than throw in the towel.

After that, Eleanor determined to be stricter, alongside which she introduced the effective cliché of song lyrics and popular TV drama to hook in her students to poetry and story shapes before gently guiding them towards the classics on the syllabus. Some were never going to be won over, however hard she tried. But she managed to keep them all in the room, and results improved sufficiently on her watch to earn her a transfer after three years to a smaller secondary with an impressive exam record.

It was in western Oxfordshire – an area she would grow to love. Flat in the south but just a few miles from the glory that was the undulating hills of the Cotswolds. And it was there, during the second term, that she was tasked with babysitting the Economics Professor from a local university ('*not Oxford – but don't be sniffy*') during a careers night when the Head of Maths suddenly went down with *explosive diarrhoea*.

'Explosive diarrhoea?' Max had said, laughing out loud at her candour and shaking her hand that first meeting.

'Yes. Paints quite a picture, don't you think? I wondered if his wife could have been a little less graphic on the phone with the excuses, but he needed this favour of me. I should warn you I have not the foggiest on economics so my introduction may not do you justice.'

And that was when she noticed that he was not blinking. Professor Maximillian Dance, senior lecturer of Economics – *who cared that it wasn't Oxford uni* – was looking right at her, without blinking. Which later, as she watched him on stage surprising all the parents with a very polished and yet relaxed presentation on the crucial place for Economics in the understanding of the world around us, she was thanking the lord for explosive diarrhoea. So that when on parting later Max wondered '*if she fancied dinner sometime*' something in her own stomach changed forever.

Eleanor determined to play it cool. And then laughed at herself as she moved her belongings into his flat within a month. There wasn't anything not to love.

Max had an energy and enthusiasm for life which was infectious and exhilarating. Nothing seemed to get him down. He loved sport. He loved cooking. He loved walking. He loved Economics. And he loved Eleanor.

He had enjoyed a very happy childhood, which on reflection was probably at the root of it all, and he was one of those rare men who actually wanted very much to get married and have a family. Forget all the commitment-phobic bollocks that had broken her heart in the past. Max was full on from the start.

They fell in love quickly and completely. And they stayed in love with only one major hiccup along the way.

Money.

Max hit a sudden and inexplicable spell when he decided that education was no place to make sufficient money to raise a family. Eleanor, unmaterialistic and with modest expectations, completely disagreed. Over this they had one spectacular falling out. It was very, very painful and Eleanor preferred to blank it.

All that mattered was they eventually resolved it.

So that on a clear, spring day in the same church in which her parents had been married, Eleanor stood in the front of the church staring at this handsome and kind, kind man – never quite believing her luck.

Until one morning baking cookies with her daughter in a cottage in Cornwall and she was brushing down the flour from her jumper.

Eleanor knew deep down that it was pure craziness not to tell Max about the lump and not to see the doctor about the lump. It wasn't a bright thing to do and she was a bright woman. But everything in her life had been so charmed until that point that she had this terrible feeling, deep inside, that all roads had been leading to this place and she needed somehow to postpone *knowing*. She did some research and tried for a time to reason that it was a fibroadenoma – both benign and quite common in women in their twenties and thirties. That could fit. But the lump, when she checked it more closely in the privacy of the bathroom seemed to go quite deep into her chest – right under the armpit. Also there was some discolouration of the breast which had been there for quite some time. A rash that she had just got used to and assumed was some kind of allergy or eczema. There was also the curious fact that she had been losing weight without trying.

Much later Eleanor would try to answer Max's heartache and exasperation at why she had delayed investigating all these symptoms – even for a week, let alone the months she actually delayed – but she just couldn't find the words or the rationale to explain that she didn't actually want to know.

Chanting in the car on the way to get that first result about the statistics and how unlikely it was to be anything serious, she was in her head writing an entirely different script – knowing already how this was going to turn out. It was more than pessimism. She actually felt that she knew. Not some psychic experience but rather a physical awareness which probably had more to do with the cancer which had already spread inside her than she realised. She just didn't want it confirmed.

And so, for Max, she put on an air of faux optimism through all the wretched tests, until they sat there and the doctor's face told them before he had even opened his mouth.

It was stage four. It was already in her liver and her lungs. It was the reason she had been losing weight and felt so tired. They were terribly, terribly sorry but her circumstance was very rare. The treatment could not be curative though there was much they could do in terms of quality of life.

Max sat there making notes – his face white as he scrawled and scrawled, pressing so hard into the page that the paper tore. Eleanor did not listen to another word.

In her mind she had already journeyed back to the front of that church. She was back in that other ward when the midwife said it was a girl. She was lying on the floor, setting up skittles. She was playing cricket on the beach. And she was collecting together all the ingredients for Easter biscuits.

And now, writing the journal for Melissa she would get these moments of extreme panic when the details would begin to jumble and she would worry about how much she should share with her daughter. All of it? Part of it?

During one writing session, she described over three full pages how she felt on her wedding day. The scent of the orange blossom which drifted into the church every time someone opened a door. Also – the day that Melissa was born. The delicious smell of the newborn that she just couldn't find the words to describe. And the story of the orange zest and the cupcakes. How they had first come to use the zest. Would Melissa remember this? Should she have written it down for her? The story. And then, thinking of orange, she suddenly got herself in the most terrible tizz – spending two full hours trying to find a particular picture of her mother visiting her in hospital on the day that Melissa arrived.

She remembered the picture as her mother was wearing a bright orange jumper which seemed to reflect on all their faces, distorting the skin tones when the pictures were developed. 'We look like oompa loompas, Mother.'

'Don't be ridiculous. The baby looks beautiful. Completely beautiful.'

'For an oompa loompa baby. Alongside your jumper.'

But Eleanor could not find the picture. She hunted high and low but it was nowhere to be found. She had mentioned it in the journal – the story of the orange jumper reflections – and so she couldn't decide what to do. To rip out the page if she did not find the picture?

All the while Max distressed… to see her distress.

'I don't understand why you need the picture today, Eleanor? We can find it another time? It's probably in a frame somewhere. Please don't be like this. I hate to see you like this.'

CHAPTER 17
Melissa – 2011

'Look – I know I said that I was fine. That we could close the whole marriage thing down but I find that I just can't, Melissa.' Sam had finally agreed to a trip. They were now on the way back from a disastrous visit to the Tomb of the Kings near Paphos.

Melissa, caffeine-deprived and distracted by confusion over the roller coaster of her mother's words had insisted they set off early. A mistake. Both overtired. Plus two days by the pool seemed to have stirred Sam into an even worse mood, the sore leg now itching unbearably in the heat.

Melissa had banked on the visit itself lifting both of them. On the website the Tombs looked impressive – a World Heritage site. She had imagined an air-conditioned visitor centre where Sam could at least rest his leg if the tour proved too much. But no. There was no centre and no coffee, merely a scorching expanse of baked earth to be explored – with mosquitoes holed up in the tombs.

Also there were no kings.

'Why do they call it the Tomb of the Kings… if there are no kings?' Sam, hobbling across the dusty pathways in searing heat, sounded at the end of his rope. On any other day and in any other circumstance, it was a visit he would have loved – devouring every word in the guidebook.

But today, after less than an hour, they threw in the towel. A quick lunch at a rather seedy cafe nearby and now heading home.

'It's doing my head in, Mel. I mean – you seem so distant suddenly. Sleeping on the sofa bed. Always looking for an excuse to sneak off. Is this really what it's going to be like now? You saying that we are OK but behaving as if you don't want to be in the same room as me. All because I asked you to marry me.'

'That isn't how it is, Sam. Look. I don't know what to say.'

'Say anything, Melissa. Anything at all. Just explain it to me. What you're thinking. What you're feeling. Why you are not only so very unsure about marrying me but have suddenly withdrawn completely—'

'Look. It's like I said in the restaurant. I just don't see what a piece of paper has to do with anything. I thought we had agreed to just leave it. See how things go. You've just had an accident, Sam. I don't think this is the time—'

'But it's not just a piece of paper, is it? It's about saying that you really want to be with someone.'

'I do want to be with you, Sam. You know that. I've told you that.'

'But not to marry me? Or even, it seems, to bloody talk to me.'

Melissa could feel her heart rate increasing. She changed down a gear but the engine revved noisily and so she moved back again into fifth. Sam looked away – out of the passenger window.

They drove on then in silence for a time and Melissa was struggling against a sick churning in her stomach, Sam now refusing to even look at her. She turned up the air conditioning.

For a moment she played the cliff-edge game. The black game she played as a kid. Imagine that you actually jump. Too late. Done it. One split second decision and no going back. She would never actually do it. Jump. Hurt herself. But it scared her that you could even have black thoughts and fears. That life, even hypothetically, could turn on split second decisions. ***Tell him***. Say it. Do things and say things that could not be undone. It was the same panic when that woman way back in primary school pressed and pressed and bloody pressed…

'Look. You know I find it difficult to talk about stuff, Sam.'

'Understatement of the year.' It was rare for him to be this harsh. She winced, breathing then through her nose, which made an unpleasant noise. She felt in her pocket for a tissue. Normally when she was struggling with anything like this, he would help. Be kind. But he was still looking pointedly away and she could see from the profile that his eyes were heavy. Like in the restaurant when he disappeared for an age to the bathroom and came back with his eyes looking just like this.

'Look. I know I'm hard work sometimes. But it isn't what you think, Sam.'

'So what is it, Melissa?'

She used the tissue, awkwardly blowing her nose one-handed. Still he would not look.

'You know what I used to think, Melissa? I used to think you are actually afraid to be in love. Afraid to let yourself be happy. I used to think all I needed to do was be patient. That what happened when you were a kid was what it was about. And that I just needed to hang in there. But now I'm thinking – that maybe we're just stuck treading water here.'

She didn't know what to say.

'So do you want to split up, Melissa? For me to move out when we get back?'

'Of course not.' She was shocked that he could even think this…

'Why say of course not as if it's obvious. When you don't appear to want to be in the same room any more.'

'That's not true.'

'OK. So how about I tell you what's true. What's true is that I watched you from the balcony this morning, taking your early swim before we left. We hadn't even said good morning, Melissa. And all I was thinking is how the hell do I make this woman happy. Because you sure don't look happy to me. You swam – what fifteen lengths, at some ridiculous hour – as if you were in some kind of rage. Then you sat by the edge of the pool with the sun right in your eyes as if you were on another planet. Not here at all. And that's how it feels right now. As if you're not even with me, Melissa.'

'My mother left me a book, Sam. A journal.' Edge of the cliff. Jump. *Say it, Melissa.* Tears pricking the back of her eyes. 'I got it when I went to that lawyer's office.' Knuckles white as she squeezed the steering wheel.

'I'm sorry?'

'When I went to see that solicitor and I said it was a mistake. A will hunter? That was a lie. It wasn't a mistake. The lawyer had a book for me. Left for me by my mother. I should have told you.'

And now Sam was frozen – his mouth gaping.

'It's a journal of recipes and letters and photographs which she put together when she was…' A long, deep breath. 'That she put together for me when she was very ill. For when I was grown-up.'

'Jesus Christ.' Finally looking at her.

'I can see now that I should have told you. But the shock threw me. I'm sorry, Sam.'

'And so this happened when? Before the restaurant?'

'No. It happened the morning after. I'm not saying it's why I'm unsure about getting married. I still can't explain that. And

I'm not trying to say it's any kind of excuse. I'm just saying it's why I'm all over the place. And all this, seeking time by myself. It's not because I don't want to be with you. I just wanted to read a bit more in private. Get my head round it before telling you and working out how I'm going to tell my father.'

'You seriously saying you haven't read it all yet?'

'No. Not yet. I'm actually finding it very…' What word would do? She tried to find one, narrowing her eyes, but couldn't.

'And your father doesn't know about it?'

'No.'

'Jesus Christ. We need to pull in, Melissa.'

'Sorry.'

'You need to stop driving,' at last he had turned to look at her.

'This is really huge, Melissa. There. That cafe. Stop there…'

Wiping at her face now. Silent tears. Relief and fear and guilt churned into one big wave as she checked the mirror.

This is huge…

Indicating to pull into the layby alongside the cafe now, so very relieved that he was looking at her again. And had said it.

The footbrake now – which she hit too hard. Then the handbrake. Picturing a Kenwood Chef mixer of white and pale blue – its surface gleaming from a damp cloth. Looking down at a single drip onto the pale linen of her trousers and thinking – that; yes.

This was really huge.

Boeuf Bourguignon

3lb quality braising steak (sounds too much – but not for hungry folk)
One large onion or handful of shallots
Pack of cubed pancetta
Two fat garlic cloves
Pack of good mushrooms – sliced
Good few sprigs of thyme – snipped with scissors
Bottle of good red wine (don't skimp!)
Seasoning + 3 tablespoons of flour + tiny bit sugar
Small amount of good beef stock, if needed

Chop the braising steak into large chunks (they shrink dramatically in the cooking) and brown in hot olive oil in a good quality casserole dish – transferring to a plate in batches. Then fry the chopped onion (or shallots) in more oil along with the pancetta and finally add the chopped garlic. Then return the beef to the dish. Sprinkle over the flour and mix everything with a wooden spoon. Don't panic at the goo at this stage. Slowly add the red wine, mixing carefully as the sauce thickens over low heat. Put in the whole bottle and add a touch more rich beef stock to cover the meat if needed. Season well, add the chopped thyme, mushrooms and half a teaspoon of sugar to balance the wine. Bring up to simmer, then transfer to oven for THREE HOURS at around 160°C. Again – this is longer than most recipes say, but it works for me. Your casserole MUST have a tight lid. If not – put some waxed paper over the top of the casserole contents to improve the seal. You don't want all the gorgeous sauce to evaporate away.

First things first, Melissa. Ignore all the recipes that say 2lbs of meat will feed six people. Who are they feeding? Sparrows? This is your father's favourite recipe in all the world and I make it for him every birthday – and trust me; when a guy likes a dish, he wants a proper, gorgeous, steaming plateful, not some dainty, little restaurant portion. So what if there are leftovers? Trust me on this. At least 3lbs of meat. In fact – as much as you can get in a good casserole dish. (I always recommend Le Creuset. Definitely worth the investment. Maybe Dad will have passed some of mine on?) But; no. I am not going to think of that as I write. Not today.

Because – do you know what, Melissa?

Even writing this recipe down is making me beam from ear to ear. I am thinking BIRTHDAYS. Your father's. Mine. *Yours especially.* Oh, but I do so love birthdays, my darling.

Your father laughs at me. Reckons I go over the top. But – I just can't help myself. Means I get three very, very special days across the year – and that's before we even think about Easter and Christmas.

I first discovered your father's passion for this dish on a trip to France. My parents used to take me for the whole summer pretty much every year so I have always loved the food. Your dad prefers holidays to be booked well ahead, bless him (and preferably Cornwall), but on this occasion I persuaded him to be brave. Just a ferry ticket and the Michelin guide.

We had such a ball, Melissa. Just moving from place to place, according to mood and how much we liked the area. And during that holiday we had some of the best food I can remember. There was this fish soup at the most unpromising looking cafe, right by the roadside. Unbelievable!

But I digress.

For the highlight of the trip was finding this wonderful, completely unpretentious hotel with a tiny restaurant which seemed to have a pot of boeuf bourguignon cooking on the stove from first light. Seriously. The smell began to seep from the kitchen even as we ate our breakfast.

Oh, I wish I had a picture of your father's face – that first mouthful! I have never forgotten it.

He tells me that mine is as good now as that hotel restaurant's and though that is definitely a lie, I will say that I think my version now comes pretty close. I've tweaked it myself from trial and error, using classic versions over the years. And this is the fail-safe one your dad loves. (You may need to thicken the sauce a bit at the end, by the way. Varies so much. Either bubble on stove top or add a bit of flour and butter paste or cornflour + water – whisking in furiously.)

Birthdays!

It is my top tip in all the world that it is impossible to make too much fuss. Yeah, yeah. Your dad says I am like a child about them – but for me that sums up everything that love and relationships of all kinds are about, Melissa.

I promised bits of advice through this journal, my darling. And when it comes to the people that you really love, it's actually quite simple. You get back what you put in.

And if you put something special into a birthday for a person that you love – well; there is just no better feeling in the world than their face when the surprise comes good. And it is just those sort of special memories – the anchors, if you like – which see you through the more difficult times. The ups and downs that all relationships will inevitably have.

Do you remember your sixth birthday, my honey? One of my favourites – though what a blessed kerfuffle I had that year over the tide tables! You were a complete water baby by this time – spending all day every day during our trips to Cornwall in your wetsuit. Rain. Shine.

I'm amazed you didn't shrink.

Your birthday being in the autumn, we had already had our week on the Lizard so Dad and I organised an extra weekend to a hotel overlooking the most amazing sandy beach.

Bear with me. This was key.

You had seen some film in which a person wrote a message in the sand – I think it may have been a marriage proposal. Something like that; can't remember exactly. Anyway. You had become a bit obsessed with it.

The hotel gave us a family suite, with you sleeping on a sofa bed in the dressing area adjacent to our bedroom. My biggest fear was that you would wake much too early in the excitement – and sure enough you did. So I played mean and said it was much too early to get up, even for a birthday girl, and that I needed to go to the gym before breakfast and presents.

I even put on my gym clothes! Is this ringing bells?

Then I set off to sort the surprise while Dad continued to play bad cop – insisting you try to sleep until a respectable hour.

I came back – around 8 a.m., terrified that the bloody tide was coming in so fast!

Then we drew back the curtains and took you onto the balcony.

It looked even better from the third floor than I dared hope. ***Happy Birthday, Melissa*** written in the fresh sand… beyond our balcony.

Other people were stirring by this time – and I remember looking across at them all smiling from their own balconies as you started jumping up and down with the excitement.

And then everyone started waving across at you and we all ended up singing happy birthday to you together from all the balconies.

Do you remember this? Please tell me you remember.

Eleanor sat back in the chair, enjoying the smile on her face. She reached into the top drawer of her dresser to find her boasting book. A small flip-style photo album of favourite shots.

There was one of the message in the sand, just as the tide was coming in to wash it away. Another of the wall and moat they built to try to divert the water for a bit. And then pictures of Melissa at the party organised for that sixth birthday once they returned home.

Eleanor shook her head, smiling, at the shot of Max with the whistle in his mouth.

We will be sued, Eleanor!

She remembered the panic on his face as she roared with laughter at him – waving his arms in frustration and blowing on his whistle – 'Six at a time! This is not funny,' as all of Melissa's friends piled onto the bouncy castle at once.

They had hired a hall so that Melissa could invite the whole class. When they booked the inflatable – the only size which would fit the hall in question – they had imagined, naively that the supplier would stay and supervise.

But no. *Not in the contract, mate.*

Instead he handed over a clipboard with a large and alarming sheet of 'rules'. No more than six on the castle at once. Be careful they don't bite their tongues. Bang their heads. Get concussion.

How she remembered the alarm on Max's face as the man then handed over a large whistle and put it around Max's neck. '*You will be needing this.*'

Poor Daddy.

'No, children, I mean it. Six at a time. Absolutely a maximum of six,' blowing his whistle and waving his arms in horror as the boys and girls, hyper from all the sugar intake, took not a blind bit of notice.

Of course no one got hurt. They all ate too much cake. They all drank too much Coke. One was sick in the toilets. But no one bit their tongue. Or got concussion. Or sued.

And one very tired little birthday girl was put to bed that night, looking so very happy.

'It was you who did the message on the beach back in Cornwall, wasn't it Mummy?'

'No. I have absolutely no idea how that happened. Some kind of magic,' Eleanor had kissed her daughter on the forehead, running her hand through her hair.

'I love you, Mummy.'

CHAPTER 18
Melissa – 2011

Melissa allowed Sam to read the first few pages of the journal only, which, she guessed, would be enough.

'Jesus Christ, Melissa,' fidgeting and then putting his hand on hers as they sat at the too-orange, too-lacquered pine table – his face white. 'You take as long as you need with this. You hear me?'

She nodded her head very rapidly. 'Thank you, Sam.'

'God. I feel like a complete arse now. Picking a fight with you.'

'Don't be silly. My fault.'

He had stood up and was pacing towards the balcony, looking out towards the pool with his hands on his hips.

'There are some really tough bits, Sam. Like the opening. And to start with, I just couldn't take it. That's why I didn't say anything. But there are some really lovely memories in there too. And some of the writing is triggering things I had completely forgotten about. I'm getting used to that now.'

He turned to face her but the sun behind him was so bright that she could not quite see his expression. And for this she was glad.

'In fact, I had this dream, Sam. The first night I was on the sofa bed. It was a recurring dream I used to have about my mother when I was a kid.'

'You've never told me this…'

'I know. I never told anyone. I didn't used to like it. I know that sounds odd but it really upset me. Then it came back when I was reading the book and I think now that I remember what it was. In the dream I was holding her hand on the beach. My mother. I think it was some birthday surprise or something.'

'Oh, Melissa.'

She smiled at his silhouette. Hands on hips against the bright blue sky – the picture broken only by the black railings of the balcony behind. Her mobile then vibrated on the table.

'Shit. Bet that's my dad. I have no idea how I'm going to tell him, Sam. It's going to be such a shock.'

Melissa picked up the phone to check the text, glancing at the journal. **Glad OK. Wish you answered all my texts! Have fun xxx Ps Would you say I'm sexist?**

She pulled a face, twisting her mouth and turned the phone to show Sam.

'Sexist? Your father? What's all that about?'

'God knows. I hope he's not in some kind of trouble at work,' Melissa sighed. 'Shit. He's done that so I'll ring him to find out what's going on. But I can't talk to him on the phone at the moment. I just can't.'

'OK. So what do you want to do then, Melissa? Today – I mean. Swim? Read. Lunch? Walk?'

'Do you mind, awfully, if I take the journal to the beach cafe? Read on a bit by myself for a while. I'll text my dad, calm him down and get my head together.'

'If that's what you want?'

'And then join me there for lunch? Say 12.30? How's that sound?'

'Sounds good to me.'

She picked up her bag, put the journal in the side pocket and then gathered her sunglasses and straw hat, him all the while watching and pretending this was not awkward, glancing instead to watch the families down by the pool through the open sliding doors to the balcony.

'I get nervous too, Sam.'

'Sorry?'

'About what's going to happen. To us. And in the journal. Every new bit I read, I get really nervous. About what it's going to say next.'

He limped across the room to kiss her on the forehead and she held onto his arm. 'I'm really sorry I didn't tell you before.'

'It's OK. I do understand, Melissa. So long as you ring me if you need me? And you try not to shut me out so much?'

She nodded.

'And what about your dad, then?'

'Oh I'll text him something bland. Talk to him properly when we get home. Face to face, I mean.'

He hugged her tightly then and watched from the balcony as she emerged from the stairwell below and walked past the pool, waving as she turned onto the track which led to the beach.

Melissa was surprised that she felt so much better that he now knew. Lighter. And unexpectedly calmer. That slightly detached sense of recovery after being shaken.

The route to the beach meandered through a small, wooded area within which locals and tourists on a budget were camping. It was a relaxed, rather hippy scene with laundry hanging on lines between trees and a range of mostly small tents with tables and chairs set up randomly in the open spaces. Melissa felt a smile on her face, wishing she was the kind of person who could cope with sleeping in a tent in that heat.

The beach cafe, being midweek, had plenty of free tables under shade, with reggae playing quietly from the bar area. Bob Marley mostly. She ordered a Coke, which they didn't have – happily settling for Pepsi instead. Melissa had always wondered at people who saw the difference.

There were several sets of young Cypriot friends playing cards at different tables – impossibly beautiful girls with perfect figures in tiny bikinis. Bronzed men. All having a wonderful time.

Melissa envied their relaxed smiles. The noise and the laughter. She imagined them having hot and very sweaty sex in their tiny tents between the trees and felt herself blushing as the waiter interrupted this thought – appearing suddenly with her drink.

She and Sam had made love precisely once on this holiday. Then she had a tummy bug. The accident. The journal…

Melissa checked reception on her phone. She watched the ocean in the distance. She watched small children covered in filthy, wet sand playing football on a stretch of beach to her right. She found her mind wandering to that moment when she was first handed her mother's book. The stretch of mahogany and the padded envelope. The stress of standing in front of the airline woman with the bloody case on the scales; to the accident. The scream of the bike. Sam's face in the car during the fight on the way back from Paphos.

Why could her life not be more carefree, like these people around her? Why did holidays so rarely turn out to be the relaxing break we imagined when we booked? Why could it not just be the scent of the sea? The scent of sex?

She blushed again.

Her mother's journal was in her bag. Waiting. It was such a relief that she no longer had to hide it. And yet she remained – yes; nervous about reading on.

Melissa took out the book and put it on the table. She stared at it for a while.

Her mother had met Sam just a couple of times when they were kids. She liked him.

Seems like a very nice boy, that Sam.

She stroked the cover. Wondered what her mother would think and say now about the terrible mess she seemed to be making of everything. Telling Sam she wasn't sure about marriage, not even understanding why.

Melissa decided that today she would just read back over the bits of the book now familiar. Yes. The cupcakes. The skittles. It took her a moment to find the right sections but the recipe headings were useful. Like chapters. She read through the pages slowly, soaking up the handwriting. The black ink. Imagining her mother at her desk, head forward and concentrating. And now Melissa could feel first a frown and then a smile breaking through. Goodness. She really did remember more of this. The skittles. Both hands up in the air when she managed a strike. Yes. That very particular sound of the wooden ball hitting the wooden skittles. And next she was conjuring a new picture. Her father coming home once – through the front door as they were playing in the hall still and her mother saying – *sorry. Haven't even thought about supper yet.*

And the cricket on the beach? Melissa put her hand up to her mouth, eyes staring. They used to visit this really wonderful beach in Cornwall. What was it called? She seemed to remember her father saying that it was where Daphne du Maurier learned to swim or something. The point being that it never seemed to be too busy, even in the early summer, so that they could claim a patch for cricket. And now Melissa was surprised to find herself really beaming as the memory grew and took clearer shape. The wind in their hair – her mother's long like her own back then.

You have your mother's hair, Melissa. Both of them tying it up into ponytails. She and her mother co-conspirators. Pulling faces and winking behind Max's back. Never very keen at all over the whole cricket scenario but not wanting to disappoint him.

If you could just concentrate, girls.

Laughing together as her father set the whole thing up ever so seriously – pacing out the distance between the stump and the bowling position. Scrawling lines in the sand.

Melissa looked back across at the boys playing football and was still smiling. And then her phone vibrated. A text from Sam to check she was OK.

Melissa replied that she was fine and would see him at 12.30 p.m., careful to add several kisses. She remembered then to send a short text to her father. **Having fun. Talk when home. x**

There was an hour until Sam joined her. She adjusted the umbrella at the table to provide more shade then sat with her hand just resting on the book, for her cold drink and then a coffee and then a second, watching the children playing and the ocean in the distance and the patch of vegetation just behind the bar where lizards darted to and fro, creating little clouds of dust as they made their own escape from the heat.

CHAPTER 19
Max – 2011

Max was now torn. He rationalised that a public place at the university was safest for this next meeting with Anna while paradoxically some element of privacy would also be necessary.

He had rather hoped that Melissa would call him after the text. That he could quietly sound her out. Melissa, with her columnist hat on, was pretty good with this legal stuff. Employment law. Blah blah. She was forever championing the underdog, hence people were always threatening to sue her. But – no. She did not ring and he had promised himself that he would not ring her. So he was on his own with this mess.

Finally, after much pacing, he plumped for the Litebite Bistro which was heaving at the beginning of term with freshers as their loans came in but even after a few short weeks was deserted – the same students now wandering around with Pot Noodles, presumably earmarking dwindling cash for alcohol.

Sure enough the Litebite was pretty much empty – only two other members of staff in one corner. Max claimed a second table at the other end of the cafe and checked his phone. No cancellation text from Anna. Good.

In the end she was just five minutes late wearing a long charcoal mac and an expression which was difficult to read. He placed a menu down in front of her as she struggled out of the coat, Max way too self-conscious to offer help.

'Thank you for meeting me again, Anna. I felt something to eat – well; that it would be a little more,' he was going to say relaxing but was suddenly worrying about every word he chose. 'Look. You know what, Anna – I'm going to put my cards right on the table here,' Shit. He really had no idea of best strategy.

'I was quite shaken up when you mentioned going to HR. I mean. I've never had any kind of trouble in that department. Not ever. And it's thrown me. Made me feel that we should talk some more. Clear the air properly?'

She employed the trick of silence.

'Look. I like your ideas, Anna. I genuinely think they have wings and I'd like to see them taken forward but I really don't have the time with all the departmental changes going on just now. Also. Honestly? The last time I got heavily involved championing a new course which required a lot of extra one-on-ones with a female colleague – well. You've probably heard the talk.'

'Deborah Hawkins?'

'The grapevine.'

'Always the grapevine.'

'So best you hear the truth from me. There was nothing improper. No cronyism. No taking advantage, I promise you of that. We were both single. And we started dating long after we started working on the project together. But honestly? I found it tricky balancing the professional and personal side of our relationship because I started worrying that people might accuse me of favouritism – even where there was none. Anyway. When the relationship didn't work out, there were a whole new set of questions and difficulties regarding that joint project. I tried my damnedest to ensure fair treatment for Deborah. But – well. I promised myself that I would tread very carefully in future when championing—'

'But we're not dating.'

'No, of course not. I didn't meant to imply a parallel. Rather that I'm a bit—'

'Paranoid?'

'I would prefer cautious.'

'Are you saying you can't work with women?'

'No. Of course not.' God, he wished that Melissa had rung. She would have warned what not to say. Christ. Maybe she would have advised against a meeting one-on-one. That this was a very, very bad idea.

'What then?'

'I'm just saying that when it comes to the sodding grapevine, I wouldn't want that history – me and Deborah, I mean – to in any way overshadow or compromise your very good ideas.'

'Did Deborah's project not get approved?'

'No, it didn't. Which was scandalous,' he sounded angry. 'It got my vote and I canvassed others entirely transparently but it was vetoed. All politics and number-crunching these days as you will know.'

'And you worried that Deborah might have thought—'

He shrugged.

And now she was smiling.

'Oh my God, Max. A professor with scruples?'

He wasn't sure if she was teasing but next she was looking down at the menu. 'I'm thinking – Panini? What about you?'

Only now did the echo confirm that she was calling him Max again.

'I hate paninis. Always burn my tongue. All that melted cheese,' he pulled the face of a cross child which made her laugh out loud. 'I always have the same thing. Baked spud with coronary.'

She raised a single eyebrow.

'Crispy bacon plus cheese. And how do you do that? The eyebrow thing. I've always wanted to be able to do that.'

She shrugged and did it with the other eyebrow.

'Now I hate you. Very jealous.'

'I'll go for roasted veg panini and skinny cappuccino,' she was passing him back the menu.

'I kid myself that I will run the bacon off later.'

'So you run too, Max?'

'I do,' he had stood up. 'Though don't even think about trying to rope me in to your charity marathon. I don't do marathons any more.'

'Pity. It's a good cause.'

'Isn't it always?'

By the time he was back at the table with drinks and a number for their food order, she was examining him intently.

'Look – Max. I really am sorry about blowing up the other morning. And I'm grateful for you explaining. It's just I'm deadly serious about these new ideas. And I really do need someone to champion them.'

'I know. And you're right. On reflection Frederick Montague was a knee-jerk panic. Probably not the best fit. How about I revisit that and see if I can line someone else up who has the time and the right profile just now. Someone flavour of the month. How does that sound?'

'That sounds much better. Thank you.'

They talked then about the running – Max interested in her training routine and sharing tips from his own experience. It had been a long time since he had taken on a marathon himself – he'd done one a couple years back, he explained, initially enjoying the timetable of the training. Something to push himself for. But in the end found he preferred to run solo, against his own stopwatch.

'I was going to pull out,' she leaned back in her chair as their food arrived. 'When my son did, I mean. But then I thought – hell. I may as well see it through now.'

'So – is there no persuading him to change his mind? Your son?'

She twisted her mouth to one side, 'Look, Max. My bloody waterworks the other day. Thank you for not mentioning it. I was a bit worried that was why you suggested lunch. That this was going to be some pastoral thing. A gentle verbal warning.'

Max could feel himself colouring.

'I promise you it won't happen again. God I can't believe that I actually did that. Cried,' she had her head in her hands.

Max could still feel the heat to his own cheeks, slurping water too quickly to counter this. 'Sorry,' coughing into his napkin – worried for a moment that it was going to escalate into a full-blown choke.

They both waited. He put up his hand to signal that he was recovering. She should go on.

'It's just we're having a few problems getting along. My son and I. Classic teenage stuff.'

'Got that T-shirt,' his voice was too high. Borderline choke. Humiliating.

'Sure you're OK?'

'Yes fine. Thank you.'

'So you have a teenager?'

'Yes. Well much older now. A daughter – Melissa. Very settled now. She's 25. I can promise you it all comes good.'

'So everyone keeps telling me,' she was beginning tentatively to bite into the edge of the panini, wincing and reaching for her own water.

'See. They always bloody burn. Paninis,' Max sprinkled more bacon over his potato and smiled.

Anna waved her hand in front of her open mouth, before gulping more water. 'I think I just underestimated things.'

'With the marathon?'

'No – the divorce. The impact on Freddie.'

Max shifted in his seat. He'd asked for this additional meeting to better clear the air between them. Calm things down. He hadn't expected this.

'Sorry. I'm embarrassing you? Oversharing. A bad habit. It's just I feel I should repay the trust. Explain myself properly. How I was, I mean, the other day.'

'It's fine, Anna. I don't want you to feel awkward.' Max really had no idea what was the right or wrong thing to say here.

'The divorce. My husband and I went for the two-year separation. I thought it would give Freddie time to adjust and that it would get easier for him. Turns out I was wrong.'

And now Max tried very hard not to let what was happening inside his body show on the outside. But he was looking at her ring finger again.

'I'm doing it again, aren't I? Making you uncomfortable, Max? Talking like this. I don't know what's the matter with me.'

'It's fine.'

'No. it's not all right. I'm sorry. I shouldn't have threatened you with HR. That was over the top.'

Such a relief. To be Max again.

'I misjudged you and that wasn't fair of me.'

She sipped more water.

'So. Anyway. I had this naive notion that a fresh start and new place would be good for both me and Freddie so I got this post and I got him into the grammar for his A levels. He seemed OK about the whole idea. Until last week.'

'And?'

'And then he decided that living here suddenly "sucks". That his new school "sucks". That doing the fundraising marathon "sucks". That living with his mother "sucks". And that he'd rather spend all his holidays living with his dad who is currently teaching English as a foreign language in Germany.'

'Oh dear.'

'I'm hoping it will all pass. A phase. He's right in the middle of A levels, for God's sake. But it's slightly taken the wind out of my sails.'

'And you like it here?'

'Love it. We've got a small place near the river. Honestly my idea of bliss. Water nearby. There are great walks – and great places for training. House is smaller than we're used to but I'd hoped Freddie would be a bit more forgiving.'

'Teenagers major in the zone of self, I'm afraid. They're all the same. Give him time. It'll pass.'

'You think?'

'Sure.'

'So – are you close to your daughter? Melissa did you say?'

'Yes. I like to think so. She's working as a journalist now. Consumer affairs. Syndicates a column for a bunch of regional papers. Quite feisty stuff. Payday loan rip-offs. Pensioner cons – that sort of stuff. I'm very proud of her. In fact she's just been offered a short contract with one of the nationals.'

'Goodness. That's a coup so early on.'

'Yes. All very promising…'

'And she lives nearby now?'

'Not too far.'

'This is just the stuff I need to hear. You see. You found a perfectly good way forward. After divorce, I mean. Most people tell me they do in the end. With the kids. That's what I keep telling myself. That it will all come good in the end.'

Max concentrated on the final slices of his baked potato, tipping some more of the salad dressing from the tiny porcelain jug onto the leaves and tomato pieces, watching the oily river catch the light against the white platter. No matter how many years passed, he always hated this bit. The point at which you had to decide whether to correct a perfectly reasonable assumption.

In the early days it had seriously offended him. The implication that Eleanor would have chosen to leave him. These days he realised it was purely maths. Most men of his age who were single again were divorced. He had mentioned that he was single when he dated Deborah so of course Anna would assume a divorce.

Sometimes he could get away with just changing the subject…

'So – your ex, Max. She still lives in this country? I don't meant to pry, it's just my ex is talking about moving from Germany to Australia. To be honest, I don't think he's sufficiently organised to pull it off but it still frightens the life out of me. Germany was bad enough but at least it's a short plane ride. Now I'm really not at all sure how the hell I should play it if Freddie wanted to go to Australia.'

'She died.'

'Sorry?'

'My wife.'

'Oh my god. I'm so sorry, Max.' The freeze frame then. The excruciating moment as they both stopped eating. Stopped moving.

'It's all right. It was a long time ago,' he smiled, doing what he had learned to do so very well – to try to smooth over the embarrassment. To imply that being a long time ago meant he was fine about it all. He always did this. Tried to suck up all the awkwardness himself, as if it were somehow his fault.

Well practised – yes; though strangely it never failed to surprise him how there was always this same tiny ping inside: this horrid little contraction of muscle which he had imagined would pass over time but had not and which he had, therefore, to overcome every single time so that the person who had committed the involuntary faux pas would not feel too embarrassed.

The muscular ping was for some reason especially strong today and Max tried to make sense of this as he ate the remainder of his salad while Anna completed the familiar cycle of discomfort which he so hated.

Max did not want anyone to feel sorry for him, least of all Anna. What he wanted was to be a man who had not lost the woman he had so loved, and given that was impossible, he wanted some end game to being this new man who over and over had to go on saying it out loud.

That they were not, please, to be embarrassed. But his wife was dead, actually.

Pavlova

4 egg whites - ROOM TEMPERATURE (medium size eggs)
8 oz caster sugar
1 teaspoon cornflour
1 tiny dash of white wine vinegar (barely a teaspoon)
Three drops pure vanilla extract
Oven at 140°C

First nag – do not even think of trying this with eggs straight from the fridge. And your bowl must be super clean. No oil or bits of yolk. Yuk! Beat the egg whites with electric mixer until soft peaks. You should be able to turn the bowl upside down without the lot flopping out. Then whisk in the sugar a bit at a time but without stopping. Also add the cornflour, a tiny dash of vinegar and vanilla. You will now have a glossy meringue. Use a metal spoon to spread this into a circle on greaseproof paper, then use a spoon to make a little dent in the middle. Cook in the oven for 1 hour and 15 mins. Next – turn the oven off but leave the meringue inside with the door open until it is completely cold. Then turn it onto a lovely dish and fill with whipped double cream and your favourite fruits – I like strawberries and raspberries mixed together.

OK. Deep breath. So the first thing to say about this recipe is – do not be afraid, which is rich coming from me as I shied away from pavlova for years and years out of sheer bloody terror. My mother made this outstanding pavlova – all crisp and crunchy on the outside and toffee gooey inside. Soon after I married, I had a bash myself and you should have seen the disaster. Dis. Gust. Ing. No idea whether I over whipped or under whipped or what. Anyway. Being such an appalling perfectionist, I threw in the towel until years later, you were moving up to a new class in primary school and Mrs Edwards (remember her? Year 5 – long, dark hair with red glasses?) asked me if I would bring or make a meringue for the Christmas party. Gawd. I should have bought one, of course. That would have been the sensible and sane thing to do. But – oh no! There followed a ridiculous few days in which I experimented with three different recipes from three different books and finally hit upon the fail-safe one above. Seriously – Melissa. This works. If you follow it to the letter, you will not go wrong. Always a show-stopper for entertaining and you can use it to make little nests if you like – cutting down the oven time, obviously. And OK you will have to walk a million miles to avoid slapping all that sugar straight to your thighs, but I am not going to waste any breath in this journal on all that bloody nonsense. Every woman has to figure out the food versus curves equation for herself and all I say is – whatever you are happy with, *be happy with*. Just don't, for heaven's sake, waste too much time worrying about what other people are happy with. Especially the frogs.

And now something less sweet. I wish I didn't have to bring this up at all but things have taken a completely unexpected turn. I had this rather odd session with my oncologist this morning. Took me by surprise and I find that I have no choice really but to mention it again.

He is a very lovely guy – my oncologist – who has accepted my decision from here to veto the more gruesome treatments in favour of quality time and so has now involved what he calls the 'comfort' team. Palliative is the less pleasant term – but whatever; they are doing a jolly good job. I am, for the most part, more 'comfortable' these days than I have been in a while. I was very lucky in that I never lost all my hair and what I did lose is now growing back so I can stop wearing the extra hairpieces to cover things up. To even everything up I decided on a crop and though you were shocked at first (do you remember – I dyed it a very dramatic blonde!) you are now very used to it and Daddy reckons it's 'very Paris chic', whatever that means. I realise that you have noticed I am not always myself and you have a lot of sleepovers at Grandma's (thank heaven for Max's lovely mum). We seem to have taken on some strange narrative about tummy trouble which worries me a bit as I suspect you will confuse it with girls' chatter over periods. But I don't think you are worrying unduly. You seem happy to me. Relaxed. Which is what I want.

Anyway – back to Dr Palmer (Hugo on a good day) my oncologist who brought up this morning quite out of the blue the question of gene testing. I knew already that he had been involved in some of the early research into all this stuff. It may well be more common knowledge in your time zone – the BRCA1 gene mutation – but as I write it is all still pretty new and only those of us sadly in the territory hear anything about it. For myself I never felt that it had any bearing on my case. There are no other cases of breast cancer in the family that I know of so how could it?

Mummy darling was lost, as you know, much too young with wretched cancer also but it was an entirely different kind. Ovarian. I had always personally wondered whether that was tragically to do with the fact that she had a number of miscarriages. The reason I was an only – born so late to them.

But my oncologist shared something which quite winded me today. I am wondering, even as I write, whether I should just kick this into the long grass until I have more information but the problem is I really don't know how much of this book will get filled. So I will share the narrative as it unfolds – hopefully ending with complete reassurance for you, which is now my absolute goal.

Deep breath. You remember that earlier in the journal, I advised you to check yourself very regularly as a standard precaution and to go straight to the doctor if you find anything unusual? I said then what I honestly believe to be true – that this wretched thing is a statistical blip only in my case. I don't want paranoia and I don't believe in my bones that what I have is any risk to you.

But Dr Palmer's talk this morning took us in an unexpected direction, Melissa….

Eleanor heard Max's key in the door and felt a strange mix of both irritation and relief. She hadn't really wanted to continue with the entry and was happy to break off and tuck the book away, even though it would inevitably now hang over her. She had been having a better day, ironically – not feeling as tired as usual – and so had felt determined to get this godawful entry done. She checked her watch – puzzled. He wasn't due home for hours.

'Darling?' His footsteps on the stairs.

'Up here. I wasn't expecting you. Everything OK?' Pretending to jot notes on her pad – Melissa's book safely tucked deep into the second drawer.

Max let out a long sigh. 'You look good today. Pinker cheeks. How did it go? With your appointment.'

'Fine. Well – mostly fine. Actually there is something I need to discuss. But what are you doing home? I thought you had seminars this afternoon?'

'Bumped them to Andrew. Half the group are out on some fieldwork anyway. Bank of England. So it's not a problem.'

'I keep telling you – you don't need to do this, Max. All this coming home early. I am fine. I will ring if I am not and they've offered the district nurse whenever I need her. It's way better when you are in work. Feels better.' The truth was she hated to see the worry in his eyes; the sense of helplessness. Clinging to the rhythm of their old routine felt better for Melissa. And better for Max too.

'Yes. Well. Like I say – only a handful of students around today so no big deal.'

'I don't want you getting into trouble, Max.'

'I am far from in trouble. I am the department's rising star, remember.'

She smiled. It was a quote from a review of one of his latest papers which had again drawn some good media attention. A slot on national radio. Max had stuck the Sunday Paper comment piece above his desk downstairs with 'rising star' highlighted in day-glow yellow pen. Melissa had added gold stars to the cutting from her craft drawer.

'So what is this bit that's not completely fine, Eleanor?'

She swung her legs round the side of the chair to face him better, pausing a moment.

'Dr Palmer – Hugo – hit me with something of a surprise today. About this new gene testing that we talked about once before.'

Max shifted from one foot to the other. They had had only one brief conversation about the gene research – in the early days when they had been bemoaning Eleanor's terrible bad luck. To be hit so young.

At that point there was no pattern in her family to suggest any relevance. Her mother had lived for five years after her diagnosis and treatment for her own cancer. There was no suggestion of a link.

But Dr Palmer had now mentioned that he was involved in more ongoing research into the possibility that the genetic flaw was relevant in both cancers. There was a second gene – BRCA2 – which had apparently been discovered and he was wondering if Eleanor would consent to be involved in that new research work?

'Why? What is he saying?'

'Well. I think he was wondering if I would consent to having this gene test as part of his new research. You know. To see if I had inherited some genetic mutation which was the reason for this.'

'But there's been no other breast cancer that we know of. I thought this testing was for clusters. For families with lots of cases of breast cancer—'

'Yes. Well. Officially they think this new test will only be offered to families with a very obvious incidence. But it's this new departure. The ovarian cancer—'

'No. No. Eleanor. Do you not think we have enough going on? I don't want you having some test that you don't need to have. And what's the bloody point, anyway. Just for something for him to write up in his research?'

'You're right. I said I didn't think you would like the idea. I was just a little bit thrown by it all...'

Neither of them mentioned Melissa.

Over supper they were almost ridiculously upbeat to compensate. Max doing his funny walk for Melissa while preparing a particularly delicious risotto. It was only much, much later when she had gone to bed and Max and Eleanor were downstairs, both not listening to a play on Radio Four. When it had finished, Eleanor snapped off the radio and offered him a hot drink.

'So this test, Eleanor. This new gene thing. Did Dr Palmer say it could have implications for Melissa? Is that what he was saying now?'

Eleanor turned on the corner lamp which shed a warm glow across the two rear walls of the sitting room. By the time she had turned back into the room, Max's face in contrast was white.

'Please tell me he's not now saying that Melissa could be at risk?'

CHAPTER 20
Melissa – 2011

The water was absolutely beautiful – clear and warm. Melissa watched the froth wash over her toes and felt the pull of the sand beneath both feet as the wave retreated. She stood still until the next much stronger wave took her by surprise.

'I'll laugh if you go over,' Sam had retreated from the water, still nervous over his injured leg, sandals in one hand.

Melissa now joined him and they moved further back to the drier, firmer sand to sit down with Sam stretching his bad leg straight out in front of him.

'God – I love this part of the day. Before it gets too hot. Should get up this early more often,' Melissa was now leaning back on her straightened arms, head tilted to the sun with her eyes closed.

'Yeah. Me too. The heat later really makes this bloody leg itch.'

'Fancy breakfast at the cafe?'

'Good idea…'

It had been so much better since he knew about the journal. She had shown him some more carefully-chosen sections. The entry on the biscuits and the boeuf bourguignon recipe. Melissa was still cautious, but they were beginning to talk a little about some of the memories her mother's writing had stirred. She was surprised by how much this helped.

In fact, she had been making a few jottings since she remembered about the box of equipment in the garage. Melissa had been noting down all the little scenes unlocked by the recipes and her reading. The little comments her mother made when she was cooking. The sound of the jam bubbling. That image of the damp cloth in her mother's hand as she so proudly cleaned her Kenwood Chef. The writer in Melissa had wanted to try to put down on paper her shock at all this; that food and cooking could trigger this, especially in someone like her who had in the past been so very disinterested in the kitchen. A part of her wanted to share these jottings but she wasn't quite sure how.

'Listen, Melissa. I've been having a think. About the journal. How about we cook all these recipes in sequence when we get back?'

Melissa sat up straight, not entirely surprised they were thinking about the journal at the same time. 'You serious? Me? Jam – and pavlova? I don't think so…'

'Oh come on, Melissa,' he had turned towards her, trying to read her expression. 'You're not as bad a cook as you make out. And you must surely want to? Have thought about it?'

Melissa was looking back at him closely. 'You're right,' she brushed sand from her legs. 'I do want to try them; of course I do. In fact I've been thinking a lot about all the stuff they've stirred up,' she was remembering that time on the balcony. The very transient but strong sense of what it felt like to have her mother in the room.

'But I want to get it right. I don't want to rush it. And I'm worrying about how to tell my dad.'

'I get that. And I didn't mean go hammer and tongs. I just mean try a few of the recipes. See how you feel. I expect it's what your mother hoped.'

Melissa was just about to share her idea about writing something. She didn't want to trespass on her family's privacy, of course – and she wouldn't do anything until she had finished the journal, spoken to her father and cleared her head. But she was thinking that it would be really nice to create some kind of open platform to share what her mother had called 'stories at the stove'. Maybe some kind of blog? Yes – a forum to both share and honour the way food and the kitchen could so surprise. *Unlock things.* She couldn't, surely, be alone in the powerful feelings her mother's recipes had triggered. Perhaps she could encourage other people to share their own stories too?

Melissa was just working out how to bounce this idea past Sam when his phone rang. He pulled a face. There had been very few intrusions. Just one minor query from the office – a hiccup over listed building consent over another chapel conversion which only Sam could sort.

Melissa watched his eyes widen as he listened.

'Yeah. And I love you too, mate. But you sound as if you could do with some coffee. Where are you, Marcus?'

Melissa frowned. Sam's older brother.

He listened for a little longer, interrupting where he could. 'Look. It's lovely to hear from you too, buddy, but I'm on a beach. In Cyprus. You need to get yourself some coffee and get some kip. Yes?' He listened some more, frowning and then widening his eyes in turn. 'OK. Yep, I hear you. But I'm going to have to ring off now, Marcus. All right? You need to go to bed, mate. Yes. Yes. And I love you too.'

He ended the call but then began to dial immediately.

'Sorry, Mel. But I'm going to have ring home. He says he's at Dad's. Drunk as a skunk.'

'Are they all right. Your parents?'

'Apparently.'

Sam then walked and talked for several minutes, hobbling to and fro on the sand, his face falling and putting his right arm up over the top of his head. His posture of panic.

Finally he rang off, let out a long sigh and tilted his head towards the beach bar.

'Come on. I'll fill you in over breakfast.'

Sam waited until their coffee arrived, his lips tight. Face pale. The story, when he finally shared it, was a shock. Marcus was apparently back with his parents in a state of complete meltdown after his wife Diana had suddenly left him.

'You are kidding me?' Melissa could genuinely not believe it. Marcus and Diana were the golden couple. Matching convertibles. Waterside loft apartment. Just two years earlier they had had the dream wedding at an art deco hotel on an island in Devon. They had actually left the reception by helicopter

'So much for my campaign for wedded bliss,' Sam stirred two sugars into his coffee.

Melissa blushed.

Sam then explained that his father had been hoping to spare them from the crisis until they got back. Hadn't realised that Marcus, just returned by taxi after an all-night bender with a friend, had rung Sam. They hadn't wanted to spoil their trip.

Bottom line – Marcus's company – was going down the tubes. He had taken out a second mortgage without telling Diana. And she – oblivious over the dosh and suspecting Marcus of an affair – had decided on a fling to balance things up. The rift had apparently all started within six months of the wedding. Marcus wanted to start a family and Diana very definitely didn't. They hadn't thought to discuss it properly before the aisle.

'Run off now with some guy in IT at her bank, apparently.'

'Oh dear God, no. Poor Marcus.'

'Well, according to Dad, he's been a real silly arse himself. Stuck his head in the sand over the financial mess. Ignored pleas from the bank for meetings. Right pickle.'

'Jeez. And I was always a bit jealous. They always seemed so sorted.'

'All smoke and mirrors, it seems. Worse thing is Diana doesn't yet know that the bubble's burst financially. She's banking on a healthy divorce settlement, by all accounts.'

'Well I don't want to be in the room when that chicken comes home,' Melissa raised her eyebrow as the waiter appeared with a basket of warm bread and a plate of butter and jam in a small bowl.

'I've told Dad I'll go over as soon as I get back.'

'Of course.'

Melissa examined Sam's face closely as he began to spread the butter on a large hunk of bread.

'I really am very sorry, Sam. So is there no way back for them?'

He shook his head. Drank more coffee. Swept his hair back. Gazed out at the sea. Sam idolised his older brother. Marcus could be a bit brash, she had thought when she first met him, but he had a good heart, and Melissa, being an only, had rather envied and admired how close the brothers were.

'So – do you want to talk about it? Marcus?'

'Do you mind actually if we don't. How about we talk about you and this job instead? I know you haven't had the energy to think about it – with the journal, I mean. But you're going to have to make a decision soon. Or bump the meeting with the editor.' He was fidgeting with the sugar sachets.

'Still undecided, then?' Sam caught the waiter's eye to order some more bread and two more coffees, setting the extra sachets of sugar ready by his spoon.

'Oh – I don't know, Sam. I'm still shit scared,' Melissa felt a frisson of guilt, realising that she really ought to have been giving this more thought rather than letting her mind wander with ideas for new writing projects. 'You know me. PhD in fearing the worst. No idea what to do.'

It was all so unexpected. And the fact it was a tabloid made things tricky. Melissa had rather rashly once sworn that she would never work for a red top. But she had already carved out a niche for herself as a consumer columnist, starting with freelance articles in her final year at uni and continuing during her training at The Bartley Observer.

Melissa not only loved consumer journalism but had just pipped more experienced colleagues to win a national columnist award after campaigning against Rachman-style landlords who were taking advantage of the buy-to-let boom and overcharging for under-par and in some cases dangerous accommodation. The whole rented sector had gone nuts since the housing bubble burst. Many potential home-owners were renting, waiting for house prices to fall further. Others were renting simply because they had no choice. No deposits to buy. The mathematics of supply and demand had made it a landlords' market and some of the less scrupulous were taking serious advantage.

Melissa had been exposing the worst cases in a series of columns. Her editor was turning grey over the pile of litigation threats, but Melissa knew they were all empty. She loved the territory and the threats to sue simply made her more determined. Campaigning journalism was by nature potentially libellous. But she researched each case meticulously, publishing only when she was sure of the defence of 'justification' to keep the paper's own legal team happy.

Very soon trading standards and then the police became involved. A student was burned badly when a faulty immersion heater exploded in a property owned by one of the landlords she had been exposing. The tenant had complained many times about the immersion heater and Melissa had taken up the case in her column but the protests fell on deaf ears.

The story made national television news with Melissa interviewed and quoted across television, radio and the national press. She immediately started to get headhunting calls – the best of which was this offer of a one-year freelance contract to launch a national campaigning consumer column for the tabloid. But Melissa was worried about the reputation of the red tops. Also her future.

'What I'm worried about Sam is that it's running before I can walk. That I will balls it all up, get myself fired and be left with nothing at all.'

'Just to look on the bright side,' Sam was smiling.

The truth was Melissa was scared of freelancing. The financial uncertainty. She was very much an ideas person, which was good for freelancing. But for all that, she also liked the certainty of a monthly cheque. Yet others on the Bartley Observer were green with envy – arguing that the lights were going out on the local newspaper industry anyway. What did she really have to lose?

'You know what I think. That you should just bloody well go for it. Take the contract,' Sam locked eyes as she stirred her own coffee. 'I mean – look at Marcus. So much for being financially sorted. Reckon there's nothing safe these days. You may as well take a risk, Melissa. Might just work out fine.'

She held his gaze for just a moment then took a deep breath and looked away toward the beach as the waiter arrived with their second basket of bread and more coffee. For just a moment, Melissa suddenly had a new thought. Maybe the London editor would like the idea of the blog too? Melissa narrowed her eyes and felt the frown. *No. Too personal. And I'm not qualified. Don't know a thing about food. Don't be ridiculous, Melissa. One thing at a time.*

'Oh, I don't know. We'll see. So – Marcus then. Was he very drunk?'

'Well, let's just say he phoned me up specifically to tell me how much he loved me. That I was his best friend in the whole of the world.'

And then he clinked his coffee cup to Melissa's. 'Happy holidays, eh?'

Melissa tilted her head 'Is he going to be all right? Marcus?'

'God knows.'

CHAPTER 21
Eleanor – 1994

'So you don't think this gene trial wotsy – this new work Dr Palmer is doing – has any real knock-on for Melissa?' Max was checking his tie in the mirror. They had not talked of this since Eleanor's last appointment which had so winded each of them. Separately. Secretly.

'Didn't seem that way but I'll ask him again today. To clarify? So what sort of day have you got ahead?'

'Usual. And you won't let him talk you into it. No more tests, I mean. Just for his international buddies.' Max had made it clear this was non-negotiable. Unless there was something involving Melissa, he wanted no part of it. *Look, I have gone along with you – not telling Melissa. Preparing her. So I need you to go along with me on this? Yes, Eleanor?*

'I can come with you, if you like. In fact I'd like to.' Now he was sitting on the edge of the bed, undoing the top button of his shirt beneath his tie. Eleanor felt something inside her shift. It was the idiosyncrasies. Doing up his shirt, putting on his tie and then undoing the top shirt button afterwards. Putting his tea cup down alongside the saucer after the first sip – never back on the china, for a reason he had failed to adequately explain. Something to do with drips. Tearing paper napkins into long matching strips when they were out for coffee. Always firing the central locking device at the car twice.

Always scanning a new room for flies. Always forgetting something.

All these things killed her because they had once upon a time annoyed her and now with every repetition she asked the same question.

How many more times?

'I'd honestly rather you go to work. I'll be in and out in five minutes today. No point you disrupting your day.'

'And you promise you won't be talked into something.'

'I won't be talked into something.'

He kissed her on the mouth, closing his eyes and doing what he always did these days, leaving his lips touching hers that little bit longer. One second. Two. Three

'Go. You'll be late.'

'Right. I'll ring.'

'Just go.'

She heard him march then into Melissa's room to wake her, listened to her daughter's response – *Go away, Daddy* – then his footsteps on the stairs. The jangle of keys. The front door. She waited. Two minutes and the key was back in the lock. Swearing.

'Left a book. Sorry. '

There was the sound of scrabbling about, more swearing and then finally the slam of the front door for the second time. Eleanor smiled.

'You awake still, Melissa? Come on into Mummy's bed.'

Melissa was like Max in the mornings, needing a period of adjustment. Trying to pitch for cooperation in the form of breakfast, teeth or dressing until she was through this zone was entirely counterproductive. So this was the preferred sequence. Max would wake her. Eleanor would pause. Then Eleanor would call her through to do her hair quietly in her bed, by which time Melissa would have surfaced sufficiently to face the day.

It was not only practical but for Eleanor now a highlight; the silent brushing of her daughter's hair as she sat, hugging her knees with her chin resting on the same. Half asleep still.

Melissa had what Eleanor liked to call suggestible hair. It would quite easily be dried straight and silky – calmed and straightened with the application of heat. But left to dry naturally it had a soft curl. Shiny, dark hair with glints of autumn in the right light.

'You have lovely hair.'

'You always say that, Mummy. Every day.'

'Ponytail?'

Melissa merely shrugged through a yawn and so Eleanor gently continued, wrapping a black velvet hair tie from the bedside table around her wrist and raking the brush through her daughter's hair – stroke after stroke.

'So have you got used to Mummy's short hair yet?'

Another shrug.

'Well it's very easy to look after, though I think we should keep yours long. Much too beautiful to cut – not until you are very much older.'

She could feel her daughter yawn again as she took the hair tie from her wrist and carefully wrapped it twice around the ponytail to secure it firmly.

'Ow.'

'Sorry, darling. There. That's done,' she then hugged her daughter tight. 'We should teach Daddy how to do your hair.'

'I don't want Daddy to do it.'

'Well. Maybe he would like to. Just sometimes.'

'I'd have to get up earlier.'

Eleanor laughed. 'No, darling. You wouldn't have to get up earlier.'

She made pancakes as a treat with lemon and sugar and just thirty minutes later watched Melissa disappear across the playground, turning for a final wave.

How many more times?

Eleanor had an hour before her meeting and so fired up the computer to see what she could find out. Max was the computer whizz in the house. She the dinosaur. Recently he had been trying to explain the new internet search function but she had been cynical – a wet blanket, certain it would all be the death knell for proper libraries and intellectual integrity. But now Eleanor needed it and so struggled to remember the instructions Max had given her. She tried a few keywords as he had explained. The gene names. BRCA-1 and BRCA-2. A number of pages were slowly listed and Eleanor began to read – her heart sinking.

She had no idea that things had come this far. But the more she read now, the more she understood why Dr Palmer was interested in her case.

The latest work seemed to be suggesting that the faulty gene they had found could be carried silently, not just by women but by men too. Eleanor was an only. Her mother had no sisters – only two brothers. So what did that mean? For the risks? For their gene tree? That the only two women in the tree for three generations had got 'unlucky'?

The article she found suggested only families with multiple cancers pointing to a link or gene fault were likely to be offered counselling and testing in the future. This wasn't yet widespread. Mainstream.

Eleanor turned off the computer and took out her journal for Melissa. She had been pasting in old family pictures and a very basic family tree with some anecdotes from her mother. She turned then to the back of the journal where she had started a new, separate section on motherhood.

Eleanor realised that a young Melissa would have very little interest in this part initially, which was why she had put it at the back. She remembered herself at 25. Goodness – parenthood drew such a line in the sand.

The before. The afterwards.

It also divided your world into two sets of people. Those with children who understood. And those without who did not. It was not a judgemental thing – suggesting that one group was better or worse than the other. Just a fact.

Until you had paced a house in the early hours with a colicky child, you did not know. Until you had watched a nurse put a needle into the arm of your baby, half wanting to punch them as your child howled, you did not know. You might guess and you might imagine how all of this might feel, but you could not know.

And so she was writing this section on parenting because she hated to think of Melissa's future. A mother without a mother. A mother with no maternal compass.

Also, it was quite simply the loveliest part to write. Practical tips on the colic and the teething and how to survive the madness of no sleep (*remember that sleep deprivation is used as a form of torture; it is normal to feel insane*). Brutal honesty about the moment when the sheer tiredness of those early days made you ask wicked questions of yourself. The shameful daydreaming over whether you had really done the right thing. Whether you would ever again feel in control of your life? The hallucinating about the old days. Long baths and reading books.

But always in the end....*the joy, Melissa*. The indescribable joy. That smell. The ache of your arm as the baby slept in the crook of it. The sound of the sucking as they fed. The eye contact.

Goodness. She had almost forgotten that. The eye contact.

Of the lurch inside every single time your child caught your eye, from the playground, from the front of a school stage or from a climbing frame in the park.

I get that pull, that lurch, over you, my darling girl. Every day. And one day, I hope that you will know exactly what I am wittering on about.

Because, I promise you, it will suddenly become what you live for …

Shit. Eleanor checked the clock and realised she would have to hurry. Too often it was like this. Tired. Hurrying. Late.

She phoned the oncologist's secretary to reassure that she was on her way – ten minutes late at the very outside – and then grabbed her coat, tucking the journal beneath her underwear in the second drawer down; pausing just a moment to look at the title to wonder if it gave the wrong impression? Worrying about keeping this from Max and what he would think in the future and realising also that within these few short weeks the whole idea and purpose of this book for Melissa was beginning to change.

CHAPTER 22

Max − 2011

Max was about fifteen minutes early as he pulled into his parking slot and so listened to the latest on the Greek Euro crisis. The second bailout was finally agreed. A fifty per cent reduction in the Greek debt and a trillion Euro rescue fund.

Various European leaders were eloquently upbeat in their sound bites but Max shook his head. They seemed to be forgetting that Greece was still broke. Bailout or no bailout.

He snapped off the radio and turned to the back seat to discover that the green folio of assignments which he was one hundred per cent sure he had put alongside his keys was impossibly not there.

Shit.

He turned and stretched awkwardly to feel around the floor. Must have fallen into the well behind the driver's seat. But no.

Shit and damn and fuck. He had left the bloody assignments plus his feedback at home. And he hadn't updated it online. He was swearing some more, checking his watch to work out if there was time to dash home after his first lecture, when he turned to open the door to feel his body jolt half out of his skin.

'Sorry. Sorry.'

She was blushing as Max fumbled for the electric window control, heart pounding.

'I didn't mean to startle you, Max. It's just I saw the car. And I wanted…'

She was wearing running clothes. A black vest with purple stripes and charcoal sweat pants.

Max had not the foggiest idea where to look. Jesus. He thought she ran on Wednesday lunchtimes.

'I thought you ran on Wednesday lunchtimes.'

'Oh. Yes.' She pulled her head back – apparently surprised that he had remembered this. 'I do. Wednesday lunchtimes. But I'm getting myself into a paddy about this half marathon. Not ready. Easier to do the extra training here and use the showers before I start.'

'Right.'

'Look. Max. About the other day—'

'Please. It's absolutely fine, Anna. If you're happy with the transfer. With Sarah as your new mentor, then we're good.'

'I didn't mean that actually. Although we've had a meeting – Sarah and me – and I think you're right. We're a good fit. She's very keen. Very switched on.'

'Good. Good. That's good.'

'But that's not what I wanted to apologise about.'

'Look. It's fine. Anna. Please. We talked it all through at lunch. All good.'

She had her hands on her hips, looking at the ground, and then stepping back as he put the window up and got out of the car, checking his watch as if he were suddenly running late.

'You in lectures all morning, Max?'

'Yes, actually. Until lunch. Got to keep an eye on this new bailout too.'

'Of course. Look. I'm tied up this morning too. But I was wondering. Well. If you could find a window to grab a sandwich or something again later?'

'Oh right.'

'I felt terrible. The way you rushed off. Me putting my size sevens in.'

'Nonsense.'

'Look. I have something I want to ask you.'

'Oh right.'

She was smiling now. Not blushing any longer and looking him directly in the eye. 'It would make me feel a whole lot better if you could spare ten minutes. This lunchtime?'

He smiled back. 'Well,' he checked his watch, not noticing what it said. 'There's no need. For any embarrassment, I mean. But if you'd like to.'

'Twelve thirty? Same place?'

'Fine. Yes. Why not.' *To hell with the folder.*

And then she turned, waving her hand as she headed back to the main sports complex – Max watching her perfect bottom moving side to side as she jogged off.

He tried to look away but could not. Did this make him sexist? This fascination – or was it now an obsession – with Anna?

Oh, bloody hell. He wanted to ask her on a date. He really, really wanted to ask her on a date.

Three hours later and he was en route to the bistro, chanting it in his head. *Do not ask her out, Max. Do not.*

Think of Deborah. Think of the fallout of that fiasco.

A perfectly lovely woman. A whole year and then suddenly she had assumed that things would move on. He had not thought it through; got so used to Sophie and the no-strings agenda he had completely forgotten that was what other people expected.

He had decided to be five minutes late for Anna – picturing himself strolling up to her at the table. *Sorry. Had he kept her waiting?*

He had never been very good at sitting on his tod in public places. Even with a newspaper, he felt exposed. Eleanor said that he hummed when he was nervous, though Max never noticed this. *You OK, darling? You're humming.*

Don't hum, he said to himself as he checked his watch – five minutes late exactly –turning the corner towards the wide entrance to the Litebite.

She was already sitting at the same table they had used the other day – the menu in her hand, and what was sweet and made him feel guilty as he watched her for just a moment before she looked up, was that she looked uncomfortable herself. Picking up the menu for a moment and then placing it back in the little stainless steel stand. Checking the clock on the wall. Then her own watch.

'Hello, Anna. Sorry I'm a tad behind. I always hate sitting waiting. Have you been here long?'

'Just five minutes.'

'So do you know what you want? I'll probably order my heart attack again. Bit pushed for time so best I order straight off.'

'No. My idea so my shout today,' she stood up.

'No please.'

And now it felt a little farcical and they did the dance over the bill, Max worrying that it was sexist to insist and so he sat down 'Baked spud again with the bacon and a cup of earl grey.'

'Milk?'

'Full cream, please.'

A few minutes later and she was back at the table with the drinks and a ticket for their food which she slipped under the metal menu holder, smiling.

'So the bailout then. Anything interesting on the radio? I missed it.'

'Not really. More of the same.' Max smiled. 'So – it's going to work out with Sarah, you think? I'm glad. Should have thought of her in the first place.'

'Yes. She's very nice. In fact that's why I've ambushed you again.'

He raised his eyebrows.

'I've invited Sarah for a little supper. Tuesday. And I was wondering if you would like to join us? A handover, if you like. More my way of apologising properly for my meltdown.'

'Well – that's very kind. But there's no need.'

'I don't want to put you on the spot – obviously. But – well, it would make me feel better. About the other day.'

'Right.'

'So – you'll come? I've promised Sarah paella.'

'Oh well. If you're talking paella,' Max smiled but was non-plussed. He hardly ever socialised with colleagues. Not his bag.

'I'll email you the address. Only twenty minutes.'

'Well – that's very kind, Anna.'

She sipped her cappuccino for a moment and then twisted her mouth. 'I expect you get a lot of people. Putting their foot in it. About your wife, I mean. I'm truly sorry about that.'

'No need.'

'So – Melissa. You said she was a consumer columnist. How did she get into that then?'

'Chance really. She wrote a couple of features on these pay-day loans. Got a lot of letters in and took it from there. Works with trading standards now and health and safety tip her off too. Feisty stuff.'

'Good for her. Local paper did you say?'

'Yeah. Writes for the whole group.'

'I'll look out for her byline.'

'She's away at the moment, actually. Holiday. Cyprus.'

'Lovely.'

'Yes. I haven't been but I hear good things. Though I rather fancy they're next with the Euro mess.'

'You think? So how long's she away? Melissa?'

'Just a few more days now. She's got to make a call on this contract offer. Job versus freelancing. Tough call.'

They were both talking much too fast.

'So you two must be very close? After losing her mother, I mean.'

'I like to think so. Though I struggle to get her to return my texts. I do try to let her live her own life now, of course, but the worrying doesn't stop.'

A waiter called their number then and so Max held up his hand – aghast as she bit almost immediately into her panini.

'Do you have an asbestos tongue or just a death wish?' He was meantime using a knife and fork to cut open his potato wider – steam pouring from the middle.

'So what's it like when they first go off to uni, then? I'm dreading it,' she was gulping water to cool the first mouthful.

'Tidy.'

She laughed.

'No – really. It's a big adjustment. I found it quite hard. But you get used to it in the end. So has your son decided where to apply?'

'Oh God. Let's not go there. Terrible when you're on the inside, isn't it?'

'Awful. Melissa picked Nottingham, which worked very well for her. A good uni but it wouldn't have been my choice.'

'And did you manage to be diplomatic?'

'Good God no. We didn't talk for a week.'

She was laughing. 'So not only me, then. The conflict?'

'It always blows over, Anna. At least – that's my experience.'

And then it was suddenly awkward, each concentrating just a little too hard on their food.

'So – paella. That a signature dish, is it?'

'Something like that.'

'I should probably mention that I'm allergic to seafood.'

Her face fell – panini frozen in her hand so that Max felt it very strongly.

'Sorry. I was kidding.'

The lurch.

'Oh right,' she looked disorientated and was frowning.

'Love seafood actually.' Wishing so much that he could take it back. Not even funny.

What the fuck, Max. Why the fuck did you say that?

CHAPTER 23

Melissa – 2011

And so now Melissa was very much ready to get home. Sam's leg was starting to heal but still itching furiously, forcing him to stick to the shade by day and still interrupting his sleep. Marcus was on the phone constantly. And the journal, which she took most mornings to the beach cafe, seemed suddenly to be taking a turn she was not expecting.

Melissa had for a few days enjoyed sharing her mother's words with Sam – especially a central section in the journal which was so upbeat and funny. It had lifted both their spirits. Eleanor called it the 'Culinary Catastrophes' chapter – listing stories of burned offerings and hilarious mistakes. She had found a picture of an early birthday cake for Melissa which was supposed to be a caterpillar and had been nicknamed 'slug' by Max.

It looks like a turd, Melissa. Seriously.

There was the story of an early roast dinner which ended with Eleanor hurling the whole pork loin in the bin 'because it smelled very strange'. The roast potatoes that just would not crisp. The first attempts at bread. 'Is this supposed to be flatbread, Eleanor? Or is it a Frisbee?' All of these stories Melissa enjoyed, not only for the picture it was re-painting of her mother but also because it made her feel less worried about trying the recipes as Sam had suggested. Eleanor counselled against perfection which struck a real chord.

What's the worst that can happen? It goes in the bin? So what? We bake, we learn, we get better…

Melissa had made a few more jottings, exploring the idea of some kind of blog.

But then came the entry with the pavlova recipe which had started to unnerve Melissa. Not so much the pictures it had stirred but the new reference to her mother's oncologist. When she was about sixteen, her father had brought up the question of gene testing, mentioning quite casually that he would like her to look into it in more detail when she was older. There was nothing at all to be scared about, he said. Her mother's condition was never confirmed as any kind of hereditary risk or anything like that, but research had made giant strides since Eleanor's death and Max felt that when she was older they should perhaps discuss it again.

Melissa hadn't wanted to and so he hadn't pushed it. Only now was she beginning to get this new and bad feeling in the very pit of her stomach. So much so that she had now stopped reading forward – choosing instead to re-read the early parts of the journal. The cupcakes. The biscuits. The skittles. The cricket. She had been talking over these recipes and memories with Sam over supper and had in this upbeat stage, suggested making a meal for her father instead of a restaurant dinner as her belated birthday celebration. Perhaps his favourites – the cheese straws and the boeuf bourguignon? Yes. It might help as she told him about the book.

And then Sam had surprised her at a taverna one night with a confession. He said it was the whole Marcus thing which had made him do some serious thinking about openness. And that he needed to better explain why he had suddenly proposed. Sam said that he wanted a family. He knew more than anything that he really wanted to be a father one day. He said that he had made the mistake of assuming Melissa would feel the same way, at least down the line, which was why it was a shock when she hadn't immediately accepted his proposal. But it had shaken him now to hear what had gone so wrong for Marcus and Diana. That they hadn't resolved the parent thing before they booked the church.

Sam told her that he had started a design file in work with plans for them to buy a detached cottage and double it in size. His dream to marry old stone with the foil of a magnificent glass and steel extension. He had been compiling pictures and ideas before he proposed. A surprise for her.

'I think what I'm saying Melissa is that I need to be completely honest. I know you said you want time to think about the proposal. About marriage. But while you're thinking, I feel I should be honest too and tell you that I can't imagine a future without becoming a father. I know you're young still. And I don't mean now. I don't even mean in the next couple of years necessarily. But it is what I want.'

Melissa had sat silently for a time.

'Say something.'

And so it was at the same restaurant they visited on their first night in Cyprus, with children again playing in the fountain that Melissa realised something. Gave shape, quietly and deep inside, to precisely what she was most afraid of.

It was a fear of not growing old. But most of all the fear of not being there. For people who *needed* you.

'It's a really big thing, having kids, Sam. A huge responsibility.'

'I know that. But we'd be good at it. I know we would.'

'Not everyone can even have kids.'

He didn't reply. And it had been left there. In the air. An unfinished sentence.

So that Melissa did not now share with Sam her new worries over the journal. That she was feeling more uneasy about why her mother had kept the book from her father. OK, so they hadn't agreed on whether she should have been prepared as a little girl about Eleanor's illness. And yes; it was meant to be girly, this journal. Maybe Eleanor wouldn't have been comfortable with Max reading all that. But there was still something else.

Some little nag which Melissa could not shake off as the tone of the journal seemed to be changing.

And now, on the penultimate day of the holiday, with Sam off buying postcards, she flipped right through the book to finger more carefully the couple of pages about two thirds through which were stuck together. She had noticed this before, assuming her mother had made a mess or error and rather than tear them out had glued them. At the back of the book there was also an entirely separate section – about a dozen or so pages about motherhood under various headings. Tips and anecdotes and other bits and pieces which she had flicked through but not read in detail.

Now, thinking of the children playing in the fountain and what Sam had said, she brushed past the section. A frisson of discomfort.

There was also a 'heritage' chapter alongside the disasters in the middle of the journal with a detailed family tree and some old black and white photographs of Eleanor's grandparents and other relatives.

Melissa had decided it was time to be more methodical. And brave. To work through the book – front to back - rather than jump around, reading things out of context. She wasn't full on afraid about what was coming next, but she was on edge now. She knew definitively that there were no other breast cancer cases around any relatives (she had checked) so she had bumped the issue. It was the reason she had batted away her father's conversation when she was younger. But it unnerved her that her mother had raised the breast cancer gene thing in the journal at all. She wasn't aware that it was even known about when her mother died.

Melissa put on a jug of coffee – the machine spitting and hissing as she sat down at the small table on the veranda with the book.

Deep breath.

The next recipe was for pavlova – one of Melissa's favourite guilty pleasures and she found herself re-reading the notes in greater detail, determined to give it a go when she got back. And then.

And now something less sweet.

And there it was again.

The oncologist…

I have honestly not wanted to make a bigger thing of it than that. I consider myself very unlucky to have got this bloody thing – a statistical blip. Paranoia is the last thing I want for my beautiful girl.

But Hugo's talk this morning has rather changed things I'm afraid. I have just had to break off to talk to your dad and I made the decision not to write any more or to worry him until I have more concrete information. But now I don't know what to do for the best.

To be honest? I was hoping, darling girl, that I could just rip the last few pages out and rewrite them without any of this stuff going any further. But that is not how it has turned out.

Oh, Melissa. This book was meant to be a help to you. A guiding hand. Me helping you and supporting you as I wish that I could have done in person– woman to woman. But suddenly everything is out of my control. And I really don't know what to do. Whether to rip this whole thing up and start again with a letter, spelling out this new information exactly as I have it. Whether to talk to your father and leave it with him?

So my oncologist – Hugo Palmer – has thrown me, talking about this newer research and statistics on the faulty gene stuff. He seems to be hinting that my cancer and gran's ovarian cancer could be linked after all. I don't see it, myself. I mean – gran never had breast cancer. Your dad is not only sceptical but cross. Reckons it's more about lab rats and researchers going after gongs. He wants absolutely nothing to do with it.

But I'm worried, Melissa. You may well already know more about all this – but bear in mind that as I write, the gene research is still quite new to us.

Anyway, Dr Palmer has said that if I would like to check our family situation, he can arrange for me to queue jump and have the test as part of his new research. The problem is there's no 'unknowing', obviously. Also the faulty gene test takes a bit of time… and I don't, of course, know how that may pan out.

Your father will worry himself sick if I add this to all that he has to deal with at the moment, so what I am thinking now is that I will try to arrange to have the test quietly. Then if the result comes through as negative, as I obviously hope, then I can confirm to you that you have absolutely nothing to worry about.

At least not from me….

Oh God. And here is the other big thing I really need to talk to you about, my lovely girl…

Melissa closed the book and sat very, very still. Every instinct in her body was telling her not to read any more.

Not today.

She put the book carefully back into the zipper and returned it to the shelf in the wardrobe.

Then she went to the pool and swam thirty lengths of breast-stroke, dipping deep beneath the water for each new breath and holding each lungful for longer and longer with every cycle until she could feel a pounding in her ears and her chest pleading with her to surface.

CHAPTER 24

Eleanor – 1994

Eleanor sat at her dressing table, head hanging forward. *Think, Eleanor. Think.*

The choices were now very simple. She either had to confide in Max or take the chance that the result would come through in time.

Shit. Why did it all have to go off piste?

Hugo had spent a long time explaining why he felt she was a candidate for the test and his new research. He didn't want to alarm her: of course he didn't. But the truth? Future guidelines were likely to suggest testing a cancer patient as the best first step to try to identify any faulty gene running in a family. So if she wanted true reassurance – for Melissa's sake – then yes – he would support her having the test as part of his new research. The plan was to write it all up in a new paper which would provide a better pathway to advise women and their consultants in the future.

What was especially difficult for Eleanor was the edge of almost excitement to Dr Palmer's voice.

'I'm sorry, Eleanor. I get fired up because we think this may be ground-breaking. Really help people.'

'I know that.'

'I didn't mean to imply that this is not terribly difficult. A decision about this test – even for research. Given your circumstance.'

'It's all right. Really. There's no need to apologise.'

He added, as the sample of blood was taken by a nurse, that he would do his very best to hurry the labs but that side of things was somewhat out of his hands. It was likely to take a few weeks at the very least. Sorry. But he could not give an exact date.

Eleanor looked at her face in the mirror. At the hair – now grown into a very presentable style. At the sunken eyes and the tiny frame which she tried these days to conceal in baggy tops.

Every day she seemed to have less energy. Dr Palmer said this was to be expected. She had been prescribed appalling energy drinks – thick and gruesome milkshakes – and he had bumped up her 'comfort package', urging her to spend a few days in hospital for some additional tests. But she was determined – no. She would go into a ward only for the final stint. As few days as possible. It was what she had agreed with Max.

And now for the first time in ages, Eleanor began to cry. *Let it out, Eleanor. Have a good cry. You'll feel better*. Eleanor listened to the echo of the voice and even as she felt the wetness unchecked on her face, realised that she was not crying over her cancer. Or even for Melissa. She was crying for the first time in years for her mother. The mother who always believed that a good cry was good therapy. Missing her so suddenly, so deeply and so unexpectedly that it completely overwhelmed her. Three years it had been since they lost her and she had thought that she was over it. Stronger. Used to it.

Five, maybe ten minutes passed and then Eleanor pulled four tissues from the box on the dressing table. She was not at all sure her mother was right about the crying and did what she could to patch up her face. Max had phoned to say he would be leaving early and would pick Melissa up from school en route to save Eleanor the drive. He was doing this more and more often – leaving early to spare her driving twice in a day and in truth she was grateful. Though she did not want him to pull out of work completely yet, she did some days get very tired and panicky in the car.

She ran the brush quickly through her hair and made a decision. No. She would not worry Max with this yet. She would wait for the result. She would *not carry the gene*. She would then write in Melissa's book that it was all fine. Nothing to worry about. And Max would never even need to know.

And then she went downstairs and took ingredients out of the cupboards. Flour and butter and salt and from the fridge the punnets of strawberries bought at the farm shop yesterday, checking also on the large pot of clotted cream.

She made the scones first, adding extra cream of tartar so they rose plump and proud. Then she took down the heavy pan from the shelf above the cooker – shocked at how difficult she found it to manage it, needing to break the move into two; lifting it to a lower shelf to catch her breath and finally back to cooker level.

She made the jam from memory, needing just two saucer tests before the wrinkly skin test confirming that it should be just perfect.

Every now and again she had to pause, to fight the panic. Drumming her fingers on the worktop; stilling herself by imagining a future Melissa making these same moves in a different kitchen. From her book.

Yes.

Two hours later there was the key in the door and she moved the plates on the table, adjusting the cutlery. Their faces were all she hoped.

'Oh mummy. You've done a cream tea.' Melissa could not contain her excitement, swinging her school bag against the wall. 'Like Cornwall.'

'Hand wash first, darling.'

'I just did them.'

'Well how about you do them again just in case you remembered wrong.'

Melissa pulled a face then ran through towards the cloakroom as Max tilted his head.

'You are overdoing it, Eleanor.'

'No lectures please, professor. Not today.'

He kissed her on the top of the head, face changing as he felt the shrinking shape of her shoulder beneath the jumper. She clutched at his arm, hanging on tight for a moment before sitting down as Melissa reappeared, hands dripping.

'So how about you tell Mummy what you did in school today.'

Melissa shrugged.

'Let me guess?' Eleanor pulled a face of mock reflection. 'Nothing?'

CHAPTER 25
Max – 2011

Max looked at the bed, mortified.

On the duvet lay two discarded shirts – one rejected because it was clearly a tad too small, which these days did him no favours, and the second for a reason he still could not fathom.

This was ridiculous. He was behaving like a teenager.

Max scanned the clothes in his wardrobe – his eye drawn to the turquoise shirt at the end of the row. He glanced at the photograph beside the bed.

God, you look good in that colour, Max.

Eleanor had been very into colour. She had had her 'colours done' once – whatever that meant. She came home with a little Filofax type folder with samples of fabric which were allegedly exactly the right shade for her complexion. Max had smiled, dreading to think how much she had paid for such nonsense. Eleanor always looked wonderful.

She had gone through her whole wardrobe then, dividing all the clothes into sections – those she could still, apparently, wear and those which, over time, would need replacement.

So what did he think? Could he see the difference?

Max smiled. He could see no difference whatsoever. He said nothing because what he thought was the fashion industry clearly had it all stitched up rather beautifully.

For himself, Max was quite happy with a uniform – the cliché of jeans or cords – *I am sorry but I like cords, Eleanor* – a checked shirt and a jumper. Jacket if he really had to.

Eleanor had bought him the turquoise shirt on a whim, holding it up against him in a smart boutique in Oxford, declaring he was an *'autumn'*. Max always felt this particular sadness when he thought now of these little scenes for he had, back then, learned to tune out the whimsical. The white noise. Now he would give anything in the world to rewind; to be standing back there in that shop. *To listen.*

Why precisely it mattered what the hell he looked like for this supper at Anna's tonight was, of course, the question. This was no date. This was the gesture of a new colleague who was ambitious and wanted, quite reasonably, to settle in and to get on. Sarah – the other lecturer – had worked alongside Max for some three years now and was perfectly good company, if a little on the earnest side. This was no bad thing in terms of Anna's agenda. It would be a pleasant evening with colleagues. Also – despite his pathetic attempt at jocularity, he very much liked paella.

All he had to do was stop thinking about her lips. Jesus. Were we not supposed now to be equal? Professional? How was it that he could go so long in work without having these feelings stirred and then there was suddenly one face, one body…

Max sat down on the bed and checked his phone. Still no further word from Melissa. He realised he should not feel annoyed about this. And yet he did.

He picked up the picture. What was most disconcerting was he wished very much that he could talk to either Melissa or Eleanor about all this. Which was, of course, ridiculous beyond measure because if he were able to talk to Eleanor, he would not be obsessing about Anna's lips. Rather he would be teasing Eleanor about it. *Hot new lecturer in the department. Runner.*

Should I be worried?

He could hear her voice and was happy to answer.

No.

Back then – you need never have worried, Eleanor.

Max had been faithful. Always.

Which was why this was so weird and still after all these years confusing. He wanted Eleanor back but given that she wasn't coming back, he wanted to be in love again. It was why he had tried and failed to make a go of the relationship with Deborah.

He had slept with only three women since Eleanor – the regular thing with Sophie plus the disastrous time with Deborah which imploded when he suddenly realised that she wanted to get married. Worse, to have more children which had never occurred to him. Why would he want to have more children? He was middle-aged. He had Melissa. It had never honestly occurred to him that Deborah, a divorcee of 38 with a wonderful and demanding full-time job which she adored would want to have more children. This terrible and belated realisation had led to the most unpleasant unravelling. Deborah had felt that Max had misled her. It had all been terribly upsetting.

This all followed a very early liaison with a rather nice woman called Charlotte, introduced to him at a dinner party in the days when people were forever trying to pair him off. She was actually very nice and rather good company but it was much too early.

And now?

Max put on a checked red and brown shirt from his wardrobe, glancing again at the photograph beside the bed. Him and Eleanor on holiday for an anniversary. Him in the turquoise shirt.

Max checked his watch. He didn't want to turn up first. To seem too eager and most of all to have made too much of the invitation.

This is not a date, Maximillian.

Anna's place was a large maisonette in a small converted block further south in Oxfordshire and hence nearer the river. The downstairs was largely open-plan with a smart stainless steel staircase. His first thought, shamefully, was to wonder how she could afford this; his second – where the hell is Sarah?

'It's not as big as it looks,' Anna smiled as he glanced around. 'Upstairs is half the size of down here. The reverse next door. But I picked this one for the garden,' she gestured to show him, pulling back the curtains to French doors onto a modest but beautiful terrace with views to a pretty, small garden and the river beyond.

'All my life I have wanted to live by water,' she was gazing out, folding her arms. 'So I figured that if we had to make such a god-awful change – the divorce, I mean – then at least something good should come out of it.'

There was the sound of footsteps on the stairs then.

'Freddie. Come and say hello to Max.'

See. Not a date.

A tall, slim young man wearing headphones appeared at the bottom of the stairs, eyes narrowing.

'Max is the head of my new department so I am shamelessly sucking up. Hoping to buy influence with seafood. The good news for you, Freddie, is it is your favourite. Paella.'

Freddie shrugged, apparently hearing nothing on account of the headphones. And then the phone rang.

'Nice to meet you, Freddie. So I hear you're in the misery of A levels. So what subjects?' Max reached out his hand to which there was no response. Freddie studied him and only then slowly removed one earphone.

'A levels I understand. What subjects?' Max let his hand fall as Anna picked up the phone and turned away towards the window.

'The sciences.' Freddie then looked down at his mobile as a text buzzed in.

'I hear you run, Freddie.'

'Oh hi – Sarah. Are you having trouble finding me?' Anna's voice across the room sounded agitated now – Max disorientated as he tried to listen in stereo.

'They're outside. I'm sorry but I'm going to have to go,' Freddie was staring at his phone.

'You're not staying, Freddie?' Max glanced across anxiously to Anna who was still on the phone and evidently in blissful ignorance of Freddie's imminent departure. 'You'll probably want to say goodbye to your mother first?' Max put a hand up to his face, aware this was overstepping the line as Freddie scowled.

'No. Of course I understand, Sarah. Poor you. No, really. It's fine. You get yourself off to bed and see how you go. It's absolutely no problem. We'll have a glass for you. You take care,' Anna turning back towards them and pulling a face. 'She's got some kind of tummy bug, suddenly. Sarah. Can't make it.'

'Look. I'm sorry, Mum. But they're waiting outside. Gotta go.'

'What do you mean – gotta go? Freddie. What are you talking about?'

'Going over to Jack's? His dad's outside. I told you.'

'No, you didn't.'

'I did.'

'Freddie. It's a school night.'

'And you arranged guests and I arranged to get out of your hair,' he was staring right at her. 'Remember?'

Anna looked across at Max, trying very hard to mask her true response.

'Look, Mum. Jack's dad is outside. He's driven twenty minutes. I can't ask him to turn around.'

Anna looked down at the ground and back up at her son. 'And is he OK to bring you home?'

'Yes.'

'Ten thirty, then, Freddie. No later.'

Freddie rolled his eyes and then turned to Max. 'Have a nice evening. Was nice to meet you.'

'Sorry about that,' Anna now turned to the paella pan which was sizzling for attention. She splashed in more wine, stepping back as it hissed violently and moved to the fridge to fetch a bowl of seafood. Raw prawns, mussels and squid.

She shook the pan as the front door slammed shut and then reached into the cupboard above for two wine glasses.

'Will you have a glass, Max?'

'Yes. Just one. Red please.'

She poured the wine slowly, her back turned and standing still for a moment.

'Look. I am sorry about this. Not quite what I planned.'

'No worry.'

'I honestly thought Freddie was staying,' she said finally, turning to hand Max his glass then leaning back against the kitchen cupboards. 'He's either up in the cave or out these days.'

'Pretty normal for the age, I'm afraid.'

'So everyone tells me.'

'So this sucking up. I'm very pleased to see it involves seafood. A favourite. Such a shame about Sarah.'

'Yes.'

They both sipped their wine in silence. A whole minute passed.

'More food for us. Smells terrific.'

'She seemed fine this afternoon.'

'Sorry?'

'Sarah.'

'Oh right. Well – these things can come on quite quickly. Probably had something iffy in one of the canteens.'

'Look. I am really sorry about this, Max. I feel a little awkward, to be honest. Especially – with Freddie. It's not that he means to be rude.'

'It's fine. Like I say. I have the T-shirt.'

'I'm being too keen, aren't I?' Anna turned to the pan again and began to sprinkle the seafood over the top of the paella. 'With the job. Frightening the horses?'

'Nonsense. Keen is good.' And then Max used the cue to talk work. Economics and politics with reference to her plans for the new European economics module she was proposing as a year two option for students. He babbled on about the possibility of a new paper – especially with the topicality. Max could see that she was very savvy – thinking ahead. It could well trigger interest in the PR department, bringing in some media interest; would also be a hit with foreign students where so much of the budget lay these days. But he was struggling to concentrate.

Anna was tonight wearing fitted jersey trousers in a soft grey with a charcoal top – wide on the shoulders with a bright turquoise necklace which, from his recollection of white noise past, was called 'statement jewellery'. Her hair was tied up in a ponytail and she was wearing flip flops. Max was very glad he had decided against a jacket.

He gave her some feedback on her plans and then brought her up to speed regarding some of the others on the team. Who had the most influence these days. Who to avoid. And who was handling the real maths behind the scenes – particularly vis-à-vis foreign students.

He told the truth also – that for all the politics and the back-biting and the financial pressure of the new 'marketplace', he still loved university life.

'Even the students?' She was teasing.

'Yes. Even the students.'

He told her then that she had made a good career move and, on Sarah's watch, would have excellent prospects – especially if she was pitching for media exposure. Yes. The university would like that very much.

'You don't think Sarah was just making an excuse tonight?' Anna said suddenly. 'That I overstepped the mark. Too much too soon? You must say, Max. I really would rather know. It's just I can be a bit full on. I do know that.'

'Look, Anna. The truth? I'm not very good on the grapevine and I don't socialise with colleagues as much as some others – perhaps as much as I should. But Sarah, from the snippets I pick up, is very open to getting to know colleagues outside of the treadmill. She's a really nice person. I'm sure the call was genuine. Not an excuse.'

She seemed pleased with this – smiling and serving the paella with a large green salad. The dish was exactly as it was supposed to be – the seafood not overcooked but the rice with a slightly sticky crust on the bottom. They discussed the differences. Paella and risotto. Both clearly enjoying the food. The company.

And then suddenly, before Max realised, they were on a second coffee and Anna seemed agitated, checking her watch. It was just past ten thirty.

'Better just send a text.'

He could see then that she was not quite following his conversation as the next fifteen minutes ticked quickly by. No return text. No key in the door.

'Look. I should probably go, Anna. Unless I can help? Collecting Freddie for you perhaps? I've only had the one glass. As I'm driving home.'

'Well you heard him. Lift is supposed to be sorted, though I'm beginning to think I shouldn't have had that second glass myself now,' she was now standing to dial her mobile. 'Would you excuse me, Max?'

'Hello – Andy? Hi. Sorry to be a nag but just checking that you're OK to bring Freddie back. I said ten thirty to him. Don't know if he passed that on.'

And then there was a pause; Anna's face changed and Max guessed immediately.

'No. Not your fault. What are they like? I'll ring around. If you could just check if Jack knows anything. Thanks.'

'He's not there?'

Anna just shook her head, the same change in her face that he recognised from that awful time in the office when she had lost it.

'Right. Don't panic. Melissa did this to me more than once. You start the calls – to his other friends – and I'll make more coffee.'

'You sure? You don't think I should just ring the police?'

'Not my call, but – no; I would suggest a ring round first. He'll turn up.'

'And you don't need to get off?'

'I'm fine.'

And then she had her mobile up to her ear again and was pacing towards the French doors, trying friend after friend, while Max refilled the cafetière. Anna smiled thanks as he put a cup of coffee alongside her which she allowed to go cold, untouched, as she continued to phone and pace.

'That's it. I've tried everyone. No one has a clue where he is. So what now? Do I just wait? Phone the police. Go out looking?'

Max didn't want to say it. He had been listening in to the calls. Impossible not to.

'What about his father? Could he—'

'He's in Germany.'

'Right.'

'I don't want to call him about this. Not yet.'

'Right.'

'Well it's not for me, Anna. But I would give it a little bit longer. He's not replied to your text?'

'No. Still straight through to answerphone. I've left three messages.'

More pacing. More phoning. Another coffee allowed to go cold. And then as she emerged from the cloakroom, eyes clearly red, Max stood up.

'You don't think that I might have unintentionally upset him. That he might have the got the wrong end of the stick.'

'No. I don't think so. He knew I had invited Sarah. No. At least I certainly hope not. I mean – I explained. I told him yesterday—'

And then suddenly there was the sound of the key in the door and Anna's whole body changed shape.

Freddie appeared, still wearing his headphones.

'Nice evening?' Anna's face was in transition from relief to fury. It was ten to midnight.

Freddie signalled that he could not hear. Anna signalled that he had better take out his earphones.

'I asked if you had a nice evening?'

'Yeah,' he shrugged. 'All right.'

'I'd better go,' Max was whispering, gathering up his keys from the coffee table. 'A lovely supper, Anna. And it was good to talk your plans through properly. I'll see myself out.'

Anna nodded, mouthing 'thank you' and 'sorry' before turning back to her son. 'No, Freddie. No disappearing upstairs. You need to sit down and we need to talk.'

CHAPTER 26
Melissa – 2011

Melissa watched Sam limp his way through customs and started to rehearse an edited version of events for her father. She had decided to tell him about the journal in her own time over a nice, quiet dinner. But not now. Please. No big inquisitions now.

'What the bloody hell—' Max's face at the arrival gate was everything she feared.

Melissa glanced at Sam's heavily bandaged leg beneath his frayed shorts. 'It's all right, Dad. We're all right. Honestly.' She hugged her father, regretting the defensive tone.

'But what's happened? Why didn't you ring me? What on earth has happened to you?'

'Look. It was an accident. Up in the mountains. A motorbike. He's fine. Just some stiches.'

'You hired a bike?'

'No, Dad. Not us. Look. Can we move out of this cramped area and I'll tell you everything. In the car.'

'So is this why you didn't answer my texts. Are you hurt as well, Melissa? Is there something you're not—'

'No. Dad. Just Sam.'

'We're doing fine, Mr Dance,' Sam tried to smile. 'We didn't want you to worry. Just need to get home now.'

'Yes. Of course. Right.'

Max insisted on taking the handle of the monster case, frowning at the addition of the bright pink holdall which Melissa was carrying as they all turned towards the exit.

'I can't believe you needed an extra bag? With this thing?'

'Long story. Are you in the short stay, Dad?'

'Yeah. Just across the way. Follow me.'

'God it feels cold here.'

On the drive, Melissa provided the bare minimum of details, feigning tiredness. And then on arrival home as Sam moved into the main hall of the block of flats, Melissa stood in the doorway to bar her father's path.

'Look. I really don't mean to be rude, Dad. Or ungrateful. But it's been a bit exhausting. I'll tell you everything at dinner. Next Wednesday?' she was whispering, glancing behind her.

'Look I'll come in. At least help you with the heavy stuff.'

'No. It's OK, Dad. We're fine. I'll see you Wednesday.'

'And you won't cancel on me?'

'No. I promise. In fact I've had an idea. I'll text you about it,' she turned again, staring into the large hallway as Sam wheeled the case behind him. 'Just a long journey. We're exhausted.'

Max fidgeted with the keys now in his pocket.

'Well. If you're absolutely sure you're OK?'

'We're fine.'

By the time she joined Sam in the sitting room, he was already phoning home. Melissa was not surprised. He had put on a brave face the last couple of days but was obviously more worried about his brother than he was letting on. He would no doubt want to go straight over there and it was now dawning that, if so, he would need a lift. The leg still not safe to drive.

Melissa began sorting through the pile of letters in her hand and sighed. Her mother was right. It was so much easier to go with the gut; to justify an opt-out than to do the right thing. Be kind.

She went through to the kitchen to make coffee and looked around the room. There was that strange and momentary frisson of adjustment that returning home always brought. The shift from the picture of the work surface on holiday to this one. Supposedly so familiar and yet for just a few seconds – strange. She had completely forgotten quite how dark this marble was.

And then she was thinking of something else. The cardboard box in the garage. Melissa paused and pushed the thought away. No. Not today. She would let Sam rest, visit his brother and then check out the box when everything had settled down a bit.

'I'll pop to Waitrose, shall I? Get us some steaks and salad and some basics,' Melissa picked up her own car keys ready, calling through to Sam who had just finished on the phone. 'And when we've had supper, I'll drive you over to Marcus if you like.'

He came through now to check her face. 'I thought you'd be too tired?'

'I don't mind. But I'd like to pop to the shop and eat first.'

'Are you really sure you don't mind driving me later?' He was looking right into her eyes. 'It can wait until tomorrow.'

'No. I don't mind. He'll be pleased to see you.'

They drank their coffee, sorting through the post and then Melissa moved through to the bedroom to recover the grey silk bag with her mother's book from the case. She placed it in a striped raffia shopping basket, before kissing Sam briefly and setting off.

At Waitrose she went straight to the cafe, ordered a large cappuccino and, heart pounding, placed the book on the table.

Roasted squash and spinach soup with feta

Whole butternut squash – peeled, de-seeded and cubed
Half bag of washed baby spinach
Two red onions – chopped in large chunks
Small pack of good feta
Two big springs of rosemary – chopped
Good olive oil
Several cloves of crushed garlic
Two to three pints of good stock (vegetable or chicken)

Toss the butternut squash and onions in a few glugs of olive oil, sprinkle over sea salt, crushed garlic and chopped rosemary and roast for 45 mins to an hour until soft and gorgeous. Put the veg with half the bag of spinach and simmer for just a few minutes in the stock. Add the feta and allow to melt. Season to taste and blitz in a processor or with a hand blitzer. You can adjust the amount of stock to make a thinner or thicker soup to taste. Ditto the amount of spinach you use is trial and error. The colour of this is a bit dark but I absolutely love it.

I have chosen this as what I rather think may have to be the final recipe for you, Melissa. A real favourite. Simple but more delicious than it deserves to be for the work involved. It was an accidental discovery, as so many good recipes are. A friend gave me a recipe for a roasted squash and feta salad on a bed of baby spinach and one day I made too much. Loads left over. So I threw it in a pan with some stock for soup and, of course, everyone RAVED about it. So now I make this soup more often than I make the salad.

And I'm rambling.

Which I always do when I'm nervous.

The truth?

I want to ramble on for ever, my darling girl, as we are running out of time and I am finding it difficult to hold things together here, trying to work out how to end this when I still have so much that I want to say to you.

I am not done here, Melissa, but I am getting weaker. And you have noticed. Your eight-year-old self, I mean. The truth is I am quite sure you have realised for a good while than I am unwell. You are a clever little girl and children miss very little. I have said it is just ladies' tummy trouble and you do not seem to want to ask many questions. I write this not to upset you but because I wonder how much you will remember and how much I may have misunderstood.

Yesterday I did your hair in my bed in the morning and suggested that Daddy might like to learn how to do it and I sensed from the way you reacted that you have probably guessed more than I would wish.

I hope not.

But today – here's the truth. I am not feeling very well at all so I have been in touch with the lawyer by phone – explaining what must happen with this journal. He is to come and collect it very soon. By Wednesday at the latest. But I am hanging on as long as possible – *hoping, hoping, hoping…* that the test will come back.

And now – deep breath – that other thing I may now have no choice but to tell you.

You may well have noticed a few pages stuck together? I am trusting and hoping that you have not meddled and torn them open. My thinking was that you would assume some mistake. The truth actually is that I was hoping I would be able to tear them out. And this page too. But obviously if you are reading this and the 'stuck pages' are still here… Well. It's not gone as I hoped.

The important thing to say before you read them is that I love you and your father more than life itself. But even good people can carry things in their head and in their hearts that they wish they did not have to.

So separate the sticky pages very, very carefully my darling girl. I stuck them like that so that you would not flick through the journal the minute you got it and jump to the most difficult part without giving me a chance to talk to you a while.

I just hope you will remember, please, to be kind and to believe that this has all run away from me – turning out very differently from how I planned…

Melissa closed the book and looked around her. Not for the first time she felt the extremity of this shift. From the black ink and the terrible place in which her mother was writing, to the banality of the place in which she was reading.

Every single time she looked up from the page, ever since the whole theme of the book had seemed to change – to *darken* – she would feel this same shock at the normality around her. Yes. The sheer banality of it all. All these people smiling over their lattes and their cupcakes, their crosswords and their mobile phones. All these people who knew absolutely nothing of the world to which the words now took her.

For a time, in this dazed state, she watched a woman sitting with a friend, leaning in with some apparent gossip. They were in their late thirties, well-dressed and with that hairstyle that everyone was still copying from *Friends*, as if in mourning that the series was no more. One of the women was laughing and then took out a small compact to refresh her lipstick before checking her watch and signalling that they should get on.

At the next table – a younger mother with a toddler in a high chair, its flat plastic tray covered with cake crumbs. The mother took out a packet of wet wipes from a tartan rucksack and cleaned up the tray and the child's face – to loud protest.

It all made Melissa feel like such an outsider. All this normality. It made her feel angry on her mother's behalf and now it also made her feel very, very alone.

She remembered her father lecturing her once when she was a child about this very thing. Shutting herself off. Sitting ever so quietly and just overthinking.

You try to carry too much on your own shoulders. You can talk to me, you know, Melissa.

But there were some things simply too difficult to share. With people who, for instance, considered it perfectly normal. All the ups and downs with their own mothers. The fallings in and out. People who had never lost someone and assumed that after a couple of years grief would surely drift away, leaving only the happy memories behind.

Bullshit. Grief, Melissa had learned through her childhood, did not actually go away. It was the thing that had shocked her most of all and in the end set her so apart. The ugly truth that the emptiness did not disappear. It just hid itself and tricked you into believing you were perfectly fine until you turned a corner one day – and **smack**, there it was again. Like the first day she won the merit badge in school and was suddenly overwhelmed with sorrow as it was pinned to her jumper. When she got into university. Fell in love with Sam. Got the job offer. All these things that her mother **would never know**.

Even in that restaurant when Sam produced the ring, she was thinking – not just that she did not actually believe in happy ever afters, that she could not risk it – she was thinking also that she had no one to choose a dress with her. No one to wear a silly hat and cry in the front row of the church.

She could not talk to anyone about any of this because it made her feel selfish and utterly ridiculous.

It had been *seventeen years…*

It was not supposed to be like this.

And now, suddenly, after all the good things in her mother's book. After the happy memories had been slowly and preciously stirred, it was taking her to a very different place now and she was more confused than ever. No longer just cricket on the beach and happy birthdays and cupcakes and biscuits.

Melissa was feeling more and more uneasy. She was thinking about the children playing in the fountain. How there was no way she could get married and become a mother. Not when she knew what it felt like to be *left.* And – no. She could not talk to Sam about it because he would say – you could not live like that. Worrying. That it was ridiculous. That anyone could get run over by a bus.

But she wasn't just anyone. And she suddenly had no idea where the hell her mother's book was going.

CHAPTER 27
Eleanor – 1994

Eleanor read back through the last few lines of the journal and checked her watch. Just time.

She looked over to the bed alongside which there was Melissa's hairbrush and a carved wooden bowl containing her collection of hair ties. A tumble of colours and textures – polka dot silk. Deep burgundy velvet. Faux fur black. Why had she not thought of handing this ritual over to Max sooner?

She ran her finger around the two, glued pages about two thirds into the journal – just before the special section on motherhood.

Eleanor had written these secret pages only recently, using a glue stick to seal the edges. It was a risk. All a bit basic; a bit boy scout – she was banking on Melissa assuming a mistake; that she would read the rest of the journal first as she was supposed to. If it came to that…

What was contained between the two pages was the memory of what she and Max had come to call 'the madness'. It was their one cataclysmic blip in the early part of their relationship. A time when all hope of the happy, married future she had come to dream of had been suddenly yanked from beneath her like a rug on a polished floor. Whoosh. Gone.

It was Max who had started it and yet she could never quite bring herself to blame him entirely. For, like so many blips, it was complicated.

For two blissful years with Max after that first meeting at her school, Eleanor had never doubted that they would end up together. It was a 'when' not an 'if'.

Everything seemed set and everything seemed simple. Max loved his job. Max loved Eleanor. And then suddenly and entirely out of character he started stressing completely irrationally about money.

'Oh for goodness sake, Max, we'll manage. We're far better off than most.'

'But what about down the line – if we have a family, Eleanor? If you go part time. Then the numbers aren't going to crunch. Not if we want to buy somewhere half decent. Somewhere where you won't get bloody mugged. Somewhere with a decent school.'

'Jesus Christ, Max. We're still single and you're talking schools?'

'You know what I mean,' he was blushing. 'People have to think of these things. Think ahead. You can't be an ostrich.'

'But you're doing great at the university, Max. Good prospects.'

'Rubbish money.'

'Oh it's not.'

'Compared to a lawyer or a doctor, it is.'

'I don't want to be with a lawyer or a doctor. I want to be with a university professor, thank you very much. A university professor who is brilliant and respected and loves what he does.'

'And live on the breadline.'

'And now you are just being silly.'

'Really? The only reason we're so flushed now is we're both working full-time. No dependants. It's a temporary phase, Eleanor.'

This tetchy to and fro went on for a few weeks with Eleanor failing to make Max snap out of it. She tried everything to distract him, but he seemed suddenly almost depressed. This was most especially ridiculous as he was riding high at the university. One of his papers had suddenly been picked up by the local media and – out of the blue, he was invited to do his first television interview. He claimed to be nervous but turned out to be an absolute natural – bylined as an economics expert with an inside track on the savings and loan crisis in America. The subject was hot as more and more financial mess unravelled. A clip from Max's interview was used by the national networks. This in turn was used internationally.

Max was suddenly seen as a man who could make complex economics understandable. A bit of a star and ipso facto suddenly in demand.

The university was thrilled. Over the following month there were many more media approaches from national newspapers with one Sunday supplement carrying a lengthy interview on Max's take on the economic mess. Several American magazines quickly followed suit.

Eleanor could not have been more thrilled for him. Suddenly he was feted at the university with the press office delighted at what the team called his new 'currency'.

And then one fateful Thursday Max was on the phone to Eleanor, almost exploding with excitement. He told Eleanor he had booked a Michelin star restaurant that night to explain everything.

Eleanor was quietly ecstatic. The university must have given some pay rise to finally snuff out the worrying.

She wore the dress he loved most. She put on his favourite perfume. She took trouble to find matching underwear. Coy. Excited. Nervous.

'OK, Eleanor? So I have something important to tell you. And to ask you.'

Eleanor put the final forkful of mint pea puree in her mouth and tried to stay calm. She patted her mouth with her napkin and was wondering if he would go down on one knee. She glanced around. Would everyone watch?

'How would you like to move to New York with the new Communications Adviser for the Unit Two Bank of Minnitag?' Max was beaming. Ear to ear.

Eleanor had no idea what to say, the room suddenly moving. The air thicker and hazy.

'America? I'm not understanding. I don't know what you mean?'

'I got a call yesterday and they confirmed the details this morning. Offer in the post.'

'Who? I don't understand.' Aware suddenly of the pulse in her ear.

'The Unit Two Bank of Minnitag. Three times my current salary – Eleanor. Flat provided until we sort ourselves out. *Manhattan*.'

'But isn't that the one that's been in the papers. The one that's in the shit over this savings and loan crisis. All the stuff you've been doing analysis on.'

'Which is precisely why they need someone like me. Someone with a real understanding of what's been going wrong and how to put it right – especially with all the new regulation which is bound to come in as a consequence. I'm perfect to advise them. And to handle questions with the media too.'

'You are kidding, Max?'

'No. Like I say. I got the job offer confirmed this morning.'

'But it's toxic. All the savings and loan mess. You've said so yourself.'

Max's face was now changing.

'They just want you because of your profile on this. Your integrity. Your paper and your years of research. They want to use you.'

'Oh thank you very much for your vote of confidence.'

'Oh come on, Max. You must see that. They're all going down and they need someone to wheel out at press conferences as the shit continues to hit their fan. The professor from a top British university. On our side.'

'I might have guessed you would be like this.'

'And what does that mean?'

'I get this amazing offer. New York. More money than I had ever dreamed of earning. Security for us. For our future. And this is how you react.'

'But Max. You're just not thinking straight. This would be the end of your career, not the making of it. The end of your reputation.'

'Nonsense.'

'The Unit Two Bank of Minnitag, Max. Duh?'

'It's no worse or better than any other bank.'

'Which is precisely why you shouldn't go near it. Not with this whole savings and loan thing going on. I don't pretend to understand it all. But you do. And you have integrity, Max. A great academic future. You're a specialist in your sector. Respected. This would finish all that.'

'Pardon me for hoping you would be excited. Pleased for me. Pleased for us.' He was looking away; across the restaurant.'

'How can I be pleased?'

'Are you saying you won't come?'

'Max. You can't be serious about this?'

There followed the worst three weeks of Eleanor's pre-married life. Max displayed a stubbornness and blindness that she had no idea he was capable of. He stuck to his guns. He tried very hard to persuade her that she was wrong. That she was naive. That this was what all grown-ups had to do. To shelve their ideals to chase the best future for the people they loved. To grow up.

Eleanor said it was not growing up, it was selling out and it would end badly. Also it was not the way she wanted to live. She would rather have less money. In Britain. If he wanted the Big Apple and its Big cop-out salary, he would have to bloody well go on his own.

She never believed for one second that he would.

Until he was gone – realising too late that they were both capable of extreme stubbornness; each fully expecting the other to cave. This was before mobile phones, so that daily they each checked their answerphone, expecting some message of climbdown. But no. The row went right up to the line and across the Atlantic.

Eleanor took to her bed for days – phoning in sick to school with the excuse of a migraine. Every hour she checked her answerphone. A plea for forgiveness. But it did not come.

She drank too much wine. She spent hours with her closest friends, going over and over the detail of what had so suddenly unravelled. How she had lost the one thing in life that mattered? And was she right? Should she have swallowed her pride? Her principles? Gone for the money? Followed the man?

All the while knowing that she did not want to live in New York. She hated big cities. She had no desire whatsoever to live in a country where anyone and everyone carried a gun, and she hated fat, stinking banks and federal loan companies who were apparently ripping everyone off while caring not a jot for the consequences.

Eleanor ran her finger again over the pages that she had stuck together in the book for Melissa and winced at the paper cut, pulling her finger back sharply to stop the pearl of blood from spoiling the page. She then sucked the finger hard as she dialled Dr Palmer's secretary yet again – only for her to confirm that *Sorry. The test result was still not back and they were doing everything they possibly could to try to speed things up. Really they were.*

CHAPTER 28
Melissa — 2011

That first weekend home from Cyprus, they ended up staying overnight with Sam's parents to help settle Marcus, and then, once back at the flat, Melissa explained about the cardboard box in the garage and asked Sam to help her.

It took a double espresso before she was ready to face the contents – Sam diplomatically holing up in their bedroom under the pretence of working while she opened it on her own.

Melissa tried to mentally picture the items inside the box from her memory of that quick check a couple of years back when Max had first brought it over. She imagined that this would prepare her.

It didn't.

This new context, with her mother's voice in her head, made the first sight of the mixer, as she lifted it from the padding of the towel, almost unbearable. She had expected it to be tough. The uncomfortable familiarity of it. She had expected it to trigger a difficult response, just as it had a couple of years back. Hadn't she, even before the journal, sealed the box back up immediately to protect herself from this?

But she hadn't expected it to so completely break her. Sobbing so loudly and uncontrollably that Sam had come straight through from the bedroom.

'Oh, Melissa. Oh, shit. You want me to pack it all away again? Oh Jesus.'

She just shook her head, sitting on the breakfast bar stool, staring at it. The white and blue of it on her marble counter, picturing it *exactly* on that other worktop in the corner of her mother's kitchen.

'No. It's OK, Sam. I just need a few moments. Sorry. I feel a bit ridiculous.'

'Don't be daft.' He looked helpless and a little guilty, fidgeting and glancing around for a box of tissues – in the end settling for kitchen towel which she accepted gratefully.

'I'll be OK. Really. I'll be all right in a minute. It's just a bit full on.'

'Sorry. When I suggested the cooking, I didn't realise—'

'It's fine, Sam. I need to do this. It's just an adjustment.' She got control of herself then, letting out little huffs of breath and staring for a moment at the ceiling. Then she stood back up to make them both more strong coffee before bracing herself to check what else was in the box.

'You sure you're OK, Melissa?'

'Yeah. Yeah. I'm fine now.'

There were a few baking trays which would need to go out – rusted from their time in storage – but also some Tupperware boxes with plastic cutters and piping bags and the like, much of which was fine.

Deeper down there was a much larger Tupperware container with the original instruction manual for the mixer along with all the accessories.

'Do you think it will still work?' Sam was clearly intrigued as Melissa began flipping through the manual. She paused then, not sure if she was ready to face the possibility of the motor failing. The mixer being defunct. But Sam could not help himself, wiping down the surface of the machine and cleaning off the flex before plugging it in and turning to Melissa for her approval. She did a little shrug and finally nodded.

Sam flicked the switch and there it was. The familiar noise of the motor and with it the echo of Eleanor raising her voice as she talked over it.

Will you pass me the bag of sugar, honey?

Melissa put her hand up to her mouth.

'That's amazing. So how old would you say this is?' Sam, the engineer, was now in a different gear, impressed by the longevity, muttering about quality build and wanting to try out all the attachments, but Melissa was no longer listening. Inside the shock was now turning into something else entirely. She was thinking – what a relief that she had not sent the box to the charity shop. So relieved – yes; and so pleased that she had this now.

Dear God.

Her mother's Kenwood Chef mixer.

Which, amazingly, still worked.

CHAPTER 29

The next day – Sam's final off work – they cooked the cupcakes together, then the biscuits and finally the butternut squash soup recipe, which was outstanding.

The mixer was going great guns but Melissa was still disorientated and hence very protective of the journal itself. There was no way she was ready to hand it over to Sam to read freely – fearing especially that he would notice and comment on the pages still sealed together. So she used the cookbook stand made of Perspex – designed to slot the journal behind the protective and transparent shield. It meant Sam, who took on the role of commis chef, could not turn the pages. She caught him a few times reading the jottings visible alongside each recipe. His eyes saddening. But he was sensitive enough, especially after her reaction when unpacking the mixer, not to push it and so remained unaware that the later content of the journal was changing in tone.

At least he was right about the cooking itself, which proved surprisingly cathartic. The cupcakes recipe in particular. It was a very generic, pretty basic recipe, but when she was zesting the orange, Melissa felt the strangest, quite overwhelming sensation – her expression of puzzlement immediately noticed by Sam.

'What is it?'

'I'm not quite sure.'

'Is the orange manky?'

'No. It's fine. It's—'

Zest of an orange (crucial – remember?)

Melissa had a new tantalising glimpse – this time of sitting on a stool. Yes. A white, painted stool alongside the kitchen table. There was an orange on a white, porcelain plate in front of her and she had the sense of her own voice whining. She looked up, narrowing her eyes. Trying to remember why she was moaning and what exactly her mother was doing…

'Just a memory. Something from when I was a kid. I can't quite place it.'

Sam smiled and then winked. Melissa took a deep breath and turned back to the bowl – today rubbing the flour and butter between her fingertips. She was now also making the cheese straws ready for the following evening. The Wednesday supper with her father.

Max had been bemused at first when she messaged suggesting that they have dinner at her flat. Sam, on his return to work, had a supper invitation that same evening with senior colleagues. He was rather nervously hoping it would be a formal offer to join them as a partner. So Melissa had decided for certain it was the night she would tell Max about the journal. And there was no way she was doing that in public…

Max had phoned and protested: 'But it's not a birthday treat for you if you have to cook, Melissa? No. I'll book us a nice restaurant.'

'No, Dad. Please. I want to. Come round for 7.30.'

She had been a tad anxious, given her very basic skills, over trying the boeuf bourguignon recipe but Sam came up with the very sensible suggestion of cooking it the day before. Casseroles were apparently always better cooked ahead, allowing the flavours to 'gel' before reheating. And if it all went horribly wrong, she could try again.

Melissa had an extra week off work, during which she was supposed to make a decision over the freelance contract, so she had plenty of time in hand. And in fact the recipe worked out just fine.

Eleanor had specified a heavy, quality pot and so Melissa was delighted to find a large Le Creuset casserole dish at the bottom of the cardboard box. Small wonder it had been so heavy.

She could not quite believe the cooking time suggested in the journal. Hours. But the smell which filled the flat was unbelievable. As was the finished dish. Sam, when he sampled it, pulled a face she had never seen in their own kitchen before.

This is seriously good, Melissa. No kidding.

And now – finally here was Wednesday. Her father looking just a little bit uneasy, evidently wondering what was going on.

'Cheese straws? Good God, Melissa. I love cheese straws!'

They were sitting on opposite sofas – Melissa trying to appear relaxed, with her shoes kicked off and her feet up, hugging a cushion to her stomach.

'These are really good. Phooo,' he took a glug of wine. 'Hot, mind. Just how I like them.'

'I made them myself.'

'You are kidding me?'

'No. Honestly.'

Max pulled a face.

'You know your mother used to make these for me. One day she played this trick. Put in practically a whole jar of cayenne. Nearly choked to death.'

Melissa smiled. Max glanced away.

'You can stay over, you know, Dad. If you fancy. I mean, I'm assuming you've spent ridiculous money on good wine. Shame for you not to enjoy it.'

'I'm fine. Will get a taxi if need be. See how we go.'

Max always picked good wine. The two bottles he had brought sported impressive mesh covers. It would be wasted on Melissa but she was pleased to see him savouring each mouthful.

'So what's going on here, Melissa? I thought you didn't much like to cook?'

'On holiday we had such terrific food, Sam and I decided it was high time to make more effort. We've made a pact to do better. Might even go on a course.'

Max pulled a face of both surprise and approval. 'Very good idea. I'll drink to that. Something is certainly smelling good in the kitchen tonight,' he reached forward for another cheese straw.

'So come on then, Dad. What was all that stuff when we were away. *Am I sexist?* You're not in any kind of trouble at work, are you?'

'No. Anyway. It doesn't matter now…'

'Yes, it does. Otherwise you wouldn't have brought it up. Sent that text.'

'You could have phoned if you were that interested?'

'Sorry,' she was blushing. 'You know what I'm like. Especially on holiday. And we got a bit distracted with the accident nonsense.'

Max took a deep breath and leant back. 'OK, then. So here it is. I married a beautiful woman. I like beautiful women. I am beginning to worry what that says about me.'

'It says that you are a normal, hot-blooded male and that in marriage, you got lucky,' Melissa poured them both water from a large jug in the centre of the coffee table. 'Seriously. What's this about, Dad?'

'Oh. Eggshells at work. Political correctness. I don't know.'

'So you are in some kind of trouble? Put your foot in it?'

'No, not exactly. But think about it. I spent your whole childhood telling you that you are beautiful.'

'Which was lovely, but not actually true.'

'Yes it is.'

'No it isn't, actually. On a good day and with the wind be-hind me I do OK. But I'm not beautiful.'

He raised his eyebrows.

'Look, Dad. Liking beautiful women and thinking your daughter is beautiful is one thing, but from where I'm sitting, you don't judge all women by what they look like all of the time. When it's not relevant. In their jobs, I mean. In everyday life.'

'No of course not.'

'There. You said – *of course not*. But the fact is some men do, Dad. Some men grade all women all the time entirely by what they look like. Work and play. And if they don't like the look of them, you sort of see their eyes scanning the room to find someone better looking to talk to.'

'Oh don't be ridiculous.'

'I'm not. That's what sexism really is. Deciding that women don't count, not even for conversation, unless they're pretty. It's completely different from finding someone attractive and want-ing to date them. Or marry them. Or – you know,' she managed not to say it.

Max pulled a face.

'You OK, Dad? Really?'

'Oh. I don't know. Mid-life crisis probably. It's just so dif-ficult these days being a guy and worrying about saying the wrong thing. You know – everything so politically correct. In the workplace. Bloody minefield.'

'But we need – *politically correct*. Keep the gropers in their place. We only just got the vote remember.' Her tone was teas-ing.

Max pulled another face. 'I knew I shouldn't have brought this up.'

'Anyway. Never mind. So long as you're not in trouble at work,' she clinked his wine glass and then disappeared into the kitchen, calling him through soon afterward to serve the boeuf bourguignon with dauphinoise potatoes and a green salad.

He was genuinely stunned by the meal. Repeated over and over how amazing it was. That it was the best decision ever for she and Sam to get more serious about the kitchen. *Unbelievable, Melissa. The best I have tasted since…*

A few times she caught him staring at the casserole dish and frowning but he didn't say anything about it.

She hadn't bothered with a pud, offering cheese instead which he said he might try later. Needing a break. And so they moved back into the sitting room with the second bottle of wine.

'And now my turn to ask you something, Dad.' A pause. 'Was there ever anything between you and Mum that you didn't tell me about, Dad? Anything difficult. A blip when you were first together.'

Melissa had not read the stuck pages. Not yet. She had got up early to go swimming every single day since their arrival back from Cyprus. She had enjoyed the cooking. She had felt more hopeful about that. More connected to her mother and her past. But she had decided that she would not read the sealed pages until she had spoken to her father. Still a bit scared.

'Why on earth do you ask that?' Max's face was suddenly ashen.

Melissa took another large mouthful of wine and reached for a cushion for comfort.

'I don't really know how to tell you this, Dad. But I've had a bit of a shock.'

'What kind of shock? What do you mean?'

He was now tapping his foot on the wooden floor.

'I got a letter on my birthday from a solicitor's office. Turns out Mum put a book together for me. As a present for my twenty fifth birthday.'

Max went white. The foot tapping stopped. There was stillness for a second and then his whole body moved slightly – the wine glass nearly spilling in his hand.

'It's just a girly book, Dad. A bunch of recipes and photographs and woman-to-woman gossip. That sort of thing.'

'No. No. She never said anything to me about this. I don't understand. Why would she not tell me about this?' He was shifting in the sofa as if it no longer fitted his shape.

'Like I say. Just a girly thing, Dad. She wanted it to be between us. She probably thought you would think it silly. Sentimental.'

'But how on earth did she get this to you, Melissa?'

'Through a solicitor. Some law firm her family had used for years.'

'No. She never said a thing. Not a word,' looking away as if not hearing her replies. 'And she wrote this when?'

'While she was unwell, Dad.'

Max took in a deep breath while Melissa continued to fidget with the cushion.

'So why didn't you tell me straight away? Can I see it?' he was looking round the room as if trying to work out where it was.

'No. I haven't read it all yet.'

'You are kidding me?' He had stood up now, physically agitated and still looking about the room.

'Sit down, Dad. Please. Look. It arrived at a pretty hairy time. I'd just told Sam I wasn't sure about marrying him.'

'Sam proposed?'

'Yes, Dad. He asked me to marry him. Well – not marry now. Obviously. Get engaged but I panicked. Asked for time to think about it. Not only because I am far too young but because I'm not sure I want to marry anyone. '

Another deep inhalation as Max finally sat back down.

'Which appears to disappoint you. As I rather feared it might.'

'Not disappointment, Melissa. I just feel... I don't know.' Still he looked winded.

'I really didn't know how to tell you, Dad, about the journal. But she left me recipes. Some of them your favourites.'

And now his face was changing. Fitting the puzzle together. Looking down first at the floor and then at the empty plate from the cheese straws and finally back up at Melissa who just nodded.

'You're not cross?'

'No, I'm not cross,' he took a long slug of water. 'I'm just a bit shocked. I'm just not understanding why your mother wouldn't have told me.'

'I think she felt you had enough to deal with.'

'Yes. Well,' he now stood up again and walked over to the window, turning away from her. 'Dear God. You know what? Shit. I do feel quite angry actually,' tossing the napkin still in his hand onto a side table. 'I mean, why the hell didn't she tell me this? She didn't write me a bloody book.'

Melissa said nothing. Just waited.

'Sorry, Melissa.'

'No. It's OK, Dad. Look. I knew it would be a shock. But she does nothing but praise you in the book. Embarrassingly so. I think she was just worried about me growing up. Without the sisterhood. A woman's voice.'

'So what's in it, exactly? This book? I would have read it straight through. Cover to cover. One sitting. I don't understand why you haven't finished it.'

'I'm finding it quite hard, actually. Emotional. And not great timing with me just having upset Sam. I didn't want to tell him either at first. I mean – I'd just told him I wasn't sure if I ever wanted to get married so it seemed a bit selfish. You know. *I don't think I want to marry you but – hey could you just help me through this big, emotional shock.'*

'So is there someone else, Melissa? Are you splitting up? You and Sam? Is that why he isn't here tonight?'

'God no.'

'So what then? I mean is he OK. With you putting him on hold?'

'Not really.'

'Oh, Melissa. But I thought you loved him?'

Melissa sipped more wine, tightening her lips as Max finally walked back across the room and sat down again. 'I do love him, Dad. I just never saw myself as someone who would need to get married. I'm just not sure I'm the type.'

'But why ever not?'

And then there was this terrible pause and Melissa could see something slowly register in her father's eyes, looking again at the empty plate on the table. The crumbs from the cheese straws.

'Look. The book was a shock, Dad, initially but then I started to see it as quite comforting. Also surprising. Mum explained why she didn't want me to know about her illness. And it's weird but also very nice too. To have her write to me, grown-up to grown-up.'

'And so there's a lot of writing in this book. Not just recipes and photos?'

'Yes. Quite a bit. '

'And what exactly does she say about me?'

'Only wonderful things.'

'So can I read it, Melissa? Please?'

'I don't know.'

'What do you mean, you don't know?' he looked tense.

'I need to finish it in my own time first. Which is why I'm asking you about when you were first together. You and Mum. In the bit I'm reading at the moment she mentioned that you had some kind of blip or something.'

Max faced changed. The foot tapping started up again.

'And she's written about that?'

'I think so. It's the bit I'm going to read next which is why I wanted to ask you first. So this blip, Dad?'

'Look. It's a time I don't really like to talk about Melissa. I made a bit of a prat of myself.' He poured more wine for them both.

'I'm listening.'

'I wasn't earning a lot when we were first together. Your Mum and me. And I got a bit caveman. Worrying about providing for a family.'

'How very old-fashioned of you.'

'Sexist?'

She smiled finally and his eyes relaxed a little.

'I know. Silly. But I loved your mother very much and I wanted to look after her. And I know that sounds quite patronising and yes, quite probably sexist, but I don't mean it to be. I wanted to protect her. Look after her. And the family I hoped we would have.'

'I'm not understanding what that has to do with a blip.'

Max sighed. 'I got offered a big job in New York. Controversial bank. Big money. You mother thought it was a sell-out. That they wanted to buy my integrity. My status.'

'And did they?'

Max took a long slug of wine. 'Yes. As it turns out, that is exactly what they wanted.'

'So what happened?'

'I got stubborn. Went to New York. Your mother stayed be-hind.'

'You *split up*?' Melissa could hardly believe the tone of her own voice, squeezing the cushion tight to her stomach.

'Yes. I know it sounds unlikely. Ridiculous. But for a very short time. Yes. Your mother and I split up.'

'Good God.'

'My fault entirely. For being stubborn and stupid. So let that be a warning.'

Melissa felt herself colour. 'So what happened?'

'I thought she would follow me. She thought I wouldn't go.'

'So who caved?'

'Who do you think?'

Melissa tilted her head.

'Your mother was completely right of course. Took about two weeks for me to face up to it. They tried to dress it up, of course, but it very quickly became apparent what the bank wanted of me. To help them talk away some morally bankrupt shenanigans.'

'So what did you do?'

'I quit and came home with my tail between my legs. No job. No nothing.'

'And?'

'And your wonderful mother took me back without a blink. Stood by me and supported me until I got another temporary lecturing contract. Until I got back on my feet and my old uni had the good grace to take me back full-time.'

'And it made you stronger?'

'No. It just made me shit scared, Melissa. Realising that I could have blown it. Lost her for good. Right at the very begin-ning.'

Melissa examined her father's face closely.

'I'm sorry. I've upset you.'

'No. It's OK. It's just all a bit of a shock. Unexpected.'

'I know.'

'Though it does feel a good thing, Melissa. For us to talk like this. About your mother, I mean.'

And then Melissa felt her shoulders relax slightly – relieved to know, at last, what was written in the sealed pages.

'You think that's what I'm doing with Sam. Making a big mistake? The marriage phobia. I thought you would understand. Me being quite young still.'

He stared into her eyes.

'You are young still, Melissa. But I like Sam. Probably more than I like to let on. So if you love him, you go carefully,' he picked imagined fluff from the knee of his trousers. 'And if this whole uncertainty or panic or whatever is because of what happened with your mother and me. At the end, I mean. Well – you need to know that I wouldn't change a thing. If I could go back, I would do it all again. Get married all over again.'

Melissa looked again really closely at his face.

'Which is why you're still resolutely single.'

'That wasn't fair, Mel,' he took a slow, deep breath. 'I had my slice of happy.'

'And who says we only get one slice, Dad?'

CHAPTER 30
Eleanor – 1994

'The thing is I'm not really ready,' Eleanor was holding the book in her hand, examining it very closely.

'I'm so sorry.' James Hall, the lawyer sent by the firm at Eleanor's special request, stood awkwardly alongside the sofa. 'I thought they said twelve o'clock.'

'No. Sorry. I didn't mean that. And do sit down. Please.'

He sat down. Tried to smile.

'So am I understanding this correctly? You want to place this book in the care of our practice, to be given to your daughter when she is twenty five, did you say?'

'Yes. That is possible, I assume? You can organise that?'

'Yes. Of course. But we will need clarity,' he was looking across at the book, 'of how precisely you would like that to happen. In the future.'

'I need you to make a few checks before the book is passed to Melissa. On her health and her father's. I've written it all down. And I will pay now and also put some money into an account. To cover all the future costs,' Eleanor was handing over a piece of paper which Mr Hall read through carefully.

'But as I say. The timing is very difficult. I'm not really ready but my doctor…' Eleanor paused to brush the arm of the sofa. 'Look. I am probably going into hospital a little earlier than I had hoped and so I need to give this to you today,' still she was holding the book tightly. 'Confidentiality is crucial here.'

'Of course.'

'My husband doesn't know about this.'

'I see.'

'Sorry. Would you like a coffee? I wasn't thinking.'

'No. I'm fine. Though if you need a drink yourself?'

'No. No.' She was self-conscious now. Aware of how she must look to him. So very thin.

There was a much longer pause then, during which Eleanor opened the book to illustrate the pages stuck together.

'There is a section in the book. This bit here,' she showed him exactly, 'which I was hoping to edit out. Rip out actually – before I handed this over. But I'm waiting for some information – some test results which will decide whether I need to make that edit.'

Mr Hall frowned.

'Yes. I know it all sounds a bit complicated and a bit clandestine. It is quite complicated actually.'

'So – what do you want to do? Do you want me to come back later? Or tomorrow?'

'No. The thing is I need you to take the book today but I would like to stay in contact by telephone from the hospital to decide whether this section should be removed before the book is put into storage.'

'I see.'

Mr Hall then explained that any special instructions would need to be drawn up officially and he could courier a copy later that day, but Eleanor became suddenly very distressed.

'No. No. I don't want anything in writing. My affairs. Well – Max will obviously be given access to everything and it is important that this remains confidential. Oh – sugar. I'm making this all sound very cryptic, aren't I? Look. It's a test result on my health that I'm waiting for. I really don't want my husband stressed out any further. Not unnecessarily. I'm wondering if I will be able to make arrangements for that result to be conveyed to you via my doctor?'

'I would need to look into that. There would be issues of confidentiality and consent to resolve. I am sorry if this all sounds unhelpful, but we have to follow procedure to the letter. Boring. But that's the way of the law.'

'Yes. I see that.'

Eleanor began to pinch her bottom lip.

'How about we spend some time now, Mrs Dance? Trying to draw something up – at least about my taking the book immediately. Your wishes as they stand right now. Today. Then I can make some follow-up inquiries regarding your other suggestion and get back to you by telephone. Vis-à-vis this test result.'

'Right. Yes. That's a good idea,' only now did Eleanor feel the roughness to her palm where she had been stroking the arm of the sofa too hard. Over and over. 'Let's do that. Yes. That will have to do for now.'

CHAPTER 31

Max – 2011

Max had slept badly ever since the meal with Melissa. He tried very hard not to think about the journal. What it might look like. Say. He also tried very hard not to think about Anna.

But, despite his very best efforts, the lurch was happening pretty much every day now. Sometimes in the car park as he clocked her arrival. Sometimes on the department as he saw her checking her watch and scurrying to a seminar. But the time it struck hardest was when he did not expect to see her at all – caught suddenly unawares. Turning a corner in the corridor. Across a canteen. Leaving the office in early evening when he had presumed that everyone else, Anna included, was long gone.

Max had decided it was lust and that it would pass. And then she turned up one morning with this stinking cold – hand up to her face, embarrassed by two cold sores which had appeared on her top lip. Ugly, crusty lumps. Red, raw nose and coughing and hacking also.

Still the lurch.

'I'd give it ten feet,' she was holding up her hand to halt him. 'Should have stayed home but busy schedule.'

'We could have fixed cover.'

'Yeah I know. Like I keep saying. Way too keen.'

'Would you like a coffee later?' he hadn't known he was going to say this. They hadn't sat down together since the supper that was not a date. 'At ten feet. Obviously.'

She laughed. 'Sure. Though I'll probably make it Lemsip. Just let me infect a few more freshers first.'

'My office? Eleven?' He was reaching into his pocket, for what he had no idea.

She checked her watch. 'OK.'

He bought two small packets of biscuits from the cafeteria en route, agonising ridiculously over which kind she might prefer – shortbread or bourbons? – and was upset that she was already waiting for him.

'Sorry. Am I late?'

'No. I was early,' she was filling the kettle in the little kitchenette alongside the office. 'Hope you don't mind me taking over but I badly need decongestant.' She reappeared to pour the Lemsip powder into a mug on his desk as Max set up his cafetière.

'So how are things with Freddie? I've been meaning to ask.'

She blew out a long puff of air, stretching out her bottom lip so that the upward flow lifted her fringe. 'Of course I went completely over the top. Assumed he was dealing crack cocaine. Turns out it was very much simpler.'

'Oh?'

'A girl.'

'Ah.'

'Her parents were away. An opportunity not to be missed – obviously.'

Max smiled and then immediately apologised but Anna was grinning too, throwing the Lemsip sachet into a bin. 'Takes you back, doesn't it?'

'So you two are OK, then?'

'Yes. We seem to be. Apart from the new panic that he'll get her pregnant. He's at the obsessed stage. First sex I suspect. But I can't be cross. Rather remember that myself. And at least he's telling me the truth now.'

Max poured the boiling water.

'And she's very pretty.' Anna had her hand up to her mouth again, first to conceal and then to actively point at her cold sores. 'Memo to self. Do not invite son's gorgeous new girlfriend around when you are impersonating Godzilla.'

'Can I repay the favour, Anna?' Max hadn't known that he was going to say this either, his vocal chords and brain apparently now disconnected.

'Sorry?'

'Supper.'

'You are offering to cook for me, Professor?'

'I was thinking of a restaurant actually.'

He let this hang in the air. Dangerous, unplanned words.

Her face said immediately that she was absorbing the significance. A restaurant made it a date.

She sipped her drink. 'Can we wait for the cold sores to go?' The lurch.

'A week should do it.'

'OK. Sure,' he was topping up his coffee, then looking her in the face, wishing that he had the courage to tell her to put her hand down. To stop worrying about how she looked because he really hated the embarrassment in her eyes. 'You tell me when's good.'

'And how's Melissa? After the holiday? Has she made a decision on that new contract? Writing for one of the nationals, wasn't it?'

'Yes. A consumer column for a tabloid. She still hasn't decided. She's had a lot on.'

'Oh?'

Max thought of the book again. How just last night he had lain in bed trying to imagine Eleanor sitting there writing it, which was not what he wanted to think about. Not here with Anna.

'I'll tell you at dinner.'

Anna was looking closely at his face and appeared concerned suddenly.

'You OK, Max?'

How did this work? How could it possibly be all right that he wanted to talk to Anna about Eleanor?

'OK. You tell me at dinner, Max. When I am looking less scary.'

And then very soon they were scurrying off to their next seminars, Max resisting the urge to glance back over his shoulder to watch her leave.

Half an hour later as he was just getting into his stride on the introduction to quantitative economics with a group of very promising second years, there was the screeching interruption of the fire alarm. Max turned away from the whiteboard. He hadn't got the bloody email. Typical.

Max hated fire drills.

He waited for the long shrill bell to break into the familiar sequences of three – the cue that this was a dress rehearsal. It didn't.

Shit.

'OK. Everyone. Fire drill.'

So this was not a drill?

'Our exit route is right out of this room and then the fire door is directly opposite. Gather your things. Nice and calm. Sorry about the intrusion.'

'So it's a drill?' several voices at once.

'Doesn't matter what it is. We have to behave as if it is real.'

'Can't we just ignore it?'

'No. Sorry. University policy. More than my pension's worth. Up you get. Nice and calmly. Turn right and then the fire door opposite. Lucky for you – it's so close. Out. Quickly. Come on. All of you. Then I have the excitement of proving that an economics professor can actually count.'

Max listened to the mumblings and grumblings, urging them to hurry. He counted the heads. Stood behind the group as they snaked right and then out the door onto the grass. *Eight. Nine. Ten.* 'Our rendezvous point is the green opposite the library. I'll see you there in just a mo.'

And then Max felt his heart beginning to race as he checked his phone, calling up the departmental timetable to check where she was. Shit. Seminar room eleven. Third floor.

Shit. Shit. Shit.

Max turned the other way and headed back to the main stairwell where Alistair Hill – one of the caretakers and departmental fire wardens – was standing with his arms outstretched, barring the way.

'Other way please, Professor Dance.' There was smoke on the stairwell. Max could now see it quite clearly.

'So this is not a drill?'

'No. Not a drill,' there was crackling on Alistair's walkie-talkie, pinned to his belt. Also his mobile phone was ringing.

'So what's happening?'

Alistair answered the phone and the walkie-talkie in turn, holding up his hand to halt Max's inquiries. A panicked, staccato conversation, impossible to decipher from one side only. Finally he put both back down, looking across at Max again.

'Kitchen of the main cafeteria. Faulty equipment. Fire brigade on the way.'

'So what about the people upstairs?' Max was glancing up the stairwell, trying to work out which route they could take. The rooms were directly over the cafeteria. He was trying to remember the last time he had used the rooms himself. Was there an external staircase? A fire escape? He couldn't remember. Never paid enough attention in all the bloody fire briefings.

'I'm sorry. I'm going to have to ask you to turn around, Professor Dance. Go the other way, please. We have this all under control.'

CHAPTER 32
Melissa – 2011

There was a part of Melissa that wished she was back in work. She missed the rhythm of it. The in-tray overflowing with letters from pensioners, ripped off by smooth-talking con artists. The noise of the keyboards tap tapping all around her. The furrowed brows as deadlines approached. The strong coffee and the raised voices. Journalists liked a good debate, when time permitted, and she was missing that.

But no. All around her was now too quiet. Melissa was still on leave from the Bartley Observer to make the decision over the contract. Sam meantime was suddenly crazy busy. As expected, he had been offered a partnership and was putting together a financial package to buy into the business. His niche was to be converting and extending listed properties, for which he had a good track record, having just led a project which made a feature in a Sunday supplement. But there was a lot to sort suddenly. A lot of networking. Meetings with the bank. Interviews with the trade press. Also there was the challenge of supporting Marcus. He and Diana had already consulted lawyers and the mud was flying thick and fast. Sam's dad was helping out financially – setting Marcus up in a rented flat while he tried to sort the financial mess.

All this left Sam wearing dark bags under his eyes, with Melissa, in contrast, juggling free time at the flat. She was supposed to be using this space to prepare for a final meeting with the editor of the tabloid.

Melissa had put together cuttings from her consumer success stories and jottings for new campaign ideas but she was now distracted – unable to get the journal, the cooking and the seeds for some kind of blog out of her mind. She was still wondering if she dared pitch this also to the editor. The idea of sharing her own memories stirred by the cooking with an open invitation for others to do the same. She was well aware that there were many experts writing brilliantly on food but that was not what she had in mind at all. She wanted to write about the surprise of the novice. The continuum. The nostalgia and the importance of recipe twists and special memories handed down from generation to generation.

Alongside this, she was also distracted by a new and secret worry – spending hours online checking out the BRCA1 and 2 cancer gene.

It was not until Melissa began looking into it properly that she realised just how much she had misunderstood.

Max had raised the subject with her only once and very tentatively – saying that when she was older she might want to talk it through with her GP.

Did they not know about this when Mummy was ill?
It was new, Melissa. All very new.

In her teens, Melissa had no desire whatsoever to look into it. All she knew was that women with the faulty gene had both breasts cut off. Good God. She remembered once standing in front of the mirror naked and feeling very faint.

Now she read page after page online. Very quickly it became apparent that the research had come a very long way since the time that her mother fell ill.

The faulty gene was indeed linked to both breast and ovarian cancer – just as they supposed back in the 1990s – but it was not straightforward. A cell needed a number of 'mistakes' in a genetic code before it might become cancerous. Being born with a gene fault didn't mean you would definitely get cancer… but it certainly increased the risk.

Official webpages of leading cancer charities explained that BRCA1 and BRCA2 – discovered around the time Eleanor fell ill – were the first breast cancer genes to be clearly identified. Anyone carrying them had an increased risk – estimates varying between 45% and 90% – of getting cancer in their lifetime. Options for treatment ranged from the extremity of a double mastectomy to the watch-and-wait scenario of regular screening.

Genetic testing was now an option for anyone with a strong family history of breast cancer or the associated ovarian cancer. To be tested via the NHS these days, you usually needed a living relative with cancer who could be checked first to verify if a gene fault was at play – and more importantly to pinpoint which one.

Melissa at first thought this closed the subject down for her. But more research revealed there could be flexibility depending on the family tree. Also the NHS route, though preferable, was not the only option. Further Googling revealed the inevitable. Genetic testing now had a booming private market. Melissa, with her journalistic hat, was immediately uncomfortable. She imagined frightened women having this test when they did not really need it – also without considering the full consequences.

But it did mean that she potentially had an option to be tested without going through her GP – and without anyone, by which she meant Sam and her father, knowing.

Further reading confirmed Melissa's risk factors did not look good. That her mother and grandmother had died relatively young from linked cancers was the big red flag – especially in a family dominated by men. Melissa was also surprised to discover that men could be silent carriers of the gene fault. In either case a mother or father with BRCA1 or BRCA2 had a fifty-fifty chance of passing it on to their children.

The reason experts liked to examine the blood from a living cancer patient and relative first was because it allowed them to try to isolate very precisely the gene fault in play. This then made subsequent 'predictive' testing of any relatives much more successful and accurate. Testing without the blood from a living relative was possible but not ideal.

UK Guidelines recommended expert counselling but some online companies were happy to take your spit by post and return a test within eight weeks. Melissa had no idea on accuracy.

She took a break from the screen to make strong coffee and set her mother's book in front of her. She put her hand flat on the cover and tilted her head to the corner of the room, picturing her at her desk – fountain pen in hand.

She felt a huge surge suddenly of compassion for her mother – facing all of that on her own. Melissa pressed her lips very hard together and suddenly knew for sure.

Like remembering a fact that was the answer in a quiz – that name not quite taking shape. That person just on the periphery of your vision.

Absolute clarity suddenly.

Melissa had realised for some time – from the early days of reading the book – that she had been angry deep down at her mother for not saying goodbye. But that was no longer it. Not any more.

All this confusion over Sam. She had imagined that what he said in the car in Cyprus during that row was perhaps right after all. That she was simply against marriage because she was *afraid*. That she didn't believe in happy ever afters, scarred by what she and her father had gone through. But now she was understanding better.

It was about the children playing in the fountain. About the *parent* thing. It had hit her when Sam confessed just how much he wanted to be a father. Melissa had always guessed Sam might like to have a family but now there was no pretending she did not know how very *strongly* he felt.

Since being offered the partnership, he had been excited about the extra money he would be earning. And had been emboldened to show her on his home computer all the design plans he had been putting together for the so-called dream family home.

It was almost as if Sam now felt that the sharing of the journal had solved any problems there had been between them.

And yet here was the paradox. If anything it was now making things worse.

Melissa felt her pulse in her ear every single time she thought about it.

She could not change her mind now and marry Sam, even if she wanted to. Because how, on earth, could she have a baby. If she took the test, it would come back positive and if she had a baby – one day in the future – there was the strong possibility the poor child would have to go through exactly what she had been through.

And no way could she do that to Sam. Or the child. This was no longer about some irrational fear of dying young. This was about science. Genes. Facts. It had been different for her mother because she didn't know any of this when she got married and had Melissa. But knowing of the risk changed everything for Melissa. Gave her a responsibility she didn't actually want.

Melissa ran her fingers around the stuck pages two thirds into the journal – realising why she had not wanted to read them earlier. She was sure now that it contained, not just the story of her parents' 'blip' but the results of her mother's test also. That Eleanor had danced around it all to prepare her as gently as was possible… for the worst.

She closed her eyes and tried to remember it. A rabbit biscuit cutter. Standing outside that bathroom in Cornwall. All impatience.

And then Melissa took a very deep breath and opened the book.

CHAPTER 33
Eleanor – 1994

Eleanor had a clear idea in her head of how the final bit would map out.

And then, shortly after handing over the book to the lawyer, she woke up on the floor. How long she had been out cold she had no idea. Eleanor was not wearing her watch and assumed a few minutes, but by the time she had dragged herself across the carpet to a position where she could see the clock, she was shocked to see that more than twenty had passed. She was also shocked at the colour of her skin. Yellow.

Max was at the university – a drive of forty-five minutes. She had pressed him to go, day after day, unable to bear his worrying and determined to keep things as normal as possible for as long as possible for Melissa. The district nurse was now checking on her twice daily and Eleanor felt this was safety net enough. But she had miscalculated.

The pain in her lower stomach was almost unbearable. She shuffled a couple more feet towards the phone and dialled first for an ambulance and then to speak to Dr Palmer. He was in his office and the secretary put her through straight away.

'It's time,' was all she said. There was a pause and then reassurance that he would liaise with ambulance control and speak to the ward – set everything in play. A side room. Was Max with her? When did she dial 999? Was she sure she would not prefer the hospice?

Eleanor had batted away all hospice support on the grounds that Melissa would very quickly work out what was going on. Writing the book meant she was now no longer certain at all that she had got this right. She told Dr Palmer that she didn't know what she thought any more about the hospice and he said that he would make sure their hospital nurse made contact on the ward. To at least discuss it.

'Is there someone with you, Eleanor? Have you seen the district nurse this morning? You're not on your own?'

'I'm fine. All in hand.'

By the time the ambulance arrived, Eleanor had managed to sit herself on the chair in the hall – a small bag at her feet. Just the basics. With every item, imagining Max slowly unpacking them. Pyjamas; washbag; books.

She had decided to get the nurse to phone Max once she was settled onto a ward. It was two o'clock. This sudden and complete weakness had overwhelmed her. She had honestly expected some more time to adjust and to make plans. So – what now? She would get Max to pick Melissa up from school and ring his mother to take over. Yes. Eleanor imagined that she could make it a bit tidier. Less stressful for everyone. She was feeling guilty. For not listening to Max who in recent days had wanted to stay home with her. Now she was thinking that by the time he caught up with what was happening, she would at least be settled. Comfortable. Calm.

Tidier.

She also wanted to speak to Dr Palmer and the lawyers about what to do about the test results. All before Max arrived.

———

'You can't go back in there, professor.'

'I bloody can. One of my staff is up there. A seminar. Half a dozen students.'

'We need to leave it to the fire brigade now.'

Max tried to barge past the caretaker but he was having none of it.

'I can't let you do that, professor.'

Max took a swing but missed.

'Jesus Christ. Professor Dance!' the caretaker was in shock. But he was a muscular man and in less than a minute had Max in a tight hold – one arm twisted up his back.

'Now. I realise you're upset. And I'm very sorry about this. But we need to calm down. And leave this to the professionals. Yes?'

Max struggled without success.

'I'm the head of the department. I'm responsible.'

'Yes. I know that. But I'm in charge on this one. Now. Can I let go of you? Are you going to calm down and let me walk you to the exit? Yes?'

———

'She's in a coma.'

'What on earth do you mean – she's in a coma. I need to speak to her. She was perfectly fine this morning. Doing OK. What do you mean she's in a coma?'

'Things deteriorated very, very quickly, Max. It's her liver. And her lungs. There's a clot. Look. She was blacking out. We had to do something for the pain.'

'But she will wake up?'

Dr Palmer had met Max on the corridor and walked swiftly alongside him to Eleanor's side room. It was five o'clock. His mother now with Melissa.

Her skin was all the wrong colour – but Dr Palmer explained it was the lungs they were more concerned about. He was wittering about the rarity of Eleanor's case. How the tumour spread and organ system response was so very difficult to predict. Every case was—

Max wanted him to shut the fuck up.

'She was fine this morning.' He was thinking now that he should have stayed home. Never mind what Eleanor wanted…

'The important thing now is that we keep her comfortable.'

'I had no idea she had lost this much weight. She wouldn't let me see her,' Max was standing by the bed as Dr Palmer checked the display from the machines. 'This is my fault, isn't it? I should have insisted. Brought her in sooner. She wouldn't even let me help her with her bath. I tried. Believe me, I—'

Dr Palmer put his hand on Max's upper arm. 'None of this is your fault, Max. It was important to let Eleanor do this her way.'

Max put his hand up to his mouth, feeling giddy suddenly. Dr Palmer helped him to sit on the chair alongside the bed.

'Pain. You said she was in pain?'

'We are giving her everything, Max. It's OK. She wasn't uncomfortable for long.'

'So she was distressed?'

Dr Palmer looked across at the nurse.

'We did our best. She wanted to stay awake to speak to you. But it got too much for her.'

'Was she distressed?'

'She wanted to talk to you about something. It was upsetting her. But she's calm now. She wasn't distressed for long, I promise you.'

'So she will wake up?'

Max watched Eleanor's chest rising and falling – this terrible pause with every third breath.

'I will get to speak to her again? She will wake up?'

———

The fire brigade used an extension ladder to reach the upper seminar rooms. There were five terrible minutes of panic when they could all see the students and Anna up at the window – the smoke in the room evident and the faces terribly afraid. And then the paradox of calm and everyone pretending it had been no big deal.

The students watching from the lawns filmed it on their mobiles and then clapped. The students who were moved to safety via the little platform changed demeanour the moment they hit the safety of the ground. It had been a lark. A triumph for Facebook.

Max watched Anna insist on being the last to be accompanied on the little platform down to safety.

'It was the deep fat fryer,' he heard someone whisper alongside him. 'Hadn't been cleaned. Health and safety are gonna have a field day.'

Anna watched him from the platform as it was manoeuvred slowly down to the ground, her hand cupped over her cold sores as Max had to sit down on the grass.

CHAPTER 34

Max had always known what the biggest test of his love for Eleanor would be. Not losing her. That felt exactly as he had feared – like ripping flesh from his bones. Just much faster than anyone expected. Four hours in the hospital. A clot on the lung.

You have to wake up, Eleanor. I'm not ready.

But no. Even that horror was not as bad as it could get.

With Eleanor's father on the way from France and Max's mother holding the fort at home, only now came the true test.

Driving home to Melissa.

This terrible, terrible journey during which Max had to muster every ounce of his physical strength to overcome an unexpected fury towards the woman he so loved for leaving him with this task.

OK, so they had had their weeks of 'normal'. But Max was sure Melissa knew, deep down, that something very big was up. And to the very end he had tried to get Eleanor to change her mind. To prepare Melissa. To let her see the counsellor. To buy some special book and do the memory box. To say a proper goodbye.

But – no. Eleanor would not budge. *I can't do it. Please don't make me do it, Max.*

For those final few days during which Eleanor was so obviously deteriorating, Melissa thought it was appendicitis.

'Is it her appendix, Daddy? Tabatha's mummy had her appendix out last summer. But she didn't get a very big scar. Tiny.

She showed us,' she had said just that morning when he left her at school. 'If Mummy has to have her appendix out, will she show me her scar?'

His own mother had also disapproved of the secrecy. And when he turned up now at the door – straight from the hospital, he could hardly bear to see her in her pinny and her slippers – slumping down into the seat by the telephone in the hallway.

She had wanted to come upstairs to Melissa. To help him do it.

But Max shook his head. He didn't want anyone else in the room.

In her bedroom Melissa was plaiting Elizabeth's hair – a tatty rag doll. A gift from his father when she was three.

'Is Mummy home with you?'

Max sat on Melissa's bed.

'No. Listen, honey. Daddy has some very, very sad news, darling.'

'Was it her appendix?'

'No.'

Melissa's body tightened and she began to undo one of the doll's plaits. To needlessly repeat the task. Plaiting the left side of the hair all over again. Pulling hard at the strands of nylon.

She said nothing.

'Sometimes things happen, my darling, which are very difficult to understand. And also to explain Melissa.'

'Is Mummy having another baby?'

'No. Mummy isn't having another baby.'

'I don't mind. I won't be jealous. I promise.'

Max moved closer to his daughter and put his arm around her shoulder, fighting the surge of panic. The adrenalin through his body.

'The thing is Melissa. God has decided that Mummy needs to be in heaven with him.'

And now Melissa was completely still. As if anaesthetised. Rigid. Saying nothing.

'Mummy has gone to heaven, darling.'

And then Melissa moved her head very strangely. A sort of twitch of her chin. She did it over and over – like a tic which Max had never seen before.

'I think I'm going to change Elizabeth's outfit now.'

'You can do that later, darling. I need you to listen to me. And to understand what I'm telling you. It's very, very sad – my darling. Awful. And it hurts Daddy very much too. Right in my heart. But we need to be very brave. I'm so sorry, darling. Mummy loved you more than anything in the whole world. But Mummy has died in the hospital and gone to heaven today. And it means we can't see her any more.'

And then, after a few more seconds of complete stillness, it came.

The tsunami. A wall of it. Fists and hair and this terrible, terrible noise.

Whether Melissa had stood first or begun shouting first he would later not remember. All he remembered was the pounding against his own body. The fists and the kicks and the wailing sound.

On and on and on.

'You are a fat, stinking liar.' Kicking and screaming. And then throwing things. The doll. Her brush. Her toys. 'You get out of my room.' Throwing books and bags. And kicking at the doll's house in the corner. Smash. Smash. And then physically trying to push him out of the room. 'You get out of my room. I hate you,' kicking really hard. 'I am going to call Granny and we are going to get Mummy. Right this minute. Get out.'

Max tried to hold his daughter's arms, to stop the thrashing but was afraid of hurting her.

'I know, darling. I know. And I'm so very sorry, my darling.'

'She is not in heaven.'

'Melissa. Look at me, darling…'

'She's not.'

'Melissa, please.'

'We're in the middle of a story. Look,' she grabbed a book from beside her bed and opened it to show him the place – the bookmark – her eyes wide and pleading for this unfinished business to count.

She looked into his face for an age, tears now streaming down her own and then her arms were suddenly limp, the book falling to the ground. From the extremity of the violence to the horror of complete collapse. On the floor. As if all the muscles had suddenly stopped working.

Max in panic called out for his mother as he checked her breathing. Oh dear God, no. Leant his ear down to hear it. Her chest rising and falling. *Good. Good. That's it, Melissa. Breathe.*

And now Max scooped her into his arms to hold her tight as she came to and his mother appeared in the doorway – lifting Melissa's head gently into the crook of his arm like he did when she was really small.

'Mummy didn't finish the story.' A convulsion of sobbing now – huge waves which made her whole chest and shoulders roll. Waves of utter wretchedness right through her little body.

Simple soda bread

1lb strong white flour
2 teaspoons bicarbonate of soda
One teaspoon salt
Around 14 fluid oz of buttermilk (I have also used live yoghurt)

Sift all the dry ingredients into a bowl, make a dip in the middle and pour in the buttermilk or yoghurt. Mix into soft dough and add a dash of milk if too dry. Tip onto floured board and knead for just a minute or so. Make into a rough round and cut a cross in the top. Bake in preheated oven at 200°C for around 40 minutes. You can add herbs and seeds, if you like.

So I have added an extra little recipe as an afterthought and OK, I admit soda bread is more scone than true bread but it is simple and very satisfying – and perfect when you are mad or sad, because even the simplest bread-making is so therapeutic. Do it when you need a lift and can't think what else to do.

Now, my darling girl, it is time.

The lawyer will be here very soon to collect the book and I don't know quite what I was expecting of this moment. Closure? Certainly some sense of peace. Some uplifting message to take you forward into the beautiful life that I wish for you.

Instead I find that I have rather messed up. And yes – things, as you now realise, have gone off piste. The results of my test are still not back so – here's my thinking.

If there is time, I will try to contact the test labs and have an insert arranged for this book. That means we can rip out the 'stuck pages' and say no more about it.

But as things stand I must sign off to you with things rather up in the air.

And so – my beautiful one. When and if you have to read the 'secret, stuck' part try only to remember everything I have said to you before and to be as kind to me as you can.

Before that – lean in close and just listen.

I am not afraid, Melissa. Not for myself at all. I am not bitter and I am not angry any more. I am leaving you in the care of a man I love with all of my heart and who is genuinely the best person I have ever met. I know that he will keep you safe and love you always with every inch of his own heart. I am only sad that I will not see you grow, Melissa, and cannot be there for you.

Not enough days for us. Unfair. But know that every single one with you has been an absolute joy and I leave you more love than there are words to describe.

Try not to be sad – over me, at least. Be brave and be strong – and always as kind as you can.

I hope I have not left it too late to say goodbye to you properly and I hope you will forgive me for doing it this way.

Please know above all else that I could not be more proud of you. Any mistakes of mine which you must now judge were born of my flaws… and not a lack of love.

Go out there and have yourself a beautiful life.

My beautiful, beautiful girl.

Goodbye,

Your ever-loving mother x x x

Melissa was aware only of her shoulders moving and an absolute determination not to let any noise out of her mouth. This deep-rooted and certain fear that if she even dared to let it start…

She set the book aside on the floor and concentrated very hard. How long she struggled to maintain control was difficult to assess. She certainly wasn't sure now that she was ready for the sealed pages.

Nearly a week now since she had cooked the meal for her father and still she had not brought herself to read it. Afraid.

So should she just forget it? Cut them out? Burn them? Walk away from it all. Sam. Marriage. Motherhood…

Melissa took out a tissue and blew her nose very hard. *Right.* She flipped through the book again just to triple check. No insert.

She stood up and went through to the en-suite bathroom to first splash water on her face and next to find nail scissors which she used very carefully to part the edges of the pages that her mother had stuck around three sides.

Eleanor had made it look like a mistake. Just two pages stuck together but she had actually sealed the double pages like an air mail envelope or pay slip. Just around the very rim. Melissa began carefully to cut around the edge, opening out the pages to find the familiar writing in fluid black ink confined to the centre of the pages.

The first part recapped, from her mother's point of view, pretty much exactly what her father had told her over dinner. The falling out over the New York job. But now Melissa was thrown.

She had actually been sure the gene result would be here too. The bad news. Instead there was rambling and the evidence of tears which had blurred some of the ink.

Once your father left for New York, I was inconsolable, Melissa. I just could not believe he would go. Leave me. …

And then the shock.

Terrible, ugly words tumbling from the page.

Melissa put the book down, no longer wanting to touch it.

No.

She pushed the bedside table on which she had placed it away from her. And then felt the sudden and absolute urge to smash something. She stood up and went over to the dressing table, sweeping her arm across the top so that all the bottles and perfume, the jewellery and the favourite ceramic bowls flew across towards the wall. And then she watched the mess of glass and fragments and golden liquid oozing down the wall.

It felt no better.

Melissa stood for a time very still, watching the pool of gold taking shape on the wooden floor, and when the feeling did not change knew that she had to go.

She needed to be in a car. Right now.

Yes.

She needed to be driving.

CHAPTER 35

Sam – 2011

'What do you mean she's gone?'

'Disappeared, Max. God knows where. Sent me just one short text. Said she needed some time out on her own and I was not to worry. Now she's not answering her mobile.'

'Jesus Christ. So what happened? You guys have a row?'

'No, Max. No row. I went to work this morning. Melissa was supposed to go to that meeting about this new contract. I was expecting her home tonight to celebrate. Booked a restaurant. Instead I come home to find things all smashed up.'

'What do you mean smashed up? You saying she's been at-tacked? Dear God, have you called—'

'No, no, Max. When I saw it, I thought that too – some burglary or something. But she did it herself. Said sorry in the text.'

'Right. Shit,' there was a pause. 'We need to stay calm.'

'Oh come on, Max. I can't do calm. She didn't even go to the meeting with the editor. What does it mean? Has she left me?'

Max said nothing.

'Is she leaving me, Max? Is that what this is? Did she talk to you over that dinner? Has she been too afraid to tell me?'

'No. I don't think that's what this is.'

'I mean I thought we were OK. Better. That we were getting closer again. But I've been so busy. Shit. I mean – with the partnership offer and with my brother all over the place. Oh God, Max. I'm worried sick.'

'Send her another message.'

'I've sent her loads. She won't ring. Her text just said – please don't worry. How can I not worry?'

'I'll try as well, Sam. I'll leave a message and I'll come straight over.'

'Right. So she really hasn't said anything to you? About us?'

'No. Not really.'

'So you don't think this is it? That it's over, I mean?'

'I don't know what this is Sam.   Just sit tight. I'm leaving now.'

'Shit.'

Half an hour later and Sam was still sitting on the floor of their bedroom – head in hands, waiting for Max. Though Melissa had not known it, this was exactly the pose he took up on the floor of the men's restroom after she stalled over the proposal.

Sam did not know how to love Melissa any more than he had. He had worn his heart out wearing it on his sleeve. Maybe, he was thinking now, that was precisely the problem.

Sam had loved Melissa from the time he watched her playing with a ladybird at school in the weeks after her mother died. He never told anyone this because he knew that they would say it could not be love because he was a child himself. It was compassion most likely – at best a crush. But no. Sam knew different.

Melissa had always completely mesmerised him – even as children. There was something about her eyes. Her skin. The way that her whole face lit up with animation when she talked. Though Sam was four years older, he vividly remembered the day he realised they shared the same birthday – Melissa with her birthday badge in school. Feeling this huge surge of complete happiness. The first proper sign.

And then the 'awful thing' happened and Sam had no idea what to say or how to behave. Melissa came back to school just a week after the funeral and threw everyone off by behaving as if nothing had happened. She point-blank refused to talk about it and just shrugged when he asked if there was anything he could do. 'I'm fine. It's actually OK.'

And then, a few weeks later, he had followed her to the orchard one day, while all the other children were in the main playground and he had watched her from behind a tree. She was sitting cross legged on the ground searching in the grass for insects. And after a while she found a ladybird, talking out loud to it and repeating the rhyme.

Ladybird, ladybird fly away home. Your house is on fire and your children are gone...

Melissa lifted her hand to let the ladybird go. She repeated the rhyme as if she was just noticing the words for the very first time. For a while the ladybird did not budge and so she chanted the verse again – this time, her voice breaking as the insect finally disappeared.

Sam was certain that she was crying but had no idea what to do. He hated it when anyone cried. His mother. His cousin. Anyone. He wondered if he should fetch a teacher. Show himself? He was worried that she would be furious that he had followed her.

In the end he just waited there, secretly watching her – feeling more and more guilty and more and more helpless. It was quite a long time until Melissa had finished, wiping her face with her sleeve and raising her chin.

She stood up then and for a moment her head sort of twitched as if she was struggling to get complete control of herself. She waited until this twitching stopped and then she brushed down her skirt, tied her ponytail tighter into a band and marched back to the class.

Melissa grew prettier and pricklier with every passing year. They became friends of a sort but she began to approach everything with just a little bit of a scowl – as if she was privately furious at the whole world. Sometimes he would wait for her at the end of the street, offering to carry her bag but she said this was 'ridiculous behaviour'. Later, after she moved on to the grammar school, he would strike up conversation on the bus, but he could tell from the way her eyes darted past him that she had no idea how he felt.

Once he had actually plucked up the courage to ask her out to the cinema but she had pulled her head back into her neck in shock. Like a tortoise. 'You don't mean like a date, Sam? Don't be silly.'

And then years later fate intervened. Sam had always known that it had to be Architecture – all his life teased by his family for the permanent crick in his neck; always walking with his head looking upwards. Checking out the buildings. Amazed. Enchanted. *Look at that arch. Good God – Look at the balustrades on that one.* The prospect of seven years of study was daunting but Sam guessed correctly that it would be worth it. For the first part of his degree, he tried very hard to forget about Melissa. For a short time he thought he might be in love with a girl called Sandra. Then he thought just maybe he was in love with a girl called Madeleine. And then on Thursday October 25th, Melissa walked back into his life properly and he faced the truth.

By this time Sam was in the final part of his first degree. He had no idea that Melissa had picked the same campus.

October 25th. The happiest day of his life.

Sam now stared at the mess of broken crockery and perfume bottles strewn across the wooden floor.

The truth? He had never quite believed that she would love him back. Never quite believed that he would hold onto her.

There was something deep in Melissa which seemed not to want to let him love her. He had thought, naively perhaps, that time would change this. That she was just afraid of love.

Maybe the truth that he did not want to face was that he was just the wrong man.

CHAPTER 36
Melissa – 2011

Melissa had tried to run away to Cornwall once before.

She had waited until two days after the news about her mother and decided that she would go and find the truth. Why she imagined she would find her mother in Cornwall did not stand up to rational analysis, but the eight-year-old Melissa had so many happy pictures of her family aligned with the cottage in Porthleven that she believed somehow that if she could just get herself to that cottage, then everything around her would be all right. The past two days with all its horrors could be undone.

She had packed a bag with pyjamas and clean pants and T-shirts and had crept out of the house before her father and Granny were up. She knew that it was quite a long walk to the railway station but had deliberately selected sensible shoes and so did not much care.

It was raining hard. She remembered wishing that she had brought her other coat, but reasoned that she would be able to get a new one with Mummy in Cornwall. They would shop in Truro. She remembered it was by the water, and while Daddy went to look at art galleries and antique shops, they would potter from shop to shop and at the end of the expedition she would be allowed a giant ice cream sundae.

Yes. In Cornwall they would shop. Sort everything out.

Melissa had four pounds and eighty six pence in her piggy bank. She had no idea how much a train ticket to Cornwall would cost. The man at the ticket booth had looked at her a little oddly when she handed over her money.

'Is your Mummy or Daddy not travelling with you, young lady?'

'Not today. My mummy's picking me up. She'll pay the extra if it's not enough.'

'I see.'

The man had suggested that she wait over there by the seats and he would check the train times for her. Melissa had thought that he was terribly nice and had waited patiently on the seats for a very long time until she realised it had all been a horrible trick. The moment when Max had thundered through the doors shouting 'Thank God' with a policewoman beside him.

Max had cried, she remembered that. She had never seen a man cry before. He had hugged her so close that she could feel the cold and wet from his cheeks. And she remembered that his tears had frightened her more than anything else she ever experienced.

This time Melissa chose the car.

She decided on the route cross country – the A303 – which she had always preferred. It meant a lot of slowing down for all the speed cameras through the series of villages, but Melissa did not mind. She loved these villages. She loved the colour of the stone and the antique shops and the blackboard signs on the pavements with chalked pictures of coffee and cakes. She liked the people gossiping on the side of the road and had some fantasy in her head that in a different life she might have lived somewhere like this. Yes. One of the villages back in Oxford-shire just like these. A dog. A fire. Sam with his dreams, drawing up his secret plans for extensions and renovations. *I was thinking*

we go for the foil. Stainless steel and glass. Modern meets thatch?
What do you think, Melissa?

She listened to classical music up much too loud. She was also driving very badly – much too fast on the stretches between the speed cameras. But so bloody what.

So.

Bloody.

What.

So long as she did not get picked up by some stupid patrol car, Melissa did not care. She stopped only once for petrol, the toilet and a strong coffee – waiting until there was a sign for the good stuff.

She was conscious of a slightly strange feeling in her stomach which was not quite hunger and not quite an upset stomach and in the end let the coffee go cold in the little cup holder by the gear stick.

Just occasionally she thought about them – the wretched, putrid words in her mother's book – but mostly she managed not to think much at all. Just to drive.

Melissa estimated the journey would take about four and a half hours, but there were two sets of roadworks and so it was well past midnight when she pulled into Truro city centre. She wanted to carry on – to get as far as the Lizard – but wasn't at all sure where she would find to stay this late, so instead stopped at the first chain hotel that she recognised.

After checking in, she took out the small bag into which she had thrown just two changes of clothes and a washbag. She checked her phone to find a string of messages from Sam and three from her father.

She sent another text telling them she was sorry. Not to worry. To please leave her be. She was OK. Just needed some space. **Please.**

Then she turned the phone off again and lay on the bed.

She remembered exactly what it felt like – that small girl in the train station who felt that if she could just get on the train, she could find the right version of her life. The different, parallel version in which the wrong news could be undone and everything could be all right.

She did not cry because it was all way beyond that.

Exhaustion must have overtaken her at some point and she woke around four a.m. still fully clothed. She climbed under the covers and then dozed fitfully until six, taking a quick shower and changing her underwear before heading straight through to the buffet breakfast where she found that she was still, inexplicably, not at all hungry.

The machine for coffee looked unpromising and so she tried orange juice instead and it was only as she sat at a table drinking this, playing with a single piece of toast that she had the idea.

Melissa switched the phone back on, ignoring the new messages, and put the name of the cottage into Google. She was astonished to see the picture ping instantly before her eyes – the place hardly changed, bar the colour of the front door. The same two terracotta pots standing guard, containing miniature trees. The cottage was still a holiday let, managed now by a small agency. The website loaded very slowly, but through two or three pages, Melissa discovered it was available for short lets off season '*by special arrangement*'. There would surely not be much interest with the school term well under way.

Melissa phoned the quoted number and was astonished to recognise the name check. Mrs Hubert. Good God.

She tried to calm her voice. She explained that she was in the area for a few days and wondered if the cottage would be available on a short let. Could she pay nightly? She remembered it from her childhood.

Mrs Hubert said that – yes; with the children all back in school, quite a few properties were available on short let – a minimum of three days booking. The shoulder season rate quoted for October was perfectly reasonable. Cheaper than a hotel room. Mrs Hubert added that she now managed five cottages and *when was Melissa thinking of coming?*

'Later today actually.'

'Oh goodness,' Mrs Hubert then sounded very flustered. She liked notice to get things ready. She normally liked to prepare a little welcome tray for all her guests.

So it was definitely her.

Melissa reassured that clean bed linen and towels would suffice and no special arrangements were necessary. She would shop for basics on the way down.

Mrs Hubert said she would meet her at the cottage at 3 p.m. and would arrange for her husband to get some logs in for the wood burner. It was turning cold of an evening down by the coast. The wind off the sea. Did Melissa realise this?

She did.

Melissa then had a spell of panic as she drove the final stretch. The cottage was on the outskirts of the town near woodland and it was not until she turned the final sharp bend onto the unmade road which wound its way through an avenue of trees to the detached cottage that she realised she had done the right thing.

She remembered once that they had driven through the nearby wood en route to the pub for a meal one evening, to experience one of the most wonderful surprises of her young life. An owl had suddenly broken cover from one of the trees and led the way below the canopy of leaves ahead of them. The wingspan had surprised Melissa – also the quiet and effortless glide of the bird.

It had simply and silently led the way, softly sweeping from side to side, swooping low enough for its shadow to be caught in the headlights – reflected on the ground ahead of them.

'Wow' was all the young Melissa managed as her mother reached out her hand to silently stroke the back of Max's neck.

Melissa now turned the car into the little parking area in front of the cottage and felt almost giddy with the paradox. The pleasure and the shock of this all being the same when everything else had broken into so many unrecognisable pieces.

Mrs Hubert – older and a little rounder but unmistakable with her grey perm and her happy wave – was on the doorstep, looking out for her.

Melissa had never been so relieved to see a sight so familiar. The glossy door, now deep blue, the proud plants and Mrs Hubert drying her hands on her apron.

Melissa closed her eyes and stood very still. Terrible decisions…

…but the right place.

CHAPTER 37

Porthleven had changed surprisingly little since Melissa's child-hood. Boats bobbing. Seagulls snatching crumbs. Fishermen a-natter at their nets because the weather was against them.

She had returned with her father, just once before, not long after Eleanor had died, with Max trying too hard to make it work – imagining that the nostalgia and the familiarity would be comforting for them. It wasn't. Back then – too soon – it merely underlined the absence. The spare chair at the table. And so for future holidays they had gone to the other extreme – avoiding anything with an echo.

Now it was different. Now Melissa was glad to be in Porthleven.

Her father…

Out of season, with that scent of true autumn beckoning, it had a quietness she had not seen before and she liked it; plenty of empty tables at the restaurants and coffee shops; shorter opening hours at some of the galleries and gift shops but room in the narrow aisles to browse without the fear that as you stepped back to let someone pass, you might knock something from a shelf with your back or your bag.

Melissa had slept badly that first night and still felt physically drained as she walked – a tiredness to her very bones – but she was glad to be out. Glad for the fresh air.

She had forgotten how loud the gulls were. How loud the sea. How loud the wind as it rocked the small fishing boats in the little harbour. This was all good. The loudness drowning all the words spitting fury in her head.

My father…

For now she kept her phone off and looked out on the white horses raging in the distance. She was glad that she had at least brought a waterproof coat and a scarf and was relieved now to find gloves in the pocket also. She zipped everything up tight, tight, tight and closed the neck flap so that it covered her mouth, right up to her nose.

She set off left from the cottage and within ten minutes or so was just one street back from the harbour. From here she headed west towards the old church and harbour wall. The tide was still out and the open sea beyond – choppy and cross.

My father…

The wind made Melissa's eyes water which she liked. She followed the road past the harbour wall and took the steps down to the beach. Every now and again the wind buffeted her sideways, her coat billowing out and her hood pushed back from her head. Melissa adjusted the tie to pull the hood even tighter around her face.

On the beach, she walked past a few couples with dogs and then one family – both parents plus three small children – one in a three-wheel buggy which they were struggling to push across the sand.

Further along, Melissa climbed another set of steps back up to the road overlooking the beach. The wind was even stronger at the higher level and she leant for a time against the railings, watching the waves rolling and smashing as the parent still struggled across the sand with the buggy. She couldn't understand why they did this. Why on earth didn't they use the higher, tarmac road to head back into the town? And then she saw the mother pull a collection of plastic buckets and spades from the large silver beach bag she was carrying.

To her continued surprise, the two smaller children kicked off shoes and socks, seemingly oblivious to the weather and began to dig in a frenzy. Very soon the mother took the small toddler out of the buggy and set him on the sand to do the same. The father meantime produced a large flask from his backpack and sat on the sand to pour two steaming mugs for himself and his wife; side by side to provide a windbreak for the children.

Melissa watched the man put his arms around his wife, rubbing her shoulders as if to warm her and felt something inside her break.

She thought of Sam, she thought of what he had said in Cyprus. Of course he wanted to be a father. Why wouldn't he? It was what most men wanted one day, wasn't it?

Melissa closed her eyes.

I am so sorry, Melissa. There is no easy way to say this but there is a very slim chance that Max is not your father... I need you to read this very closely to allow me to explain – I beg you – why I have locked this inside me all these years...

Melissa pictured him.

Max who on this very beach had taught her to body board. Max who had taken her to the butchers for fat, spicy sausages for the barbeque in the evening and in the morning to the bakery along the seafront for warm rolls for breakfast and pasties for lunch. Max who had hugged her so tight in that railway station waiting room that she had thought her bones would crack.

It felt like grief. Yes. The same numbness. That same out of body sensation where you were waiting for the mistake to be rectified. For someone to come along and say – *Whoops. Sorry about that. Wrong information. Our mistake.*

It was the same feeling when she sat in the train station waiting room all those years ago, not quite understanding what had happened. Feeling that if she could just change the geography; get herself to the right place then the mistake would be undone.

Melissa leant forward onto the railing and pressed her forehead against the cold metal. What surprised her most was that she was no longer feeling rage at her mother. That had now passed. What she felt instead now was anger at whoever or whatever controlled the shit that was her life. Who was it who decided she could take this? That all the blows so far were not quite enough?

Melissa did not often swear. But she was screaming every filthy word she had ever heard in her head now.

I lose my mother and now I am supposed to lose my father too?

She would have liked to have screamed all the words out loud. **Fuck you.** To scream them into the wind. But she was worried that the children on the beach would hear.

Melissa could not bear to watch the family any longer and so turned back towards the town, walking faster this time – the wind pushing her along and almost lifting her off her feet every third or fourth stride. Back finally on the main street, she ducked into a small cafe and ordered a cappuccino, heart pounding. She sat at a table by the window, waiting for it to arrive and pretended to read the menu. She looked around the room, confused by how detached she felt. As if in some bubble.

Yes. It was if she had stepped just a little bit outside of her body and was watching herself from the sidelines.

The waitress – a pretty, tall girl with her dark hair pinned up with a single pencil – walked carefully across the cafe with her drink, watching the froth on the cappuccino, evidently worried that it would spill.

Melissa nodded a thank you. She put the cup up to her lips but winced. The smell acrid and the drink much too hot.

She glanced across at the machine behind the counter – an impressive brand. Cream and shiny proper pods and a steamer for the froth. She put the coffee up to her lips again – but no. Still too hot. Still wrong.

Melissa wished that she had brought her mother's book with her, needing to read it again. Panicked suddenly that the words were all there still in the book on the coffee table in the cottage and that if anything happened to her they would be found. Read.

She could feel her heart pounding, realising that she should have thought of this before and hurried to the counter to leave coins for the coffee plus a small tip.

'Was the drink not OK?'

'Sorry. I've got to go.'

Back at the cottage she found matches in one of the kitchen cupboards and lit the wood burner which had been set ready by Mr Hubert. It roared wild and promising but she knew to wait until it settled, using the oven glove from the wood basket to open the latch and feed three more of the larger logs.

And then while she watched as the colour behind the glass changed to the steady glow she needed, Melissa read her mother's words one final time.

Once your father left for New York, I was inconsolable, Melissa. I just could not believe he would go, Melissa. Leave me. …

… In my stubbornness, I felt that my refusal to go with him would make him stay and would save him from being hurt. I thought I was doing it for him. Out of love.

Looking back, I am not so sure I wasn't being selfish. I didn't want to live in a land of guns and I didn't want to be with a man who would speak up at press conferences on behalf of a shitty bank.

And yet I did want to be with Max.

I went to bed, Melissa. For days – no kidding. I suppose it was some kind of depression. I just closed the curtains on the world.

My two best friends back then were Amanda (who you may well know; I suspect she will keep in contact) and a male friend from my degree course who you will not know.

Amanda came to stay first and saved my life. She wanted me to see a doctor but I refused so instead she cooked soup and made me eat on a tray in bed, sleeping on a little camp bed beside me. But then she had to go on a trip for work and so she called the other friend to take over.

He was good and kind, Melissa, but with every passing day I became more and more disorientated and distraught that your father did not get in touch.

And then something very, very stupid happened. More than a week with no word from Max and one night I got drunk with this friend. No excuses. Stupid. I was weak and low and I reached for comfort.

We both regretted it badly – him as much as me, fearing I would feel he had taken advantage. I have to tell you he didn't. Six of one. Just a madness in a dark hole.

I sent him packing and after two more days, Amanda returned and I finally got up. And then just a week later – there he was. Your father on the doorstep.

We married as you know then very quickly and I fell for you immediately.

I have always felt sure in my heart and in my head, Melissa, that Max is your father. But the truth, from the dates, is there is this slim possibility that he is not.

Should I have told Max? Taken some test?

I didn't think so because I just FELT you were his. And the selfish truth? I loved him so much that I could not bear the risk of losing him ever again.

But now I realise that if you go in for some kind of testing in the future, this may possibly come out. I'm no scientist but – blood groups? DNA? Somehow?

And what frightens me is that if my gut is wrong and Max is not biologically your father, then I will not be there to explain what it really was and that my darling man and you will think such terrible things of me. Even worse than the truth.

I swear that I have **never** messed up before or since. It would never have happened but for that bloody job. But – no excuse. It would break your father's heart in half to know this, which is why I just pretended it was not so. I called it an act of love. You may disagree.

Please don't hate me…

It took a while for the pages to burn. Melissa fed the two 'secret pages' in, one after another. Then she flicked through the book to rip out any reference to them and let those pages join the flames also.

She closed the glass door and watched the secret burn. Max was not to know about this. Not ever. It did not matter what she thought. It only mattered that her father should never know about this.

Her father.

For a moment Melissa considered putting the whole sodding book into the flames but something just held her back.

And so next she got out her laptop, put in the Wi-Fi password from the cottage information folder and searched for the solicitor who had handed the journal to her. James Hall. She turned her phone back on to see several more texts and recorded messages from both Max and Sam. She felt guilty, but what else could she do?

She phoned the London office and asked to speak to Mr Hall who, by chance, was at his desk. *Of course he remembered her.*

He confided now in a low whisper that he was actually the one who had visited her mother to collect the book. He hadn't liked to say before; been worried, given the context, that this would upset her.

'Right. I didn't realise it was you who met her.'

'A lovely and very brave woman.'

'Thank you.'

'So what is it that I can do?'

'The journal said there was another letter left for me.'

Eleanor had explained this at the end of the confession. If Melissa had wanted or ever needed the name of the other man... it was contained in a letter with the solicitor.

'Would you destroy it please?'

'Destroy it?'

'Yes. I will send you an email to confirm in writing that this is my instruction. My decision.'

'You're sure?'

'Yes. I'm absolutely sure.'

There was a pause.

'Sorry. Is there a problem, Mr Hall?'

'No, no. It's just—'

'What?'

'I don't want to speak out of turn.'

'No. Please do go on.'

'It's just – this is exactly what your mother predicted.'

'I'm not following.'

'Well when your mother gave me the journal and the separate sealed envelope....'

'Yes?'

'She said that we were to keep the envelope after you were given the book and it would be up to you whether you chose to have the additional material.' There was a much longer pause now and Melissa became conscious of her own pulse in her ear as she pressed the mobile closer to her head.

'It was an unusual request as you can imagine. But what I remember very clearly is that she said you would hopefully not want the envelope at all.'

'What?'

'Your mother. She said that if she had got things right, she believed – well; that you would ask for it to be destroyed.'

'She said that.'

'Yes. I found it rather cryptic at the time. That she would go to all the trouble of leaving something additional in our care that she hoped you would want to destroy.'

Melissa held her breath, turning her head to watch the flames again.

'Did she say anything else?'

'Yes, actually. She said that she would be very proud of you.'

Melissa now moved the mobile from her ear to her chest, pressing it flat to her jumper. She looked back again at the log burner, the pages just black confetti now. She watched the draw of the fire lifting some of the charred pieces to float in the flames.

'She said that?'

Her father…

'She did.'

'Well thank you very much. I'll send that email,' Melissa conscious of her eyelid beginning to flicker, cleared her throat and needed suddenly to be off the phone. 'And will you confirm by reply when it's done?'

'I will.'

Melissa then sat, watching the flames, with the phone still in her hand, waiting for the flickering of her eye to subside.

One decision.

One to go.

She added more logs, ever conscious of some strange detachment. Like watching herself. Some out-of-body-awareness.

Yes. An **awareness.** That was the word she had been looking for.

She watched herself watching the fire and she thought, after a time, about fate and chance. And odds.

Fifty-fifty.

Melissa took a coin from her purse and placed it on the table. Heads she had the gene. Tails she didn't.

It landed heads the first time. Tails the second. Heads the third and fourth. She felt nothing.

Of course. No scope for relief or for fear unless she took the test for real.

Melissa knew exactly what Sam would say. He would say that it didn't matter. He would say that he wouldn't care if she needed both her breasts chopped off; that he wouldn't care if she didn't want children because of it.

But it wouldn't be true. Because the truth was what he told her at the restaurant in Cyprus. That he couldn't imagine life without becoming a father.

And yes; he would deny it now. And he would twist it. He would say that he felt entirely differently now because of her new circumstance.

But it would always be there secretly between them. *The truth*. And one day she would catch him watching a family on a beach…

Melissa thought then of her mother facing all of this on her own, turning to the corner of the room to watch her sitting there at the desk in her bedroom with her beautiful fountain pen, smiling at her. And then she remembered something else suddenly.

It was when she had been flicking through the journal earlier – deciding which pages to destroy. Yes. She had glanced at the final section – the part on motherhood. She had just skimmed these – much too upsetting. The recipe for banana and avocado mush. Tips on colic. *Don't buy a wooden high chair – a nightmare to clean.*

A sea of words.

Upsetting.

But there was one word repeated over and over on a page. Melissa narrowed her eyes and could see it quite clearly.

Dear God.

She rushed to fetch the book again. Skimmed the pages, licking her fingers. *Where? Where? Come on – come on.*

Recipe after recipe. A note on cots. A page on sleep and bedtime routines.

And then, there it was…

…this strange ***awareness***. I don't know how else to describe it, Melissa. But I just knew. Even before I took the pregnancy test, I knew. It was like I was AWARE – walking around in this bubble. This strange sense of detachment. As if I was looking out on the world in a different way; aware of something… I just didn't know what it was yet.

Yes. That's the word – an ***awareness.***

Why ice is so nice!

OK, so this is not really a recipe, Melissa – more a tip. I know there are lots of brilliant baby foods out there, and some think DIY is OTT, but making your own is so easy-peasy, I just have to share my method. Just make up batches of pureed fruit and/or vegetable, cool and pop the mixture into ice cube trays. Freeze and then transfer the cubes into freezer bags with labels. Defrost a few cubes at a time and heat gently to feed delicious, healthy food for babs!

Suggestions: pureed, cooked carrot; broccoli; cooked apple, pear; mashed banana + avocado is fab too (can't remember if this freezes well!). You can also freeze cooked dinners into little cubes once baby is weaned but DO NOT ADD SALT to these meals.

Happy freezing...

Eleanor had wanted it to be Max who held her hand at the end. But it was not. Laying in the hospital bed she kept going over the book – handed to the lawyer now – in her head. Over and over. All the tips and the recipes and the letters and the secrets. And she couldn't quite remember what she had written and what she had not.

'Is he on his way? My husband?'

'He's on his way.' The nurse was kind and sat right by the bed holding on tight to her hand. 'They've paged him. His mother is picking up Melissa and he's on his way.'

Eleanor realised that it was her fault. Leaving it all too long. Too late.

'I need to speak to him. To my husband,'

'Yes I know. Shhh now. You need to rest.'

The nurse watched closely as Eleanor winced. 'We need to give you something stronger for that.'

'No. I need to stay awake. I need to speak to my husband.'

Eleanor closed her eyes, furious with herself. She was trying to remember if in the baby section, she had warned Melissa about salt? Had she put that in? Would Melissa know this? Would somebody else think to tell her? Had she ever told Max that he was not to put salt in a baby's food?

The secret pages. Were they still in? Or had she taken them out?

And the test results. Where would they go now? Some filing cabinet?

'Do you have children, nurse?'

'Two boys. You?'

'A daughter. Melissa.' She kept her eyes closed but could feel the bed moving.   Drifting.

'Shhh. You really need to rest.'

'I'm afraid she will never forgive me for something. My Melissa.'

Eleanor felt the nurse's hand smoothing her hair back from her face, over and over.

'Of course she will.'

'You think so?'

The stroking of her hair was soothing and Eleanor was thinking of different hair. Melissa sitting up in bed, chin on her knees. Warm and golden brown hair in a ponytail, reaching out to feel the hair, so warm and silky in her hands that it made her smile.

'Will you tell them I love them very much?'

'Of course I will.'

CHAPTER 38
Melissa – 2011

Anyone who has ever waited for a test result that could change their life will know that there is only one thing worse – and that is watching someone you love waiting for a test result that could change their life.

Sam and Max drove together to collect Melissa from Cornwall after she sent them a text telling them simply and suddenly that she was so very sorry she had run away.

And she needed them.

She told them later, standing in the same kitchen where her mother had once been baking and innocently brushed flour from her jumper, that she had decided to have a breast cancer gene test. Sorry. That's why she ran away. She had suddenly decided that she needed to know one way or the other, given her mother's history. She did not tell them the truth. About the baby. About the three pregnancy tests from the corner chemist's which had each produced a clear blue line.

Melissa had gone to Cornwall, imagining that it might be kinder to leave Sam. To set him free of this and to make sure he would never be in her father's shoes. It was the moment she realised that love is about the person you love and not your own happiness. She could give up the option of motherhood also – for keeps. She was young and ambitious and could throw herself into her career instead. She didn't even have to have the gene test. If she wasn't to become a mother, she couldn't pass it on. She would simply have scans every year. She could take the contract in London. Try a job abroad.

And then just two days later the whole world had changed. She was leaving Cornwall with the man she would always call her father driving her car in convoy behind while she sat alongside Sam, secretly carrying his child already. It must have happened in Cyprus. She had an upset stomach for a few days which must have affected the pill. And even this early and even though she was still quite young and was afraid and would not have chosen it this way, she suddenly felt that it was no longer about her and knew for the first time exactly how her mother had felt in those final weeks. And it completely broke her heart into pieces. Because the only thing which thundered through Melissa's head, over and over as she sat in her bubble and looked out on a different world, was that her child must not have this thing.

Fifty, fifty.

Heads.

Tails.

Melissa made another very difficult call. She decided not to tell Sam about the baby until she had the gene test result. Though she had decided she would have the child, whatever the results, she wanted at least one of them to have the small chance of hearing the news in a better way. Having a child with a person you loved, even by accident, was supposed surely to be a wondrous thing. It was not meant to feel like this.

To speed things up, Melissa decided to pay for a private referral. She informed her GP, using the same clinic and labs that the NHS recommended. Just hopefully a little faster. Around four weeks. She saw a genetics counsellor twice who referred her also, despite Melissa's initial resistance, to a grief counsellor.

'There is a lot of unfinished business,' was what she said after their first session. 'How about we deal with it, Melissa?'

The genetics counsellor also made inquiries about her mother's oncologist to see if the original test result could be traced. It was a long shot but would apparently greatly help the accuracy of Melissa's test if they could know what her mother's had revealed. James Hall the lawyer was using the book from Eleanor as evidence of consent – that Melissa's mother wanted her to know the result. Melissa went along with all of this on the strict condition that Max was not to be told that her mother had secretly taken the test. Her mother had carried a lot to spare him this distress. It would not be right to tell him now.

And so they all faced four long weeks of waiting – each coping very differently but with the same exaggerated pretence at normality.

Over and over, Melissa apologised to Sam for bolting. For putting him and Max through that. She should have talked to him, she said. Shared. She knew that. But she was just so terribly afraid. All she told him was that the journal included information which suggested there was a stronger chance of a gene fault than anyone had realised.

In response Sam was almost unbearably upbeat. 'It will be fine. Negative,' a strategy which was meant kindly but to Melissa seemed somehow to diminish what she was feeling. The terrible fear. *They couldn't know that it would be fine. She might have to have her breasts cut off. How could that be fine?*

And then she would feel terribly guilty and remember that he did not know about the baby; just how much there was at stake now.

'I'm sorry, Sam. I'm just afraid.'

'I know.'

Max upped the running. Morning and evening. He took Anna to dinner – their first proper date – and tried very hard not to mention any of this and then ended up spending an hour pouring out his heart.

'I am so sorry, Anna. All this baggage. You don't need this. It is selfish and completely insensitive and unfair—'

She had reached out then and suddenly kissed him.

'I'm sorry.' She looked as surprised as he did.

'Goodness. Don't be.' Kissing her back.

And she had confessed then, still blushing and awkward, that she was flattered that he trusted her and wanted to share this. Had been drawn to him from their very first meeting and realising how inappropriate this was – *her boss after all* – she had over-compensated by behaving so bonkers. She told him that she got this odd feeling in her stomach whenever she saw him. *Ridiculous, I know – but there it is. Seeing as we're talking honestly here.*

And so there were more dinners and walks and he told her all about Sophie, then went to pick up the gift from Sophie's gallery which was a painting of him and Melissa on a beach in the rain – in the distance a rainbow of purples and pinks and clashing blues. *A tad sentimental, some might think. Not at all her usual work* – the owner of the gallery had observed. *But there is the foil that the rainbow colours are deliberately wrong. Out of sequence. Rather clever, actually. Yes. You have a rather nice piece there.*

Max put the painting on his wall and in the fourth long week of waiting, Anna began to join him running. Max knew then, running alongside her, silent but in rhythm, that if it were not for the cloud hanging over his daughter, he would be happy. Yes. He could actually imagine being happy again.

They could not know – Anna and Max – just how far they would come to run together over the years and decades ahead. Marathon after marathon.

None of this they could yet know. And so Anna would not yet stay overnight at Max's – too afraid to upset her son – and instead they lay in bed in daylight, long hours after making love because neither of them could bear to get up and go back to the world.

Marcus was in turn a surprise. The shock of Melissa's circumstance – like a wake-up call. He put in long hours to try to get his business back on track and took up his father's offer of a bridging loan plus the rental of a flat to get him on his feet. Each of the four Fridays he invited Melissa and Sam for supper with an update on his progress.

While back in her own kitchen, Melissa cooked also – slowly working her way through all of her mother's recipes. The scones, the Easter biscuits, the soda bread and with it even an attempt at the jam, which though it set too hard that first time was still delicious.

She made the boeuf bourguignon again, serving it this time with rice. And secretly she began drafts of her blog, detailing her efforts and her thoughts. The sense of connection and comfort, using her mother's treasured mixer and her little box of biscuit cutters.

Not everything went well – but she remembered the advice in the journal. We bake, we learn, we get better…

And then one day she decided to cook the cupcakes again, nipping to the nearest supermarket for cream cheese and rather dubious out-of-season strawberries for the topping. Melissa creamed the butter and sugar by hand this time, using a wooden spoon. Her mother used to do this sometimes when they were not in a hurry and she liked the sound. The crunch as you pressed the caster sugar against the bowl, coaxing it into the butter. It was on this occasion, reaching for an orange to zest, that something very special happened. So that by the time Sam came home early, with the cakes in the oven, she was sitting on the floor of the kitchen, back against the cupboards, her eyes red.

'Oh God. Are you alright, Melissa? What's happened?'

'No. It's OK, Sam. Something nice. I remembered something really nice…'

After that Melissa returned to the computer a bit too. She claimed illness for missing the appointment with the London editor and was surprised to be given a second chance. The meeting went better than she could have hoped and so she took the contract, reasoning that it did not matter now that it was only temporary and freelance. She would be giving up work for a bit soon anyway. The baby. And OK – it would mean a new career plan, to have a baby this young, but the beauty of writing was she could work from home some of the time. Freelancing would actually be better.

Through all of this the imperative – to try to stay as positive and as busy as possible. Cooking pretty much every day and sitting up to read her mother's journal over and over when in the middle of the night she could not sleep and needed to hear her voice.

Sam noticed that she had given up coffee and alcohol but Melissa used the script of a whole new healthy way of living. The worry of this cancer cloud.

The appointment for the result was a Thursday. Sam drove and Max came too although Melissa insisted that her father must wait outside the consulting room.

None of them said a word on the journey.

It was a cold but clear day with a sky so blue that Melissa felt it was somehow much too beautiful. Out of sync.

'You ready?' Sam asked as they stood outside the door on the first floor.

'No.'

Heads. Tails.

She was wondering now whether she should have opted for the results by telephone. 'Do you want me to ask them to wait a bit? Go for a walk?'

Would it have been worse or better by phone? She couldn't decide.

'No.'

Inside finally, they sat side by side, waiting for the counsellor who came through from an adjoining office. She was smiling.

'The news is good, Melissa.'

It was Sam who made the loud noise. A weird noise which wasn't a word and wasn't exactly a cry either.

'I'm sorry.' He was embarrassed.

'Don't be sorry. It's a big ask. Waiting for this.'

'You're sure?' Melissa became aware suddenly of the sky again. Through the window. True blue. Not a trick after all. She would remember it always, she told herself – this very blue and very beautiful sky.

The counsellor's voice seemed to drift away with the detail. They had tested for everything they could. This was not an absolute guarantee that she could never have a breast cancer. She understood this? But no. They had found none of the genetic flaws which science had identified so far as pointing to an increased risk.

The result was negative.

Melissa asked then if Sam would mind leaving the room. He should go and tell Max immediately but Melissa had a couple more questions.

The counsellor poured her a glass of water as Sam kissed her on the forehead and closed the door.

'Is this about your father's test?'

'I'm sorry?' Melissa had wanted to ask only if they had traced her mother's results.

'It's just your father agreed that his results should be shared with you. We phoned his over earlier.'

'What results? I have no idea what you are talking about.'

'He wanted to be tested also. For the genetic flaw? He didn't tell you.'

'But why? I don't understand. There's no cancer in his family. Why on earth would he want that?'

'He was worried that if your result came back positive, that it might be from his side of the family. That there was no way of knowing for sure that it came from your mother.'

Melissa still didn't understand.

'But that's ridiculous. Irrational. My mother was the one with the cancer.'

'We are not always rational when we are afraid.'

'And you agreed to this? Why would you agree to this? '

Melissa's heart was now racing. DNA. Blood groups. Good God. What if a parental match was part of…

No. Please, no.

'You asked us not to tell him that your mother had been tested. We had to respect that. And so in the circumstance, well – we agreed. We felt it would help him to accept the whole picture.'

'And my mother's test? Did you trace the result?'

'We did.'

'It was positive, wasn't it?'

'It was Melissa.'

She closed her eyes.

Heads. Tails.

And then a terrible thought growing and growing.

'My father's test. I don't understand a great deal about genes. DNA and everything. And I have no idea why my father did this.'

'Like I say. He didn't want your mother to be blamed. If it went the wrong way. Without being sure.'

'Right. Yes. But his test. Did it throw up anything? Well. Anything surprising?' She was afraid to ask directly – about their match – but Christ. He was standing outside in the corridor. Melissa tried to read the counsellor's eyes.

'Well there's the standard familial DNA match. You and your father, I mean. Ninety nine point nine per cent. That's what we'd expect. But there wasn't anything else unusual.' The counsellor was glancing at the computer screen now. 'As I say – he asked for his results by phone this morning and said we were to share everything with you. But nothing here. Nothing at all to worry about.'

'Please don't tell him my mother had the faulty gene.' Melissa felt relief creep through every muscle of her body. As if she had not realised until that moment just how tense so many of her muscles really were.

'I won't. Are you OK, Melissa?'

'Very OK. Very, very OK.'

She was thinking of her mother. How much she had loved her and wished that she could have taken all that worrying from her shoulders all those years ago. How she was so glad and so grateful that she had the book. Had her with her still.

Outside then after long and silent hugs with both Sam and her father, she asked Sam to wait upstairs a moment, leading Max away with the excuse of needing hot drinks. And then, once they were alone, in an alcove by the drinks machine, she cleared her throat.

'In the journal, mum said you would do a great job.'

'Sorry?'

'Right at the beginning of the journal. She said that you would do a great job, looking after me.'

Max's eyes changed – drifting away momentarily and then back, locked onto hers. Questioning.

'I should have told you that before. Because she was right, Dad. And I don't say thank you nearly often enough.' Kissing him on the cheek and then pulling back to ask him to wait just a moment – while she went to collect Sam.

'You gonna be OK, Dad?' Hand pressed against his face.

'I am now.'

Back upstairs, Sam was searching on his phone for something.

'Sam, I need you to listen to me.'

'I am taking you to lunch. No arguments. You and Max. Somewhere really terrific. Somewhere outrageously expensive.'

'Look at me. I need you to listen to me.'

'Champagne.'

She wouldn't drink champagne. Couldn't drink champagne.

'There is something I need to tell you. And you must promise not to be angry. That I didn't tell you before.'

He tilted his head.

'I am a bit young. We are probably both a bit young. And I wouldn't have planned it this way. But you need to know that I have never been more happy.'

'You're not making sense, Melissa. Of course you're happy. The test was negative.'

'No.' She reached out for his hand and placed it on her stomach.

She looked right into his face. He moved his head by way of a question, narrowing his eyes.

For a moment Melissa could imagine another face watching and listening. Warm eyes looking down. Warm sand. Running across a beach.

'We're having a baby, Sam. It must have been Cyprus. When I had that bug. It was an accident. But I'm not sorry. And I really need to know what you think. I mean, if you think the timing is tricky with the partnership now. And if you're very angry I didn't say. It's just with all this hanging over us, I was afraid… Say something, Sam. Please say something.'

'A baby?' He looked utterly shocked.

'Yes. A baby.'

'Oh my God.' He tilted his head back and closed his eyes.

'You're very shocked?'

'Of course I'm shocked.'

'Bad shocked? I mean – are you very angry? Because I didn't tell you?'

'No, Melissa. Good shocked. A baby? *A real baby?*'

He put his arms around her then and squeezed very tight – just standing stunned and squeezing tight as a secretary tried to make her way past with a pile of files.

Melissa then pulled back. 'Of course this means we have a problem'

'You mean the job? The contract? You're not to worry about that. I can keep us until…'

'No, no. I don't mean money.'

'What, then?'

'Well – it's just I find that I feel so different. Terribly old-fashioned suddenly.'

Melissa was thinking of the final chapters in her mother's book then. Not just the tips and the tricks but the joy on the page. The colic and the cots. All the ups and the down.

And one day… you will know exactly what I am wittering on about. Because it will suddenly become what you live for…

Sam meantime still looked puzzled as another member of staff came out of a side room and they had to step backwards to let them pass.

Melissa looked over the railing to the atrium below them where Max stepped into view, carrying a cardboard tray with three drinks.

She needed to say it before they joined him.

'I am going to have to ask *you* to marry *me*, Sam.'

And now for the first time ever he did the tortoise face himself. Pulled his head right back into his neck in sheer surprise before closing his eyes – a freeze-frame of utter disbelief – before opening them to kiss first her forehead and then each of her eyelids in turn. Melissa now embarrassed as another person appeared from yet another office along the corridor, watching them and waiting to squeeze past.

'Is that a yes, Sam?'

Taking her finally very tightly into his arms again just as Max, below them, lifted his little tray of drinks as a signal to hurry.

'That's a yes, Melissa.'

ORANGE ZEST ...

At the kitchen table the daughter is eating an orange. See how she breaks the segments, one at a time, placing each between her back teeth – wincing in bittersweet anticipation and then smiling as the juice bursts onto her tongue.

Beside the stove the mother is watching this and smiling also. She puts a zester in the sink then bends down to check the ovens. On the left, a tray of cupcakes is set on the middle shelf. In the smaller oven on the right, a leg of lamb is sighing into an unctuous mess of onions and wine and herbs. Look at the mother's eyes more closely now.

See how they change as she turns again to her daughter.

'When these cakes are cool enough, you can have one with your milk, then it's time for bed.'

'I'm not tired.'

The mother moves her head so that the daughter will not see her bite away an even broader smile as she picks up the oven timer from the edge of the table and pops it into her pocket. The child, eyes already heavy, will be asleep within ten minutes of head on pillow.

'Listen – mummy is going through to finish her writing. You wash your sticky hands when you've finished. Yes? Then cake, then bed.'

The mother stands, checks the timer again in her pocket then walks past the table where she smooths her daughter's fringe back from her eyes and kisses her forehead. Through the hall next, across the oak floor and up the stairs. In the corner of the bedroom there is an alcove with a big, bay window. She sits at a wide dressing table-cum-desk and glances for a moment at the tree beyond the window – straining to the left with the wind. Very soon her husband's car will appear on the drive and the daughter will run into the hall to greet him. With her sticky fingers still unwashed.

The mother opens her laptop …

Orange zest….and other stories.

By food blogger Melissa Dance

Melissa leans forward to type the date. **March 2015**. She sees Sam's car crunch across the gravel and smiles at the reaction downstairs.

And so – what to write today?

Ah yes.

Today she will share once again how this all began. How a campaigning journalist shape-shifted into the kitchen. How a precious journal sparked a memory. That sparked a blog. That turned a woman who thought cooking was just about food into a woman who can travel through time.

Today she will write about a child at a kitchen table in Cornwall who cannot peel her orange, moaning and whining for help. The mother – creaming butter and sugar and smiling – *I tell you what, Melissa. Why don't I show you how to zest before I peel it? We can try the zest in the cakes instead of vanilla? See what we think*?

Yes. She will write once more about that twist. The memory and the magic of a single, simple scent.

Zest the orange. Close your eyes. Travel back there. Right through time.
Child at the table. Orange on the plate. Reaching out with sticky fingers….
…to hold a mother's hand.

THE END

A NOTE FROM TERESA

Thank you so much for reading Melissa's story – pure fiction, of course, but the theme does come from the emotional landscape of my life and I worried a bit about that.

I lost my mother to cancer when I was 17 and for a long time I wondered whether that experience had any place in my writing life. Then as a BBC television news presenter, I was asked to start a local Race for Life to raise money for Cancer Research and there were all these lovely ladies, many with a single word pinned to their backs. *'Mum'.* It was both traumatic and comforting also and I realised, as a writer, I perhaps had something to say…

It took me a long time to find a strong enough fictional story to carry a theme so close to so many people's hearts. But once Melissa and Eleanor finally stepped into my writing room, the novel almost seemed to write itself.

My next novel with Bookouture is THE SEARCH and I will share publication news and updates on my website www.teresadriscoll.com. You are also very welcome to get in touch via Twitter or my Facebook Author page.

Thank you, again, for reading my debut. If you are able to post a review, that would mean a lot to me. Most important - I feel so very proud and privileged to be signing off here as an author at last.

With warm wishes,
Teresa Driscoll
@teresadriscoll
https://www.facebook.com/teresadriscollauthor

ACKNOWLEDGEMENTS

My journey to publication has been a long one and huge thanks go to all who have supported me along the way – most especially my wonderful husband and two sons who never stopped believing.

Massive thanks also to my fabulous agent Madeleine Milburn who finally made all this happen for me and to my patient and very clever editor Claire Bord, together with the dedicated team at Bookouture.